best dreams."

—Rich Larson, author of *Ymir* and *Tomorrow Factory*

"This novel instantly propels Alvaro Zinos-Amaro into being one of the most exciting new voices in SF. Read it now, before everybody starts asking you if you've read *Equimedian* yet."

—Michael Marshall Smith, *New York Times* and internationally-bestselling novelist

PRAISE FOR EQUIMEDIAN

"Wow. So... *Equimedian*. Alvaro Zinos-Amaro isn't fucking around. Working-class, righteously subversive post-cyberpunk that patches MIRL through MIDI and drags memory into malware. With wit, grit, heat, and bite, Zinos-Amaro hunts the most dangerous VR game of all: the human brain. Philip K. Dick is turning [these pages proudly] in his grave."

—**Jason Heller**, Hugo Award-winning author of *Strange Stars: David Bowie, Pop Music, and the Decade Sci-Fi Exploded*

"Plenty of science fiction books get the science right, but this might be the first one that gets the science *fiction* right. It's *Don Quixote* in a Möbius comic strip drawn by Philip K. Dick—for Kilgore Trout."

—**Stephen Graham Jones**, *New York Times* bestselling author of *The Only Good Indians*

"A cleverly Borgesian, reality-distorting premise enlivens this tribute to Silver Age SF."

—**Kirkus Reviews**

"[*Equimedian*] promises to reach many different types of reader with its invitation to traverse high tech, how reality is defined and represented, and the forces that would compromise, alter, or control it."

—**Midwest Book Review**

"One of the most promising of today's newer science-fiction writers."

—**Robert Silverberg**

"*Equimedian* is a valentine to science fiction, a story of maturation, and a complex view of our complex reality. You will root for Jason as he struggles, as we all must, to grow up in a bewildering world."

—**Nancy Kress**, multiple Nebula and Hugo Award-winning author

"Not only does *Equimedian* appeal to the reader in me, but the writer—stories here are not only real, but the keys to the Kingdom. *Equimedian* is weird, intellectual, warm, warped, freaky and fannish. I loved it."

—**Thoraiya Dyer**, four-time Aurealis and Ditmar Award-winning writer

"Wondrous, creepy, vertiginous. PK Dick meets Hermann Hesse meets *Black Mirror*, with knowing nods to Russ, Heinlein, Galouye and countless others, on a ride through fandom, obsession and loss. *Equimedian* is as mind-bending as it is urgent in what it has to say about the combinatory power of words to change the world."

—**J.S. Breukelaar**, author of *The Bridge*

"Alvaro Zinos-Amaro, one of the field's sharpest minds, has written a Phildickian delight. Jason, a science fiction obsessive, finds himself inside the kind of stories he's spent his life reading. As reality keeps shifting under Jason's feet, and conspiracies unfurl, we never stop rooting for him. Fans of New Wave SF are especially going to dig this."

—**Daryl Gregory**, author of *Spoonbenders*

"Zinos-Amaro's absorbing debut is—fittingly—at least three things at once: a poignant slice of life, a surreal, slow-burn conspiracy thriller, and a love-and-loss letter to the science fiction genre. I emerged from it as one does from the very

EQUI ME DIAN

A NOVEL

ALVARO ZINOS-AMARO

EQUIMEDIAN
Copyright © 2023 by Alvaro Zinos-Amaro.
All rights reserved.

Copyedits by Bret Smith and Jeanni Smith
Cover by Damonza.com
Typesets and formatting by Damonza.com
A Hex Publishers Book

Published & Distributed by Hex Publishers, LLC
PO BOX 298
Erie, CO 80516
www.HexPublishers.com

Paperback ISBN: 979-8-9862194-8-6
Hardcover ISBN: 979-8-9880827-1-2
e-Book ISBN: 979-8-9880827-0-5

First Edition: February 2024
10 9 8 7 6 5 4 3 2 1
Printed in the U.S.A.

*For my father, Richard Walter Zinos, who once upon a time
read me a story about the town musicians of Bremen, and
later handed me a passport to all the galaxies of science fiction.*

I. A Confederacy of Disappointments

ONE

I STAND IN Miss Moulin's bathroom, heat-dazed, thoughts melting inside my skull and leaking through my pores. Outside it's a hundred and five degrees; inside this musty, sixth-floor apartment it's at least five degrees hotter. The air is stale mildew. Enough dust clings to the small windowpane that I could finger-scrawl the word "Help" on it. That would be very unprofessional.

As a Codis employee I have to wear a long-sleeve uniform even in the summer. Sweat stains suck at my armpits. I turn the sink faucet, which creaks and produces only tepid water. I splash some on my face, the lukewarm drops mingling with the sweat oozing from my skin. *I'm just diluting the sweat*, I think. *Literally making more sweat.* Then I stop to evaluate whether or not I've used the word "literally" correctly. Most people take the word "figuratively" literally and the word "literally" figuratively, which causes me endless doubts about my own usage. The effort of drying off my face while thinking through this generates more sweat.

I close my eyes and imagine myself somewhere different from the here-and-now of New York, 1979. The first image that pops into my head is from DAW Collectors paperback number two-hundred and twenty-three, *Walkers on the Sky* by David J. Lake. I see Signi Signison chilling on the force-field in Melior's sky, looking down in contempt at the brutish Neathings below. Zilith has fastened mechanical wings to her arms and is going to take me for a flight, so I can soar in the sky with Signi. *Please, Zilith, take me away.*

I open my eyes. I'm not going anywhere. Zilith and Signi and Weldon and all the rest are trapped in their novel, and I'm trapped in this life, stuck in this apartment until I've finished the installation.

Still, I wonder, will the gods interfere and prevent the Nasronites from capturing their enemies? If they don't, will Signi and Zilith fight the gods? Signi is a good guy. I could do worse for a role model. I decide that as soon as I get off work tonight, I'll finish the book and then immediately start the sequel, *The Right Hand of Dextra*, which I've already procured. If two is as good as one, I'll soon be rushing to parts three and four, *The Wildings of Westron*, and *The Gods of Xuma*, intriguingly subtitled *Barsoom Revisited*. A cross-over with Edgar Rice Burroughs? Sending humans to Mars three years ago may have dispelled some of the planet's romance, but I don't care. This book series has me tingling with antici-pation.

Back in the poorly lit living room I wonder: is it really so dim, or is my right eye acting up again?

"Would you like some water, Jason?" Miss Moulin says.

I turn to face the kitchen and get a strong whiff of fried garlic. "I'm good, thanks. Let me finish up for you."

"Suit yourself." She studies the half-assembled system on her living room table and shifts uneasily. I check the time. Good—still within my estimated installation window of twenty-two minutes.

"You're getting the newer model, you know," I say, trying to pre-empt any hostility. I grab two micro-calibrators. "Very realistic."

She leans forward. "Are you just saying that?"

I scan the headset gear and tweak three settings. My right eye betrays me and I close it, working only with the left until the alignment is complete. "I'm not *just* saying it," I say. "It's true."

"Which EmuX does it for you?"

"Me?" The question makes me uncomfortable, and I consider copping out on a technicality. Leon Sobol, my roommate, has a unit, and I could imply that I use Leon's machine without explicitly saying so. But Signi Signison in *Walkers on the Sky* wouldn't lie, would he? Unlike, for instance, Jack Jacobi, the failed-novelist-anti-hero of Gordon Eklund's Ace Books special *The Eclipse of Dawn*, which I devoured a few nights ago. In a 1988-set dystopia—a mere nine years from now, I realize with a shudder—Jacobi sets out to write a highly fictionalized, self-serving biography of the detestable politician Robert F. Colonby.

One of Eklund's brilliant strokes is to include summary chapters of Jacobi's book-within-the-book, providing all kinds of moral warnings. Our current president, Frank Church, has more in common with Colonby than I care to think about.

"I prefer books," I say, remembering Eklund's descriptions of the effects of nuclear war: a wasteland America, Disneyland in ruins, and so on. I wipe my face with my right sleeve and find nothing with which to wipe my now too-damp sleeve. "I'm really in no rush to experience the future."

"What do you read?"

Here it comes. I brace myself. "Mostly science fiction," I say. She chuckles without warmth.

Time to switch strategies. "I think an EmuX would remind me of work too much. I don't want to think about my job during my down time."

"You don't like what you do," she concludes.

I crouch under the processor box to take voltage readings. It's a sensitive piece of hardware. Sweat stings my eyes. My right arm itches. I must be imagining the sensation, because it healed from the laser tattoo removal—my first and last, a lame infinity symbol—weeks ago. Miss Moulin, who I would guess is in her late sixties or early seventies, is, unwisely, wearing shorts, and from beneath the processor box my view of her wrinkled legs translates to rippling oceans of ink. The style is something like neo-baroque tribalism. The images jumble together in such profusion that I wonder if the ink weighs down her skin.

"Have you ever met one?" she blurts out.

I proceed to activate the tutorial and let it play through the empty headset, a shortcut to achieve better efficiency scores in my daily stats. "Met who?"

"A Progress Pilgrim." She speaks the words with reverence.

"Afraid not," I say. I've learned over time that when it comes to paying customers it's generally best to keep my opinions about the Progress Pilgrims to myself.

"You play the PP lottery?" she asks.

Based on her home, I place Miss Moulin on the lowest

echelon of middle class, her feet dangling into the class below. She really shouldn't be squandering her savings on the PP lottery, but I suppose it's none of my business. "Nah."

As though sensing my socio-economically blunt assessment of her life, she disappears into the kitchen for a few minutes, then returns with a soda in her hand. I finish the assembly, complete my diagnostics, and gather my tools. "Would you like to try it?" I ask.

"You do this for a living and you're not curious about the real deal?"

The inside of my mouth feels like an oven; I force myself to cook up some words in response. "At the end of the day, the Pilgrims are people, same as you and me."

She shakes her head. "You read science fiction, but you're not interested in the future. You install EmuX's, but you're not interested in the PPs. I don't understand you people."

I'm not sure who she's referring to—Codis employees, science fiction readers, the youth of today—but I'm in no hurry to find out. "We recommend you limit usage to a max of two hours a day for the first two weeks," I say. "To avoid migraines." I recite additional disclosures and receive her digital thumbprint indicating receipt.

I don't expect a tip from Miss Moulin, so once the paperwork is done, I grab my bag and head towards the door. "Have a nice day," I say. She doesn't reply. From my peripheral vision I see that it's because she's already donned the EmuX headpiece.

Disliking confined spaces, I use the stairwell instead of the elevator. On my way down I pass a couple of teenagers sitting on the stairs and holding hands. The guy's t-shirt says BIRDIE LUDD DIED FOR YOU.

Once I've schlepped my tools to the van, I check my schedule for the rest of the day. Nine installs left if I want to hit my expected performance target; eleven if I want to climb to the top of this district's curve.

Sitting in my van, I make a note that I should start packing a change of underclothes with me during the summer months.

The next four installs proceed without a hitch.

When I buzz the intercom of the fifth, a male voice says, "Who is this?" I say, "I'm here from Codis, to install your EmuX."

There's a long pause, and then he says "Come up" in a strange monotone.

Upon opening the door, Mr. Gerber's swarthy face betrays no emotion. He's wearing a too-small white bathrobe with an embroidered red "S" on the right side, right above his chest. A tat of a black-and-white castle, with red fireworks shooting out of it, adorns his chin. "Enter," he says in a flat affect.

"Cool-o-roonie." I set my bag on the floor, near his living room table, and point to the "S."

"Like *The Scarlet Letter*, huh?"

"My mom made this bathrobe for me when I was twelve," he says. "The 'S' stands for my name, Shawn."

"Gotcha."

It's gotta be my lucky day: again, no AC. Bright overhead lights dilate my pores in the hot stillness. I swallow. "I'm going to get started." I open my bag and extract components. "Where would you like the unit?"

He seems confused. "I haven't thought about that." He moves his arms up and down. "I didn't consider this," he says, sounding more agitated.

"It's okay, buddy." I power up a high-watt smile. My energy is sucked up into the black hole of his non-expression, but I keep it steady. "I can set it up right here in the living room and if you change your mind, I'm happy to move it for you. It's not that heavy."

"I've thought about it now," he says. "Please perform the installation in my brother's bedroom."

I nod. "Sure."

He stands with a placid expression.

"Excuse me," I say. "Can you show me the way?"

"He's sleeping now," he says. "We need to wait."

"Oh…" *This*, I tell myself, *is reason one hundred and seven why I really need to quit this job.* "How long is your brother going to be resting?" I ask.

"He likes to sleep during the day," Mr. Gerber says, "and work at night."

I glance at my watch, realizing I've neglected to eat dinner. A combination of hunger and exhaustion make me unconcerned about my efficiency scores, but I'm not so far gone to think that I can dawdle for hours at this guy's apartment. My supe, Mr. Wirt, would buzz me on my wrist-plex, and I'd rather talk to him when I choose, thank you very much. Not to mention how incredibly uncomfortable it would be to stand here doing nothing all that time. I'm slathered by awkwardness thicker than the heat.

"Night shift, huh. Where does your brother work?" I ask.

"In the living room."

"I see. What does he do?"

He looks at me, no hint of anything. "I'm not sure."

"We're talking about… your brother, right, Mr. Gerber? Or did I misunderstand?"

"In a manner of speaking." He crosses his arms. "I need to respect his boundaries. He hasn't shared what he's working on right now and I haven't inquired."

"If you don't mind my asking, how long has he been living here?"

"He was delivered four months ago."

I blink. "Did you say 'delivered'?"

"Yes."

"From where?"

"The clinic. His eyes were bandaged. It helps them imprint positively to see their home before anything else. If they saw the clinic, they might think that was their home."

I assume "clinic" is some sort of euphemism for hospital. But at the rate this is going, "Shawn Gerber" could be a euphemism for "alien-posing-as-human."

"The clinic," I repeat. "Was he sick?"

"No," he says. "You ask a lot of questions."

"I apologize," I say. "Simply trying to figure out how to get your product up and running with the least amount of fuss possible."

I let my gaze wander. A small metal-framed picture on the living room wall shows Shawn and his brother. Then I notice a panoply of pills and assorted medical equipment on a kitchen shelf.

And finally, I see an array of over-ripe fruit on the counter.

Holy smokes. I thought this was only a rumor.

"May I ask," I say, "what prompted you to, ah, request the delivery?"

"I'm special," Mr. Gerber says. "My doctor said a brother would help with my empathy skills."

I hear a rustling from the corridor near the living room.

A figure wearing dark sunglasses, clothed in a bathrobe similar to Mr. Gerber's but lacking the signature "S," traipses out and studies me.

"You're awake," Mr. Gerber says, evidently surprised. The man nods and closes the distance between them.

When they hug, their identical builds seem to dissolve into one two-bodied entity. They embrace in a way that makes me want to look away.

But I stare on, because I've never seen a clone before.

"You poor thing," Shawn Gerber tells his replica. "You must have heard us out here and decided to change your schedule to accommodate."

His clone nods.

"I'll get your breakfast ready right away."

Mr. Gerber proceeds as though I'm not around, and part of me wants to allow this domestic ritual to unfold without interference. But my sense of professional decorum overrides my inner voyeur. "Mr. Gerber, now that your brother is awake, I should probably proceed with the installation."

Mr. Gerber directs his eyes, visibly softened, at me. He says, "Would you like something to eat?"

I'll be darned, I think. *This really does seem to stimulate his empathy.*

"Thanks, I'm good."

He opens a cupboard beneath the sink. A strong smell of rotting bananas drifts up and makes me grateful to be at the other end of the room. He lifts the trash bag onto the counter, scoops up several helpings of runny black paste into a bowl, and mixes in some of the over-ripe fruit from the counter. The whole assemblage looks like manure mulch. As the stench fills the room, I repress my gag reflex.

"I'll let myself into his bedroom," I announce, heft the equipment, and exit the living room.

The clone's room is dark. A pervasive musk commingles the aromas of rubbing alcohol, talcum powder, diapers, and excrement. Turning on the light only provides a faint cerulean glow. I use it to locate the room's single window, which has been locked shut—with a chain.

"He's sensitive to light," Mr. Gerber says behind me, startlingly close. "The window lock is a protective measure. They can be impulsive during the first year, strangely self-destructive, and we're on a fourteenth floor."

Taking all this in, my mind recalls the clone saga of physicist Paul Swenson in the far-off year 2000. I discovered Pamela Sargent's *Cloned Lives* because Joanna Russ wrote about it in *Fantasy & Science Fiction*, and I listen to Russ always, even when I know she's talking—or yelling—right past me. Sargent shows us the rich inner lives of Paul's replicas, and she doesn't shy away from sex stuff: one of Paul's clones is chromosomally converted to a woman, and we're then treated to male-on-female intra-clone coitus. A couple of the Custodians thought the novel scandalous. But as I stand here now, surveying this nursery-prison-cell, and remembering the hug between Shawn and his "brother," I realize that Sargent didn't go far enough. This realization in turn triggers the memory of Cole Wellmann's impassioned argument three years ago that Kate Wilhelm's *Where Late the Sweet Birds Sang* was a superior contemporary treatment of the clone theme. Will Shawn Gerber's clone ever read a science fiction novel, I wonder? Which would *he* prefer?

Anyway, I'm going to be forced to reassess both Wilhelm and Sargent. The words of their stories may not have changed, but my experience in the world has changed their meaning.

"Some air circulation would be lovely," I say. "By any chance do you have a fan?"

"Yes." He regards my expression phlegmatically. "I'll set it up by the door."

"Thank you."

It doesn't work as I'd hoped. The foul smells from the bedroom mix with those from the kitchen, all of it stirring up into an overwhelming miasma. My sense of smell shuts down in self-defense.

I focus on my work. Once I've finished, I walk Mr. Gerber through the device's operation and basic settings.

Back in the living room, I see the clone finishing up a bowl of that mulch. I guess they can only eat partially decomposed food.

"Will he be able to manipulate the EmuX's controls?" I wonder aloud.

"Eventually," Mr. Gerber says.

How many more dirty diapers, I don't ask, lie between this moment and that hypothetical future? "I realize it's none of my business, but…"

"What would you like to know?" he says.

I consider the moral equation that balances the creation of life on one side with the lubrication of societal intercourse on the other. "I'm curious about your brother's… life expectancy."

"Unclear," he says. "If he makes it past the three-year mark, he might have a couple of decent decades."

Now finished eating, the clone transitions to the couch,

leans forward and begins drawing. I notice he's a tat virgin. Another manifestation of his increased sensitivity?

I cover the obligatory disclosures with Mr. Gerber and obtain the requisite thumbprint. On my way out I accidentally knock over Walt Disney's *The Black Hole* coloring book off the edge of the coffee table.

"One of my brother's favorites," Mr. Gerber says, with avuncular pride.

I make out a pack of crayons nearby. The clone seems confused, looking first at Mr. Gerber and then at me. I place the coloring book exactly where it was, and then the clone resumes the drawing he was working on.

"Sorry, my friend."

The clone takes off his dark sunglasses.

His eyes are milky-gray pupils dilated against black irises. The whites appear clouded by some kind of emulsion.

"He's thankful you put it back," Mr. Gerber says. "No hard feelings." I look away from the clone's completely penetrating gaze.

"My pleasure," I say, and duck out.

∽

When I get home that evening, Leon is in a mopey mood. "I was sure she'd say yes," he gripes.

"Elissa, from accounting, right?" I ask.

Leon puffs. Without bothering to elaborate, he dons the headgear that connects him to the virtual environment of the EmuX. I abandon hope of any civilized discourse and retreat to my room.

In bed, I remember the clone's remarkable eyes. I'm

haunted by their otherworldliness. Bizarrely silvered, with pupils that seemed dilated by our standards, those virginal-looking eyes were beautiful in their own way. Maybe, I realize, I'm a little jealous. With the luck I've had with *my* eyes…

I turn on my side. Book spines beckon. I'm drawn to an elegant black font against pristine white, my Ballentine paperback of R. A. Lafferty's *Arrive at Easterwine: The Autobiography of a Ktistec Machine*. I love that title, though my memories of the text are vague (this happens to me with Lafferty, which is a personal failing, because his stories are worth remembering in their full zany glory). I delicately pry the uncreased book loose from its stack. Ah yes. Fantastic psychedelic cover, featuring triangles within triangles, nude meditation, and a melting city of gold, by the little-known Mati Klarwein. Klarwein's cover for the likewise underrated Stephen Goldin anthology *The Alien Condition*, which is part of a different stack on the floor near the closet, is, alas, not quite as impressive, but that anthology will forever warm my heart, for in it I discovered James Tiptree, Jr.'s "Love Is the Plan the Plan Is Death."

I open up *Easterwine* at random. The story starts coming back to me. An intelligent computer—the first Ktistec machine of the title—named Epiktistes, or Epikt for short, has been created to complete three tasks: seek out a leader, find love, and locate a liaison. After about a dozen pages, I drift off.

Then I seem to be awake again, except I know I'm still sleeping. I feel invigorated, ready to take on anything. I decide to get out of bed and—

My body refuses to cooperate. Some force keeps me

pressed against the mattress, a gravitational funnel trying to suck me down *through* the mattress.

Unable to breathe, I fold in two.

My room evaporates and I float in a black space. I hover, suspended in both time and free-fall. Then I tumble down and all the blood rushes to my face.

Though a part of me knows I'm dreaming, another part of me knows the dream is somehow more real than ordinary reality. Dream gravity has temporarily overpowered real gravity, and I'm completely in its grip.

My stomach flutters and my bones jostle about. From my peripheral vision I make out strange symbols in the air. They seem to mock me with the promise of meaning. I turn to try and see them head-on, but an intense pain in my temples forces me to look elsewhere. I scream. My voice echoes in the nothingness, and I stop in mid-air.

A pale blue light coalesces into a point before me. The point grows into a circle, an aperture of some kind. I reach towards it, and it widens. I squeeze through the opening. I'm suspended in free-fall, as before, and then I plummet once more.

This second fall contains more twists and turns than the first, yet feels more controlled.

I sense observers peering at me from perches and recesses beyond my ability to resolve. I want to reach out to them, to talk to them, but I'm moving too fast on this invisible rollercoaster. There's nothing to provide traction or friction, so I can't slow down. I yell again, and again come to a complete standstill in mid-air.

Orange light, this time, beams in from above and punches a rapidly expanding circle into space. I'm debating whether to stay where I am or enter the orange gateway when I feel a shove from behind. A bag has been strapped to my back. The momentum ushers me through to the place of orange light.

My third plunge follows.

I no longer flail. I retain enough motor control for my hands to reach back towards the backpack with which I've been provisioned. My fingers sense a zipper. I'm approaching a black tunnel, and I become convinced the tunnel will send me back to the first black space to begin the cycle all over again. As I'm about to open the zipper, searing pain, similar to what I felt when I tried to read the floating symbols during my first fall, causes me to scream a third time.

I wake up.

Disoriented, I stare at the ceiling.

Motion sickness creates the illusion that my room is spinning. I take deep breaths and wait for it to pass.

Tentatively, I move on the bed. Ordinary gravity— thank God.

I wait for reality to open up a trapdoor beneath me, as it did in the three dreams, but nothing happens. The mere memory of the falls is almost enough to make me heave.

I sit up and rub my eyes, clearing gossamer dream fragments from my vision. I've never experienced dreams this real before. They were *Lathe-of-Heaven* intense. I feel like Möbius and Morpheus ganged up on me for the ultimate prank. It takes a few minutes for reality to settle solidly around me.

I should feel grateful to be back in the land of the living, but instead I feel only—disappointment. Surveying the stacks of books around me, the mundaneness of my life sinks in. With great effort I get up, trying to recover a sense of the familiar.

I half-heartedly toss some worn shirts into the laundry basket in my closet and end up stumbling over a pile of *Galileo* magazines. I'm missing the March 1978 issue, which was the second bimonthly issue after the magazine switched from quarterly publication.

Keshawn Lee from the Custodians keeps telling me I need to check out Kevin O'Donnell, Jr.'s story in that issue, called "Do Not Go Gentle," but I've never trusted Keshawn's tastes, and I don't care for O'Donnell's work. Still, not going gently is a theme that resonates right now.

I sit down, winded. All day long I was looking forward to finishing *Walkers on the Sky*, but presently it holds zero interest. In fact, the thought of reading it inspires only fatigue.

Surveying the thousands of books and magazines in my collection makes me even more exhausted. All these fictional lives, these non-existent places… where have they gotten me? I've invested so much time, so much money, so much energy in this stuff—for what?

Entertainment and intellectual stimulation are the standard answers, but right now it feels like a huge nothing. I'm thirty-eight and working for a company I dislike just to afford living with a roommate. What have I accomplished with my life except the internal glamorization of a populist, low-denominator form of entertainment?

This needs to stop.

Usually I like to lose myself in the latest novel by D. G. Compton or Michael G. Coney or Suzette Haden Elgin. Maybe revisit one of Bob Hoskins' *Infinity* anthologies (ah, the glory days of Lancer Books). Usually I avoid anything that's been nominated for a major award. (*Actual* award-winners are too pandering or self-serious.) E. L. Doctorow's *Ragtime* was up for a Nebula a few years ago, after he got his start with a science fiction novel called *Big as Life,* and Thomas Pynchon was up for a Nebula too, five years ago, for *Gravity's Rainbow.* Not for me. I'll take some good old Andrew J. Offutt over them any day of the week. Like the Dell paperback of *The Galactic Rejects.* Have you ever seen a more evocative, mysterious-looking barn on a cover? Or the Paperback Library *Evil is Live Spelled Backwards,* with that fabulous cover tag: "The Super-state controlled men's minds—but the Underground had a better weapon!" A better weapon than whatever it is that can control a human mind; how insanely awesome—

I stop myself. I'm getting swept up into it again. This is one time I can't turn to science fiction since it's part of the problem.

After some half-hearted tidying up, I realize I can't shake my sense of uneasiness about my environment and my life in general.

The three dreams hold me in their thrall.

I think of them as the vertices of an equilateral triangle. Then I realize that whatever joins them is not straight, but looped, making up one of those impossible M. C. Escher triangles—Penrose triangles, I think they're called—where following one outer side leads to another's inner side, and that leads to the outer side of the next, and now you're back where you started but on the inner face, and as you follow it through again it's the opposite as before, and so on.

I try to go back to sleep, but it's no use.

To break free from the grip of the three trapdoor dreams, I decide to make a list. It always helps. *What precisely, Jason, are you so dissatisfied with?*

Once I start answering this question, my wristplex has a hard time keeping up with me:

1. I should sell off most of my collection. I really don't need to be hauling around thousands of books for the rest of my life, that's for sure. Plus, this'll make me some immediate cash.
2. I need to manage my finances better, starting by reining in my compulsive spending on sf books and magazines. If I really want to save up—oh God—should I move back in with my parents?
3. I have to change jobs. I'm sick of working for Codis. The company capitalizes on people's desire to copy the sickly rich Progress Pilgrims. We provide an addictive product that promotes isolation and escape—no moral justification here.
4. Make more friends. There's nothing wrong with the Custodians and the Mayflies, but I need to expand beyond these circles. Particularly if I want to reduce my science fiction consumption.
5. Call Jill more often. She's dependable and kind.
6. Call my parents more often. Maybe that's a stretch, considering where we are.
7. Girlfriend?

Pfffff. Deep breath.

That's a good start.

Tension starts ebbing from my body, and the world stills.

TWO

LEON SAYS, "HEY, got a minute?"

I can tell he's standing right outside my door.

I plop down the book I'm reading, a nifty little Lafferty called *The Three Armageddons of Enniscorthy Sweeney*. "Sure. What's up?"

I open the door haltingly. Leon is clad in his characteristic lounge outfit, which consists of Union Flag jeans, a tight white t-shirt that highlights his sculptured, abstract-pattern tatted arms and chest, and a ridiculous loose gray scarf that meets his neck at roughly the same spot as the tresses of his shiny black shoulder-length hair. The ink along the sides of his face trails down his neck in a serpentine configuration of geometrical shapes. Leon's blue eyes, which I've heard at least one girl unironically describe as "dreamy," pause on various mounds of books and magazines, and his Roman nose sniffs the air.

"Rent's due in four days," he says, holding his chin in his hand. "Last month you got the days confused."

My body tenses. "Okay."

"No chance I might get it before then, I suppose?"

I grind my teeth. "I'll see what I can do," I say.

He crosses his arms, biceps swelling. "Will you clean up your room in the meantime?"

"You're not my mom, Leon."

His eyes chuckle. "Is this really how you like to live?"

My face flushes. "How's that dry spell going?"

He studies me. I imagine him staring at my right droopy eyelid. "Four days," he repeats, and then leaves.

I need to clear my head. I walk down our street and turn on Haven, heading towards the Salvation Army thrift store at 112 on 4th, where the Custodians will be holding their Thursday evening get-together.

After I pass by the store's bright-red emblazoned shield and enter, my stomach reminds me I've skipped dinner yet again. I'm greeted by Ramon Cloutier's distinctively squeaky voice, which always manages to pierce the conversational froth of any meeting.

"Hey hey hey," he says. "Look what the cat who walks through walls dragged in."

His sweaty forehead sports a nautical knot tat, presumably made in white ink years ago and now faded into a vaguely repulsive yellowish brown.

"Good to see you." I rub my hands together. "Any food tonight?"

"What are you reading these days?" he says.

Clearly this isn't headed where I want it to go. "A six-volume history of the Daleks." Ramon dislikes TV and film references almost as much as I do, which makes him an easy target.

"Get real," he protests.

My belly growls. "Fine." I remember that Ramon is a science fiction purist. "A new epic fantasy series," I say.

"Did you read the '69 October and November issues of *Analog*?" he asks. "I got this whole stash of back issues from Lorri Ebner in exchange for Spinrad's *The Iron Dream*, can you believe it? Anyway, John Dalmas has an interesting thing in those issues. A serialization called *The Yngling*, which he fixed up for Pyramid. Norse legends retold. Powerful stuff. I think it's making me appreciate fantasy for the first time."

He's getting me back now.

"Have you read anything by Cristabel?" I say, playing along. "*Manalacor of Veltakin* and *The Cruachan and the Killane* are superb."

"Cristabel who?" He takes out a notepad and adjusts his glasses.

"Just Cristabel."

"Really?"

"Yeah."

"Also mythology?"

Keshawn Lee appears in his full-bearded splendor, his black eyes staring like he's never seen me before. The tat of a setting sun on his face, made entirely in the pointillist style, seems to radiate with life.

"You dig Cristabel?" Keshawn says, dispensing with trivialities like "hello." "*The Mortal Immortals* is Cristabel's best work. We were almost called the Mortal Immortals, you know, instead of the Custodians. Cole can testify to that. The vote was five to four against. Though it was going to be the Cosmic Custodians, we ended up passing an amendment to shorten it."

"Where *is* Cole?" I ask. "Did he leave early again? He always seems pressed for time."

"Speaking of time," Ramon says, "have you noticed this

new fixation by writers? It's starting to get to me. Crawford Kilian's *The Empire of Time* is a title that sums it up."

Still thinking of food, I notice that both Keshawn's hands are full, one of them holding a greasy brown paper bag and the other a can of Point Special beer. "The new Captain Kirk Happy Meal," he says in response to my inquisitive look. He opens up the bag, revealing the yellow-purple box with its comic book panels and Kirk badge. "I think there's another one stashed in the back. Let me grab it for you." And in a puff of altruism, he's gone.

"You shouldn't read so much into titles, Ramon," I say.

"Come on," Ramon intones, sounding genuinely put out. "It's clear what Kilian is really referring to."

Keshawn returns with the bag, and I dive in. "You think he's talking about the Pilgrims?" I ask in between bites.

"What else? Kilian is just the tip of the iceberg. Think about it. Monteleone's *The Time-Swept City*, Cowper's *Time Out of Mind*—that's as explicit as you can get, I think— Biggle, Jr.'s *The Whirligig of Time*, Koontz's *Time Thieves*, Bayley's *The Fall of Chronopolis*. C'mon! You like D. G. Compton, right, Jason? *Chronocules*! They're sending us a message. The Pilgrims are up to no good." He throws his hands up in the air.

I'm in no mood to slip into one of my anti-Pilgrims rants, and fortunately I make out Cole mingling at the other end of the room. I wave him over and he approaches.

He gives me a solid shoulder pat and straightens his gray wool jacket. I notice a new tat on the side of his index finger—a quote in French, which I'm unable to translate.

"How have you been, Jason?"

"It's good to see you, man. Ramon here, by the way, says

that our writers are obsessing over time, and that it's code for the PPs."

"Just because a title references 'time' doesn't mean it's part of a conspiracy," Cole points out. "Have you even read the books, Ramon? Anyway, we don't need fiction to tell us that the Pilgrims are the scourge of the Earth."

"I'm not saying it's a conspiracy. More like a *zeitgeist* thing—and what do you think 'zeit' means? Speaking of which, how's Codis treating you these days, Jason?"

"I'm considering quitting."

A woman walks up to Keshawn—Christina?—and we all exchange nods.

"Ramon," I say, "what is it you think the Pilgrims are doing that we don't know about?"

"You install simulators, right? Gear that allows people to experience a copy of what the PPs promise?"

"Yeah. EmuX's," I say. My disapproval is audible. "Expensive, harmful toys."

"I'm sure the PPs love this fad," Ramon says. "They probably see it as a form of flattery. Wouldn't be surprised if they're in bed with Codis. That's the point. They're always going to be one step ahead of us."

"I don't think a few microseconds is such a big deal."

Cole says, "To be fair, it does give them an advantage with high-frequency trading. I'm sure that didn't hurt in their establishment of a financial empire."

Ramon continues undaunted. He begins slicing the air with his hand as he speaks. "When it comes to temporal displacement, they started small, but how wide is their lead now? It's like Zeno's paradox in reverse. If you can travel microseconds into the future, then you can travel microseconds into the future from the future into which you've already traveled, and so on, stacking up jumps into a kind of bridge. Microseconds become milliseconds, milliseconds turn into seconds, seconds into minutes, hours, days, weeks, months, years. Eventually they'll be able to manipulate us completely. We'll be *history* to them. Pliable history at that."

Ignoring Ramon, Keshawn turns to me and says, "I heard that some big-league writers are getting hooked up by Codis for free, so that they'll be more tempted to write about this kind of stuff. Have you done installs for any writers we know?"

I sigh. "Nope."

"Heinlein's allegedly tried the real thing," Ramon says. "He wouldn't mess around with a simulation. He's got someone on the inside of the PPs that let him use the equipment. Blew his mind. He wrote *Time Enough for Love* right after that."

My right eye bothers me. I turn to the woman by Keshawn's side. She's sporting her short auburn hair in a wedge, a vaguely triangular shape with a point of intersecting bangs on the forehead and heavy layers at the sides and back. Her cheeks are streaked by two apple green tats, discrete but stylish. "Hi, what's your name?"

"Christina," she says.

"Did we meet last year? When did you join this merry band?"

Christina looks at Keshawn. "I've been here a couple of times. To be honest, I'm not really into sci-fi," she says. Her tone is blunt, but she comes across as neither haughty nor apologetic, merely direct.

"I understand," I say. "I definitely need to reduce my own, uh, intake. May even sell off my collection."

Keshawn runs his hand slowly through his beard. "Christina's a scholar, Jason, getting a degree in comparative lit from Columbia, and she won't be deceived by your pretense of disaffection with our cadre. Christina, don't believe a word this man tells you. He's been a member of the Custodians—an admittedly inconstant one—for years, and his talent for dissembling is known to fandom from here to the West Coast. In fact, that's the reason we allow him to join us on occasion. A little infamy spices things up."

"You're being very gallant," I say. "The first time you found out I'd attended a Mayflies meeting you were a little more uncouth."

"Mayflies?" Christina asks.

"The rivalry between the Custodians and Mayflies is renowned," Cole says.

"And it's clearly never bothered me," I say. "Their drinks are much better, by the way. Did you and Keshawn meet at Columbia?"

"I was making use of the coveted behind-the-stacks library pass and researching something called Equimedian," Keshawn says, "when Christina's charm caught my attention."

"To get back to the question at hand," Cole says, "if the PPs are the subject of writers, it may be in the guise of social protest. You don't have to look far. Julio Cortázar wrote a comic book called *Fantomas Contra los Vampiros Multinacionales*. That's a statement."

"Cortázar is overrated," Keshawn says. "You want a real critique of the Pilgrims, Ballard's *Crash* is where it's at. Technology and desire fused. Like the headsets you set up in people's homes, Jason."

Ramon starts to speak. I feel Cole looking at my bad eye. He tugs gently on my sleeve, and we step away. Two tables down he leans forward. "Are you okay?"

Though attendance is low for a Custodian gathering, the shop is stuffy, and my clothes feel too tight. "Tired, is all."

The edges of his lips pucker up. "Come on, it's me."

"Don't take this the wrong way, but I think I may be getting too old for this stuff. In fact, this is probably going to be my last meeting for a while."

"Really?"

I heave an invisible weight. "I still love reading. But it's time for me to explore larger seas, you know?"

"Expanding your horizons is most commendable," Cole says warmly. "I'd go mad if I restricted myself to science fiction. And I daresay, I wouldn't have been published in the *New American Review*." Cole is the only Custodian whose writing has surpassed the fanzine and semi-pro levels. "But why should branching out," he continues, "mean having to give up your first love?"

"I'll be honest," I say. "I don't know how healthy my relationship with all this is. Sometimes I feel like I'm so preoccupied with three hundred years from now that I'm missing *now*."

"Ah, my friend," he says. "We could certainly all use being more present."

"If you saw my room, I think you'd get where I'm coming from."

He's clearly amused. "You forget, I *have* seen your room."

"Fair enough." I smile. "Anything interesting out there in the great beyond?"

"Oh, plenty. Though Sturgeon's Modified Law still applies."

"His Modified Law? You mean, it's worse than stating that ninety percent of everything is crap?"

Cole says, "The Modified Law states that *one hundred and ten* percent of everything is crap."

"Cute," I say. "But how could it exceed a hundred percent?"

"Because we're talking about everything that exists now—plus stuff that's being created but hasn't been released yet."

We laugh.

"Sorry, a little Pilgrim-inspired humor," he adds. "It seemed a-PP-ropriate."

I groan. "So, who modified Sturgeon's law?"

"Me," he says. "Just now. Caveat aside, I recommend Harry Mathews' *The Sinking of the Odradek Stadium*. A few years old now, but I picked it up on Monday evening last week and read it straight through."

I notice that Ramon, Keshawn, and Christina have started a new conversation of their own, and I'm content to remain on the sidelines with Cole.

I make a mental note of the author and title Cole has alluded to, but the information seems to drift away mere moments after trying to commit it to memory. "You mentioned a writer named Cortázar back there. I think I've heard the name before, but I can't remember where."

Cole's gaze softens into out-of-focus pensive. Then he says, "I think he was included in a dream-themed anthology we talked about back in the day. Dreams may be more of an obsession for writers these days than time, but don't let Ramon find out I said that. Case in point—" Cole sounds distinctly Rod Serling-esque when he utters those words—

"Sturgeon's *Case and the Dreamer*, McIntyre's *Dreamsnake*, Ballard's *The Unlimited Dream Company*, and Malzberg's *Down Here in the Dream Quarter*."

Memories of my three trapdoor dreams rush up to the surface. With bullish determination I bat them away. "To which we could add," I say, "Kate Wilhelm's *Somerset Dreams*."

"Glad you're playing along. As far as oneiric titles go, I'll also nominate Emma Tennant's *Hotel de Dream*. Probably not right for this crowd, but since you want to branch out…"

I make another mental note, hoping this one will stick around longer than the last. "Speaking of crowds, how's life in the commune?"

"Just hit six months at Pillars of Salt," Cole says. "Can you believe it?"

"Remind me, the name."

"It's from a novel by Barbara Paul. She dated one of the founders. I'm telling you, the Lower East Side never felt like such a foreign land."

"You sound inspired."

"I'm going to be writing a short book about it. I've been keeping a journal, and an editor saw it and asked me for an article. He liked it enough to request an expansion. We've already got a publisher."

"So you want my money in exchange for your answer?" I tease.

"Signed copy coming your way, compliments of the author."

I'm genuinely touched. "Thank you."

"You sounded pretty down on Codis before," he says.

"Yeah," I admit. "I think I'm going resign."

Cole studies me. "You're serious."

"They're exploiting people, and I'm doing the scutwork. The hours are long, the shifts are crappy, the customers are never satisfied, and most of them end up becoming addicted or, as we like to say, 'lifetime subscribers.' Whole thing's depressing."

Cole seems to glow. "I'm proud of you," he says. "It's not easy to leave the security of a gig like that. Got anything else lined up?"

"Not yet. Any suggestions?"

Cole looks down. "Wait a minute. This doesn't have anything to do with Shanice, does it?"

"Nah. This is me coming to certain realizations about the path I want my life to take."

He straightens his jacket. "Good."

"It's kind of ironic," I say, crossing my arms. "After our breakup she ended up marrying a PP." I uncross them. "Smart move, I guess. I doubt she would have been satisfied living an ordinary life."

"Are you guys still in touch?"

"No." I clear my throat. "The truth is, I sent Shanice wristplex messages a few times in the aftermath of her moving out, and then again when I heard she was engaged. Okay— more than a few times. An embarrassing number of times. Never heard back. Anyway, none of that has to do with the need I feel to change up my life. I need to get my head on straight and figure out what's right for me. That's all."

"Glad to hear it," Cole says, nodding.

A man gambols over and takes the lull in our conversation as an invitation to join in.

He sports a sparse, blonde, asymmetrical moustache. "Hey guys. I'm Glen. Wondering if you've read anything by William Kotzwinkle? Leiber reviewed this book of his called *Doctor Rat* in which the narrator is a lab rat whose mind has gotten screwy from running through too many mazes. How about that? The rat says things like 'Death is freedom,' and he tells young rats who are being chilled in a thermos full of ice not to worry, they're about to be castrated is all, like him."

Cole whistles. "Lovely."

"This is my cue," I say. "I'm taking off. Cole, you've got my number."

He gives me a bear hug. "And I'm not going to lose it," he says.

I begin to walk away. Ramon catches up with me and proffers his hand. I shake it briefly.

"I was wondering," he says. "If you decide to actually part with your books…"

"Yes, Ramon," I say. "I'll make sure word gets to you."

He blinks. "We Custodians will make you a reasonable offer. More importantly, we'll take care of your stuff. You have a decent collection," he elaborates. "Wouldn't want it to be broken up. You know what they say: haste makes for an apocalyptic wasteland."

Keshawn intercepts us. "Take care of yourself."

"Thanks. You do the same," I say.

I turn around and step outside the thrift shop, a hollowness in my gut.

On my walk home I keep my head down. I set myself a deadline for massively downsizing my collection: one week. The feeling in my stomach turns to nostalgia. A book dealer once told me that instant nostalgia is a luxury that belongs exclusively to the young, because when you're older the only nostalgia you feel is sweetly fermented. Well, youth certainly isn't my excuse.

Maybe instant nostalgia applies to the immature, too. Or the despairing.

THREE

SATURDAY MORNING I wake up feeling weirdly hung over, not from alcohol, but from my trapdoor nightmares.

I leave the apartment in a hurry, making my way to a Brooklyn dump called Jackson's in search of literary bargains. They have none. From there I visit an antique shop that sometimes carries old magazines, and I score three issues of *Vertex*. One of these has a rubber-stamped address of another shop I've never heard of. Something about the address—106a Court—calls out to me, and the name of the store, The Curio, immediately appeals, so I decide to venture forth and explore.

As I head over, I wonder if the place is still in business; the magazine with the stamped address is over ten years old. My speculative excitement grows with each step, and I recall a plethora of "magic shop" stories I read as a teen. When I reach the address, I find that the place still very much exists. I'm both underwhelmed and completely satisfied by its dingy exterior. Dirty storefront glass reveals the diffuse glow of a faint bulb inside, and the building itself, drab and gray, suggests decrepitude. *Herein may lie wonders*, I think.

A surprisingly young man behind a makeshift counter

formed by columns of books watches me approach. To get to him I have to navigate a long, narrow passage between walls crammed from floor to ceiling with books.

As I draw near, he sets down a green, jacketless hardcover with a faded title on its cracked spine, and his gaunt face regards me coolly. "What're you looking for?"

He's probably fifteen years younger than me. How ridiculous that he should have at his command this vast emporium. "Excuse me," I say, "are you the proprietor?"

"I'm his son." He scowls. "What do you need?"

I'm reassured by his response. Nepotism is one of several satisfying explanations for life's inimical unfairness and requires no further thought. "Do you carry science fiction?"

"Upstairs." He points in the direction of a rickety staircase and resumes his reading.

"Would you mind holding on to these?"

I place a bag on the counter, containing my purchases from earlier in the day. "Receipt is inside," I point out.

Wordlessly he takes the bag, which disappears behind the counter.

Up I go, emerging on an even dustier second level overstuffed with books and coin cases and mismatched plates and decorative tiles and incomplete silverware sets and what appear to be broken lamps. After a few valiant heartbeats I study the bookcases, organized in no apparent order. Deep inside this crammed, dusky labyrinth, between stamp-collecting catalogs and railway manuals, I hit the mother lode: three bookcases sagging under the weight of obscure science fiction magazines and paperbacks, again in no decipherable order. I roll up my sleeves and begin the treasure hunt.

Within minutes, I claim two issues of *Odyssey*.

Until now, I'd never even heard of this magazine, but these two specimens, the first with its bright golden Kelly Freas cover, the second with its seductive magenta backdrop and stylized ships, steal my breath the moment I spy them on one of this bookstore's endless shelves. And now that I've scanned their contents, my fear of glossy-but-calorically-empty product has been allayed.

The nonfiction has its hooks in me. The first issue, dated Spring 1976, includes "Charlie Brown's Fan Scene," as well as book reviews by Ted Sturgeon and Bob Silverberg—and there's even an interview with Zenna Henderson. The second issue, from Summer 1976, has more reviews by Silverberg, another fan piece by Charlie Brown, and essays by Ackerman, Pohl and Goldin. Looking at the fiction listings, the only author who grabs my attention is Thomas N. Scortia, whose collection a few years back, *Caution! Inflammable!*, won me over with its Aztec-infused tale "The Goddess of the Cats." Senora Martin and that mermaid mural—sigh. Those two exclamation marks pack a punch, too. Take that, feeble single-exclamation-mark *Dorsai!* and *Cryptozoic!!*

The magazines are dusty but are otherwise in acceptable condition, their covers mostly uncreased. They possess the scent of unrealized potential, and they bear the eccentric touch of Roger Elwood, a loony and obsessive editor. He pumped out fifty-five anthologies from 1972 to 1978. I once heard it said that Elwood showed up at a convention where a fan was seeking signatures for his copy of Clute's *Encyclopedia*—"The Book"—and when Elwood, who'd never heard of the volume, saw that it contained an entry about him, he proceeded to use the convention hotel's staff-only photocopier to make himself a copy. Apparently he also once threw cellophane-wrapped sandwiches at the audience of a Lunacon in an attempt to get folks to attend one of his talks. Still, some of Elwood's misconceived, thoroughly warped projects, like *Androids, Time Machines and Blue Giraffes*, which Elwood edited with TV publicist Vic Ghidalia, have a certain charm. All of which is to say that despite Elwood being more blemish than medallion, I have a soft spot for him and his work, and it inclines me to like these two magazine issues bearing his imprimatur.

The issues' greatest virtue is probably that they don't take up much room. I have to think of this now, because once I walk out of here and head back to the apartment, I'm going to be confronted by the reality of my upcoming downsizing. If nothing else, though, I should buy them as a memento of this experience.

I finish rifling through the current shelf, but the rest of it turns out to be pretty mundane. I keep going.

Time passes in a kind of fugue. Titles start to blur together. Three shelves yield nothing, and I feel my energy wane. But there's a shot of pick-me-up on the very next shelf, Kenneth Bulmer's *On the Symb-Socket Circuit*, which I started reading two years ago, loaned out at a Mayflies gathering, and never received back. Less intriguing but also coming home with me will be Ernest Callenbach's *Ecotopia*, Geoffrey Simmons' *The Adam Experiment* and David R. Bunch's *Moderan*. I examine them as best I can in the weak light. Is my treacherous right eye acting up again? Two of these paperbacks have hole-punched covers, but are otherwise intact, and the third looks unread. I set them aside along with the magazines.

Again, the shelves after this are mostly junk, and the

pendulum swings back toward exhaustion. I need fuel. I advise the young man behind the register that I'll be back shortly to continue scouring the place for more manna. "Knock yourself out," he says.

On my walk I pass a Hardee's, a Perkins Pancakes and a Bob Evans eatery. I opt for the latter, order one of their "farm-sized" chicken and noodles dishes and leave half the food on my plate. My wristplex tells me about half an hour has passed since I left the Curio, and I hustle back.

I receive a surly nod from the cashier and head back to the literary ossuary, now as before, deserted. I've barely resumed my efforts when I make out three hardcovers by William Kotzwinkle—isn't he the writer with whom that Custodian was so enamored? I'll admit that this trifecta tempts me. *Hermes 3000*, an unusual Pantheon hardcover, has a pristine jacket, and though *Fata Morgana* and *Herr Nightingale and the Satin Woman*, both issued by Knopf, are ex-lib, their worn jacket sleeves can be peeled off without difficulty, as can their spine stamps. The presence of this Pantheon edition puts me on high alert for more British goodies, and this attentiveness pays off when I find a pile of *New Worlds Quarterly's*. Anthology number 8 in this series, edited by one Hilary Bailey, has two stories—"The Broken Field" and "Black Hole"—by Nigel Francis, a writer I like, and also two tales by Robert Meadley, whose titles— "Conversations at Ma Maia Metron" and "Love at Lost Sight"—immediately captivate me.

And so it continues, until the clerk downstairs calls out, "Fifteen minutes to closing time!"

"Be right down," I yell back.

I kick into hyper-mode, assessing and re-assessing my

stack of intended purchases with frenetic diligence. I feel guilty about spending any money at all on this stuff, but the store owner clearly has no idea what some of this is worth. Leaving the principle of the thing aside, the books and magazines are in superb condition, and their combined expense won't make a dent on anything except my grocery money. Besides, if I'm going to reduce my collection to its absolute essentials and sell off most of it, I should allow myself these last additions, which will no doubt enhance the collection's overall resale value.

I sweep the over-stuffed shelves one last time, and as I turn around I notice a flyer sticking out from the middle of the last bookcase.

The flyer's color and sheen distinguish it from its surroundings. Printed on a glossy sheet in deep azure, and neatly inserted atop the book row, it looks brand new.

"Closing time," the clerk hollers.

"One second!"

I pull the flyer out and glimpse a word printed in a sleek, minimalist, white font: EQUIMEDIAN. Beneath it is a phone number. I fold it in four and stuff it in my pocket.

I wend my way down the creaky staircase, both arms loaded, clutching the goods tightly to my chest to keep them from toppling over.

As he rings me up, I take another look at the flyer. The word "Equimedian" sounds familiar. Where have I heard it before?

Ah yes, Keshawn Lee. In the Custodians meeting he mentioned researching it at the Columbia University library.

I deposit the flyer on the desk. "Do you know what this is?"

"What?" asks the clerk. "No rebates or coupons, if that's what you're after."

"I found this among the stacks," I say.

"Congratulations."

"Looks brand new."

He continues with his arithmetic.

"It wasn't in the science fiction section when I went out for food. I would have noticed it. But it was there when I came back."

"You're a regular Jules de Grandin."

"My point is that someone left this flyer here during the short time I was away."

"You do realize you're not the only customer who's been in here today, right?" His tone wordlessly adds "*Thank God for that.*"

"Do you happen to remember who went upstairs when I was gone? I was away for maybe thirty-five minutes."

"No clue," he says.

"Try."

"I just did."

I wave at the cash register. "I'll pay you twice whatever you were going to charge me if you try harder."

His forehead stiffens. "Sorry."

Defeated, I refold and repocket the flyer.

He bags up my purchases, in a manner more haphazard than I'd like, and I pay and leave.

Two subway lines later I'm back at the apartment. When I walk in Leon is standing at the edge of the kitchen.

"Hey," he says.

"Hey."

"Wow." He points at the bags. "And that is?"

I stop. "None of your business."

He jeers and juts forward. "More books, isn't it?"

"Don't worry about it," I say.

"Jason, I really don't care what you read or how you spend your time," he says. "But I *am* seriously concerned about the clutter. And the hygiene."

"I'll have your rent on time," I say. "What I do in my room is my concern."

I walk to my bedroom, set the bags down and close the door. I sit on my bed and catch my breath.

I'm surprised by the apartment's stillness.

It's gloomy. Invasive.

The silence is *loud*.

The trapdoor dreams float up to my consciousness and swim around in my thoughts.

To avoid them, I start unpacking my haul. The very first book I pick out of the bag has a gash in the cover that I could have sworn wasn't there when I bought it. The next two paperbacks have obnoxious lime-colored price-stickers that I hadn't noticed on the rear covers, which, as I find out by clawing at them, won't come off without peeling away part of the book. The next stack of magazines is mostly okay, though they appear older and more frail than they looked under the Curio's dim lights. I lay everything out on the bed and do a quick count: seventy-two paperbacks, six hardcovers, and forty-three back issues of rare magazines. I should be shivering with pleasure, with a sense of accomplishment, but as I take a cold, hard look at the display, I mumble, "This looks like a pile of trash."

What was I thinking?

I grab a couple of items at random and hold them up

to the light. The artwork hues and the aged tint of the pages seem to change before my eyes. I squint and look only through my good eye, the left one.

My breath catches in my throat.

The world looks slightly blurry. Recently I've been seeing these web-like "floaters" and there are more than the last time I checked. Holding the books up much closer, they finally resolve themselves into detail and texture. My eyesight appears to have worsened—a lot.

Each thud of my heart tolls disappointment and self-chastisement. I feel myself slouch.

I have barely enough willpower to slide all this junk off the bed and toss it into the bags in which I dragged it up here.

I sit for a while, hearing things I don't want to hear, whispers from the relentless demon of self-doubt.

I turn off the lights and lie down, fully clothed, and something brushes against my right leg. I reach down and pull out a flyer from my pocket.

Its surface shimmers.

The letters on the flyer spelling out EQUIMEDIAN emit a faint light. The letters become bioluminescent creatures, roaming through the coral sea of my bed, swimming towards the island that is my life. The creatures lodge themselves in my mind. The phone number right below the word *occupies* me.

Without turning on the light, I reach toward the phone on my night table.

I dial the number.

"An invitation to personal freedom," the phone whispers. "The dream that soars with the eagle. Balance, symmetry, and mental poise: enlightenment awaits."

This is followed by a click. Oxygen rushes into my lungs.

A female voice says, "Hello. You have, I assume, received one of our select invitations." Her voice has a cadence I can't quite describe.

"Yes." I sound clumsy, uncertain.

"At which location were you given the flyer?"

"It wasn't given to me. Not exactly."

"Ah," the woman says. The voice's magnetic calm is undisturbed by my admission. "Then it was left for you. Where was that?"

"A store called the Curio," I say.

Over the phone I hear a wristplex tapping and buzzing. Then her airy voice continues: "Yes, very good. According to our records, in the science fiction section. Delighted that you've decided to try us out. May I have your name?"

"What is this about?"

"In order to answer all your questions, we just need to confirm we have the right person."

"Fine," I say. "Jason."

"Jason, may I assume that you're interested in our services?"

"Depends—what are they?"

"We provide free instruction in certain techniques of meditation that will allow you to minimize stress in your life," she says. If a voice could ever sell you on an idea, hers is that voice. "It is the first step on a longer road towards self-improvement. We offer personalized treatments, including a complimentary orientation at one of our offices to ground you on our approach."

"I see. And after four or five of these sessions," I say, leery, "you'll recommend a book or two recapping the insights, and that'll be $14.95. Or you'll tack on something else."

"We don't sell any instructional materials," she says, unoffended. "That is part of Equimedian's policy."

"Then explain to me, what's in it for you?"

"We're a non-profit, Jason. We believe in helping humanity for its own sake."

If what she's saying is true, does that make me a charity case? How did they find out about me in the first place? Why was I selected? "So you help people out of the kindness of your hearts."

"Essentially."

"You must have other motives," I insist.

"The dream that soars with the eagle, Jason." She laughs. "I'm being a bit dramatic, of course, but I enjoy that line from our marketing campaign."

"Not very informative."

"Equimedian functions along many parallel tracks," she says. "We enjoy sharing meditation techniques with high-potential individuals to drive broader societal changes. We believe that all significant change stems from within, but not everyone is capable of a transformation. We would be happy to review those details with you during your orientation."

"I'm going to be very clear," I say. "If I show up—and I haven't decided yet—I won't buy *anything*, and I won't do anything that feels uncomfortable."

"Of course. I want to reassure you that if you change your mind, it's no trouble at all. No obligation, no commitment. We can reschedule or cancel any appointment as needed."

"All free of charge."

"Absolutely," she says.

"You're not a front for some church or other, are you?"

"We are not associated with any religion," she states, confident but not arrogant. "We do not endorse any particular theological views."

"How about political ones?"

"Politics are about community, and as I mentioned before, we do believe strongly in improving our global community."

"Ah," I say. "That's it then. You're going to peddle Marxism. Or free love. Or some New Age crap. You're going to tell me that the energy field of certain thoughts can be harnessed to connect telepathically with dolphins."

She chuckles.

I realize that, compared to her relative calm, I'm starting to sound over-the-top. "Let's come back to this question. Who picked me, and why?"

For the first time, a pause that feels unintended. "Your name was referred to us. We were told you are an avid science fiction collector."

I try to think of who could have gotten me involved with this group. Maybe it was a practical joke by one of the Mayflies or the Custodians. Some of them definitely have a twisted sense of humor. Ramon, perhaps?

"You said before you go after high-potential individuals," I say. "What makes you think I fit the bill?"

"That's something we look forward to confirming in person. Our orientations are a kind of two-way interview."

"Why can't I just come by whenever I decide?"

"We prefer to provide a specialized experience and wish to ensure we have the right staff ready for your individual orientation."

"What if want to bring a friend?"

"Sure," she says. "We'd be happy to include him or her."

By now I've worn myself out, weary in the face of her continued politeness and affable professionalism. This is where things stay for several seconds. Finally, I break the détente: "Once I make the appointment, I'm going to tell my roommate where my friend and I are going, and when. Should anything happen to us, he'll alert the authorities."

Empathy on the edge of sadness colors her voice. "Jason, if you have any doubts whatsoever about your safety or about our intent, it would be best for you not to visit us. Nothing good can come from such discomfort, and we wouldn't want to use up your valuable time."

This I didn't expect. Into my momentary disorientation she lands the following words: "May I ask you a question?"

"Okay," I say.

"Do you have any experience with lucid dreaming?"

"No," I say. "Why?"

She says, "This type of activity can correlate with heightened states of cognitive development and intelligence."

"Really?"

"Yes," she says. "Not unusual among our candidates, but not definitive one way or the other."

Memories of the three trapdoor dreams settle over me like a second skin. With great effort I manage to peel them off. "What's your name?" I ask.

"Quiana."

I scribble it down next to the new phone number.

"I hope I've answered your questions in a satisfactory manner," she says. "Is there anything else with which I can assist you?"

"If I decide to make the appointment, do I just call you back at this number?"

"Yes," she confirms. "I hope we'll see you soon, Jason. Enjoy the rest of your evening."

And it's over, flat dial tone of the receiver pressed too hard against my ear.

I hang up. If I called back this instant, would she pick up again or would I get through to someone else who would offer me a different flavor of the same spiel?

I play back our conversation in my head and feel myself entering into a reverie, somehow more susceptible to Quiana's words now than while we talked. A nonprofit organization that promotes anti-stress techniques and undertakes social activism: is that so bad? Contrast this with my own behavior, such as this weekend's book-buying binge.

My genre affliction has reached its terminal stage: either I kill it, or it kills me.

I stare at the invitation.

I turn on the light, and the flyer's luminous effect disappears. An ordinary piece of paper, I tell myself.

Whatever waves I was riding break.

Yet the spell lingers.

FOUR

"REMEMBER THE TIME he presented the award on roller skates?" I ask.

I'm at a Mayflies gathering, in a crowded seventh-floor apartment. The windows are open to a surprisingly cool night breeze, and the drinks have been flowing with similarly unanticipated brio. I've vowed to make only a brief appearance so I can retire from this fan group as I did from the Custodians, but alcoholic lubrication and a general sentimental haze of camaraderie have induced me to stretch my stay from ten minutes to an hour, to another hour, to whatever comes beyond.

"Do *I* remember? Front row seat, my friend," Toby Fux declaims, punctuating the words with his trademark impish smile. On the right side of his forehead, in monotone shades, a small tat of the world map has been distorted to double as a flock of birds.

We've been talking about the Mechanismo, an award voted on by fanzine writers for best non-professional reviewer or commentator upon the field. With one notable exception, which involved the now-dispersed frou-frou contingent of Orange County fans, it's been given out annually for forty years. The individual we've been relating anecdotes about is one Gordon Darcy, an irrepressibly rowdy Falstaff of fandom who for the better part of two decades found increasingly theatrical and bizarre ways to dole out these silly awards.

"I miss Gordy," Pam Santos says. Her inkshow is quite pedestrian; a series of small glyphs along the bridge of her nose, and a slightly faded unalome, the Buddhist symbol for the journey to enlightenment, on her chin.

Toby and I exchange glances that attest to a shared depth of experience.

"To Gordy." I raise my glass.

Toby and Pam join me. We drink.

As the blend of vanilla-sweet Italian liqueur, vodka and orange juice slides down my throat, I suspect that the sense of loss we're feeling is not due to the remembrance of Gordy's last days as an embittered, thrice-divorced, couch-surfing alcoholic, but to the realization that what ultimately killed him was the field's growing *past* him. There was a day when the world of fandom appreciated an impromptu broadsword fight among writers at a convention, and there was a day when it didn't. That transition did something to Gordy's soul, and he faded away.

At this moment I feel a weird kinship to him, as though I too will disappear into some endless crevasse. All evening I've been holding on to the illusion that safety is being ensconced in this apartment, away from the troubles of the universe, but now the illusion starts to slip away from me. Successfully dodging Leon for the last day, I'm not eager to go back home any time soon.

"Does anybody these days write the kind of stuff he did

so well?" Pam wants to know. "Madcap fantasy, but logically worked out."

"Nah," Toby says. "He was one-of-a-kind."

"There are still inventive writers out there," I say, somewhat meekly. "Keshawn was raving about this new oddball satirist, John Slad-something."

Toby's eyes detonate with recognition. "For once, Keshawn has it right. Sladek! He's wild! *The Steam-Driven Boy and other strangers* is a fantastic collection. *Keep the Giraffe Burning*, also brilliant. If you're a fan of the paranoia and surrealism of *The Prisoner* you have to check out Sladek's *The Müller-Fokker Effect*. That's paranoia." He moves his head and sips his Tequila Sunrise.

I finish my own drink in one hasty gulp, set down the tall empty glass at a nearby table, and stare at my soon-to-be ex-compatriots.

Pam smiles at me.

Good time for a refill. At the makeshift bar in the kitchen, I ask for a Tom Collins and am promptly served one. *I was right*, I think, *about this bar being better than the Custodians'*. I take two generous draughts of the gin, lemon, soda, and syrup concoction and rejoin the group, with a fan I don't recognize in tow.

"I do believe more people should experience Sladek's work," Toby is saying. "He's not a trivial writer. Not a great writer, but far from trivial."

"Hi. I'm Gary Stanek," the fan who's just joined us says. "You know what they say about great novels. They wield their craft to break your heart. Bad novels, on the other hand, break your heart because they have no craft to wield."

"Whoever said that is a pompous dolt," Pam says. She

adds, "Bad novels don't break your heart at all. They are, by definition, too shabbily constructed, too ineffective, to have that kind of power. Bad novels simply bore you. They're merely dull, misshapen verbal objects."

"If only their authors could be tried on that account," Toby says.

"But aren't they?" I say. "By us readers? We reward them with dismal reviews and poor sales. Eventually they starve and go away."

The last sentence ends up sounding more autobiographical than I'd intended, and I pick up my glass again.

Pam notices things. "You look preoccupied," she says.

My feet itch and my right eye throbs. I set the glass down.

"Jason, what's going on?" Toby says. "You haven't been quite yourself tonight. Talk to us."

"Okay, fine," I say, breathless. "I'm a day late on my rent. Leon and I have been butting heads. I can't stomach my job. And I think I'm through with science fiction. I can't... I just can't keep losing myself in it. I need to step away from all this. Including, for a time, you lovely people. It's not personal, you understand. I need—space."

"If money's the issue," Toby says, "I'm sure some of us would be willing to pitch in." He casts a look towards the others that manages to be inquiring, solicitous and propitious all at once.

Pam's the first one to jump in. "For sure," she says. "No idea you were in a tough spot. We'll all contribute, right guys? I'm sure Larry wouldn't mind helping out, and—"

"I'd prefer it if we didn't get the whole of fandom involved," I say.

"Just us then," Pam says.

Toby says, "How much are we talking about?"

"I'm short about ninety bucks," I whisper. "But it's not just about the money. I really do need things to change. That's the bottom line. The money problem is not the cause—it's a symptom."

Toby reaches for his wallet. "One step at a time. Here's a twenty."

My skin pricks with heat, a rash of it that spreads from my earlobes and face to my arms and legs. "I can't," I say. "I don't even know when I'll see you again."

"It's not a loan. It's a gift," Toby says. He puts the money in my hand.

"Toby," I say. "You really—"

"I know, I know," he says. "Be quiet. This is what community's about."

Pam pulls out some bills from her purse and hands them over. A few others join in, including Gary.

A wad of cash in my hand, I shake my head, not wanting to cry. "Thank you."

"Jason…" Pam says.

"It occurs to me," Gary says. "I have several PP lottery tickets I have no use for. They were a gift from my mom. They're yours if you want them. It won't cost you anything to transfer them to your name at a local center." He proffers them and smiles.

It seems rude to reject the gesture, particularly since I don't know Gary very well.

Now is not an opportune moment for me to share my opinions about the PPs. Besides, I can always toss out the tickets later.

"I really appreciate the help," I say, accepting the tickets and putting them in my pocket along with the cash. "And I'm sorry about everything," I stammer, and wave my hands. "I'm… going to call it a night."

Toby says, "Are you sure about this?"

Pam says, "Maybe you could hang around and we could play a game of Mouse Trap or Rebound. A little light entertainment might be just the thing."

I pretend my wristplex has buzzed me with a message, so I have an excuse to look away.

"See you guys around," I say.

I turn and without glancing back march toward the door.

Outside, the sounds of the party filtering through to the corridor, I pause and lean against the wall for a few moments, trying to regain my sense of self.

Feeling sturdier, I decide to walk the twenty-five minutes home. At the fifth or sixth crossing, waiting for the light, I look up at the sky. The smog is too thick to provide a clear view, and I can only make out indistinct haloes of light. At the next crossing I try again, and I see those same spread-out blurs of light—and my stomach tightens as I realize they're not stars, but floaters at the edge of my field of vision.

Closing one eye at a time, I determine that these floaters are in the left.

My so-called good eye.

By the time I'm on my street my steady clip and the hardening coldness of this new predicament have sobered me up completely and pushed me into a kind of uber-reality.

I fumble with the key in the lock of our door and curse myself. Inside it's dark and quiet. Apparently Leon's not home—thank God for small favors. Nevertheless, out of habit I creep towards my room and shut the door gently behind me. I head straight for the dresser near my bookcase.

I open up the second drawer, and behind my broken electronic Simon game board, behind the socks and the little pile of diaries stretching back to my twenties, I locate the small metal tin where I keep valuables. In it I deposit the money and PP tickets the Mayflies have gifted me.

I'm still a little short on rent, but I'm much closer than when I went out this evening. And the way to close the gap is staring me in the face—look at all these books and magazines. I'll select choice items and take them down to a couple of book dealers I know. That's what I'm going to do.

In bed, I can't seem to wind down, so I pull up the wristplex list I made last week about the things I wanted to accomplish. I start feeling bad almost instantly—but then I get to item number 5 on the list: *Call Jill more often. She's dependable and kind.*

Not a bad idea. I check the time. Not yet nine, and this is the weekend. I dial her number.

"Hello?" she says.

"Hey, Jill."

"Jason! I was starting to worry about you."

"Well no need; here I am."

"How are things going?"

I sigh. "Do you have a few minutes?"

"Sure, sure. Let me get the hot water off the stove. You know me and chamomile. Be right back."

When she returns, I make good on my threat and unload about everything. "I'd like to think this is all part of a growth phase," I say at the end of my little recap. "As opposed to a midlife crisis."

She chuckles. "Don't commit either way just yet," she says. "Tell me more about your eyes."

"Okay."

"When did the problems start?"

I take a breath. "Are you sure I'm not interrupting anything?"

"I'm sure." I hear her sip her tea. "Talk to me."

"Well, I've needed glasses since I was four, and when I was six, I required some surgeries on my right eye…. Anyway, the outcome was less than perfect, and I rely on my left eye for everyday tasks."

"And that's where you're having issues?"

"Yeah," I say. "I'm very near-sighted, which I'm told increases the odds of what they call a retinal detachment. Floaters are a bad sign. They could indicate an imminent PVD—a kind of detachment."

"Jason—"

"Then again, it's not unusual to have more floaters as you get older." Coincidentally, my deterioration started shortly after I finished reading *Backflash*, the third volume in Laurence James' Simon Rack series. When the fourth volume was published, I refused to read it merely because its title inspired angst. Who knows, maybe that title isn't meant literally, but I'm too much of a sissy to find out: no *Planet of the Blind* for this reader.

"Is everything else normal?"

"Eyelid's been acting up a little too."

"That was a long pause." Jill's tone shifts. "It's worse than you're letting on, isn't it?"

"What do you want me to say?"

"Jason, given that you pretty much depend on your left eye to function, I strongly suggest you see an ophthalmologist right away."

"It's not that serious."

"Says Jason Velez, who studied ophthalmology at which school again?"

"Hey, it's *my* eye. I'm the one seeing through it. That should confer upon me *some* level of expertise."

"You'll get credit when and only when you make the appointment." Then she speaks more gently. "It all makes sense now, everything you've been talking about."

"Wait a second. You're saying my issues with Codis, my decision to quit science fiction, is somehow related to my eyes?"

"Don't you think it's at least plausible that your anxiety could be making difficult things worse? It's probably amplifying ordinary doubts into wrenching uncertainties. Once you get your eyes checked out things might not seem quite so dire."

There's no trying to dissuade Jill when she gets like this, and why should I? Her intentions are good and her logic sound. Besides, there's no downside to getting my eyes checked, though I'll have to stay with Codis until then to make sure I have medical benefits. If the ophthalmologist discovers a problem and action is needed, I won't be able to afford treatment without insurance.

"You're right," I say. "Maybe I've been putting it off."

"You're welcome. I'm glad we talked about this."

"Thank you. I am too."

"Can I ask you something else?"

"Ask away."

"You mentioned downsizing your collection."

"Correct."

"Our library could use some donations," she says.

"Perfect," I say. "Two birds with one stone. And I'll have the pleasure of knowing I'm corrupting the impressionable minds of Brentwood High."

"I was also thinking you could use some help. I know from personal experience how hard it is to get rid of stuff. After Dean and I split up… Anyway, when you do it alone, all these memories surface, and you hold on to things for the wrong reasons. I'm happy to assist with the culling."

Scanning my shelves, I can't argue with her. "Okay. I'm going to take you up on it. When would be a good time?"

"Hang on." I hear rustling paper. "What are you doing tomorrow morning?"

"It's Sunday," I say. "Probably sleep in, have a late breakfast, waste the day and then berate myself for not having accomplished anything."

"Change of plans. I can be there at nine. And I'll bring some breakfast."

"Jill," I say, leaning back. "Why are you so nice?"

"You've known me since kindergarten," Jill says, "which is long enough to know I'm not that nice."

"True."

"Have a good night."

"You too."

❧

The following morning Jill arrives in a light green skinny rib vest and a high-waisted pair of dark denim flares and, as promised, she comes bearing gifts: a croissant for her and one of my favorite breakfasts, a raisin "Brooklyn jawbreaker"—a type of bagel—with cream cheese for me. I put on a pot of coffee. I notice she's changed her thick ash-blond hair from the last time I saw it: now she's sporting it in a long feather cut. Her pale gray eyes, framed by fine spider-web tats that radiate from her eyebrows, and illuminated by some secret inner vision, regard me with kindness. But I can tell she's also on a mission. We exchange pleasantries over breakfast in the kitchen and then perform a quick inventory of the bookshelves and piles in my room.

She whistles. "You've added a lot of books since the last time I was here."

"Way to rub it in."

"Let's shoot for three hours and see how far we get," Jill says.

"Works for me."

After I go over the criteria I'd like us to use to decide which books to set aside for possible removal, Jill begins on one of the major shelves, and I opt for a small tower of books adjacent to the night table.

Immediately begin the difficulties.

The first thing I encounter is the tetralogy of *Quark* anthologies edited by Marilyn Hacker and Chip Delany, except in my case it's a sad little trilogy, since I'm missing volume three. Do I set aside volumes one, two and four and make a note to hunt down three, or give up the lot? *A landmark anthology set*, I tell myself. *Keep it for now*. I change my mind and decide it has to go, then change my mind again and re-add it to the books to keep. Moving on. Here's a cluster of anthologies co-edited by David Gerrold and Stephen Goldin: *Protostars*, *Generation*, *Alternities*, and *Ascents of Wonder*. I flip through each volume's table of contents. *Protostars* has a Tiptree story I don't remember reading, called "I'll Be Waiting for You When the Swimming Pool is Empty," and a story by a writer who's become popular of late, Edward Bryant, that I should probably check out before I do away with the book. Cole Wellmann actually met Bryant last year at a convention into which real Russian vodka had been smuggled, and he told me the man was warm and friendly even when acerbic, and that his chuckle was like gravel. "Hell of a short story writer," Cole said, and based on that alone I need to give Bryant a chance. Reading these two stories shouldn't take long, maybe twenty or thirty minutes. I can do it later today, so I set them aside. *Generation* and *Alternities* go hand-in-hand, both of them neat, tight Dell paperbacks with vivid covers and single-word titles that slant diagonally towards the upper right-hand corner. The former contains not one but two Tiptree's, I see, as well as two Bryant's (one a collaboration), and the latter, another Bryant, plus a story titled "Womb, with a View" by an author—Steven Utley—who has also been recommended to me. Next up is an Ace double containing work by Neal Barrett, Jr. and K. M. O'Donnell. Is K. M. O'Donnell the guy Keshawn keeps harping about? No, wait, that was Kevin O'Donnell, Jr. I scan the K. M. O'Donnell novel, *Dwellers of the Deep*. Looks like bitter stuff. I remember now that Cole was not particularly impressed by it. Thought it was self-indulgent: look at the suffering artist, the terrible conditions a writer must work in, blah blah blah. Now it comes back to me, too, that Cole thinks Kris Neville is better than O'Donnell, Jr. and O'Donnell put together. What was the name of the Neville collection he recommended? Oh yeah, *Mission: Manstop*. I think I have that somewhere. I rummage through the pile on the other side of the bed and locate my copy. There, preserved.

I glance at the clock, disheartened. Fifteen minutes in, I've barely made a dent.

Meanwhile, Jill has gotten through almost half her assigned shelf.

She sees me struggling. "I think we need new criteria to help make faster decisions."

"You seem to be moving swiftly." I'm afraid to ask which of her piles is comprised of keepers and which of discards, since one clearly outsizes the other.

"Here's a thought," she says. "Let's set aside all anthologies for now and deal with them later."

"I like it." With two rapid scoops I move the anthologies from the pile-in-progress to the bed and leave the novels and short story collections behind. The remnants include books with titles like *The Adolescence of P-1* and *The Masters of Solitude* and *The Doppelganger Gambit* and *The Secret Galactics* and others whose mere brush against my consciousness evokes rich memories of the dusty places where I found them, the crazy things I imagined they might be about, what my pals gushed about them. The web of associations becomes a net, tangling me up on my journey of relinquishment.

"Something else," Jill says. "Maybe you should keep at most one novel and one story collection per author—at least for now."

I balk at this. One novel and story collection *per author*? Science fiction tends to attract prolific types—it's not unusual for writers to generate twenty, fifty, or even seventy books. How can I possibly decide *which* novel or short story collection to retain? I grumble and decide on a little experiment.

I remove novels from various shelves populated by partial or complete author bibliographies.

"Two books max per author seems harsh, but you may be on to something," I tell Jill. "Things to consider: publisher prestige, cover blurbs, artwork, whether or not I've already read something by that person." To that I silently add: how I respond to random passages, what reliable sources have told me, canonicity in the genre…

"If you really want a fresh start, you should probably give up most books you've already read. Because let's be honest, you'll probably not re-read them."

"True," I acknowledge.

With this latest declaration we proceed to eliminate large chunks of my collection. Most of the Golden Age stuff can be tossed out, along with many of the 50s "classics" and even some of the 60s titles. Within thirty minutes we have enough books to fill at least five boxes. I have to hand it to Jill. I couldn't have done this without her.

"What do you think?" I say, marveling at the display. "A box is for you. Let me set this aside, let's see—"

"My students are going to be very happy." She grins. "And I'd say we've earned lunch; you can give me the books after."

"Deal," I say.

FIVE

"BRAINS BEFORE BEAUTY," Cole says, opening the door of the PP lottery office for me.

"If you insist," I rejoin, crossing the threshold.

The inside of the office is too brightly lit, and the recycled air carries an antiseptic, vaguely nauseating flavor. Cole and I exchange looks. Our view is occupied almost entirely by a white counter, behind which stands a man keying something directly into a screen we can't see, recessed in one of two columns that protrude from the counter's edges.

"Welcome," the man says, pausing his work and making eye contact with both of us.

He holds his gaze longer than might seem tactful. His preternatural tan competes with cultivated stubble for the real estate of his broad chin and jaw, and his sideways-slicked hair has been fixed recently. He wears a navy-blue corduroy suit over a black shirt. His face is tatted with a trompe-l'oeil showing the skin being opened to expose mechanical circuits within. I shiver a little. "Are you here to purchase tickets for the lottery?"

"Actually," Cole says, "we already have tickets. My friend Jason got two from a friend and he'd like to change them over to his name."

Part of the reason I agreed to come here is that Cole volunteered to do most of the talking. My job is to take mental notes. Cole thinks he might get an article out of this that he can sell to *Harper's* or *Esquire*. Considering his encyclopedic knowledge not only of science fiction, but more broadly, literature, science, and history, I don't think his designs are unrealistic. He needed a credible reason for the visit, which is where I come in. Because we have similar feelings about the PPs, I know what kind of piece he's going to write, and I'm happy to support him. Underneath the sleeve of his gray silk shirt, his wristplex is actively recording everything being said. Such a move is not strictly legal, but he'll be smart enough to paraphrase things in his essay.

"I'm happy to help," the man behind the counter says.

A rectangular section of the counter in front of me becomes translucent, and the surface displays writing in a dark blue font, with a virtual keyboard right beneath it.

"Please complete the following questionnaire if you'd be so kind," the man instructs.

I hesitate and then glance at the first question. It asks for my age. The next one, my occupation. The one after that, my address.

"This is getting a little personal for my tastes," I say, lifting my hands from the virtual keyboard.

"Ah," the man says. "I understand. Those questions are merely intended for informational purposes. Feel free to skip them. To complete the name transfer, the following form is required."

The screen now asks me to enter the name of the individual for whom the tickets were meant, and then my own name. Fighting my instinct, I type in "Gary Stanek" and then "Jason Velez."

"Please thumb-sign."

I do so.

"The tickets, if I may."

Cole places them on the counter, which returns to its solid egg-shell white.

The man runs some kind of scan on them with a device behind one of the columns. "The transaction is complete," he says. "If either of these tickets should win any prize in the next lottery, you'll be notified at once Mr. Velez."

"When will it take place?" Cole inquires.

"Three weeks from now."

"And how much do tickets cost, if I wanted to purchase some right now?"

"After a brief background scan of—"

"Never mind. Just for kicks, what are the odds of winning?"

"I'm afraid I can't disclose that," the man replies.

"Look, we're well aware that the odds of winning an ordinary lottery are lower than those of being hit by lightning while simultaneously being devoured by a shark," Cole says, and smiles. "Are you saying they're even lower here?"

"We prefer to keep information about our lottery confidential."

"Something else I'm curious about," Cole continues, unfazed. "How are the winners chosen? With something like the Lotto, the means are obvious."

"Our approach is superior," the man says. "We use computers to generate random numbers."

Cole leans forward, resting his right arm on the counter.

"Hold on a minute," he says. "You mean to tell me the winners are chosen by a computer program?"

"In essence."

Cole pauses for effect. "But it's been proven mathematically that computers are incapable of generating *genuinely* random numbers." He glances at me, relishing the moment.

"Quite so," agrees the man. "At least, in the case of classical computers. The PPs rely on quantum computation to circumvent that problem. The technical details are beyond my humble intellect, but by measuring the movements of photons through microscopic, semi-transparent mirrors, the PPs are able to create true random number combinations. I suppose one could argue it's simply a more sophisticated form of Lotto after all." He smirks in a self-satisfied way.

"For which we have to take your word," Cole says. "Why not make things more transparent to the public? It's not like you couldn't use some positive publicity."

"The lottery offers ordinary people the extraordinary possibility of living outside of their present circumstances— of getting a peek around the corner of time itself. It's the ultimate invitation to personal freedom, don't you think? It should begin with a certain mystique and sophistication."

Something about this answer sets me on edge.

"Simplicity is the ultimate sophistication," Cole replies. Then he says, "Have you ever played?"

"Unfortunately, my position here bars me from participation," the man says. "What a shame," I mumble.

Intuiting my discomfort, Cole says, "Thank you for your time."

We begin to move away from the counter when a beep

sounds from behind the right column, and the man's tone changes in a subtle way.

"Mr. Velez," he says. "I've just received an alert. There's a communication for you."

Cole does the frowning for both of us.

"What kind of communication?" I say.

"It appears to be a voice message, left by one Shanice Vega."

I'm not sure if my face suddenly pales or becomes flushed. All I know in that moment is that my response involves the rapid redistribution of blood-flow across my body. "Did you say Shanice Vega?"

I turn to face Cole, as though somehow the familiarity of his face will make this news less startling.

"That's correct," the man says. "I can play it for you here or download it to your wristplex."

Shanice. After all this time? Possibilities dart through my mind, increasingly implausible, insensibly wishful. I realize I'm too stunned to make a decision regarding the means of the message's conveyance.

Cole comes to the rescue. "I believe Jason would prefer the download."

"Yes," I say a moment later. That sounds right. I certainly don't want this creep listening in.

He dials various codes in the screen to his right, and says, "It's been done. The message is on your device."

A soft alert buzz on my wrist confirms it.

"In your experience, is this unusual?" Cole probes. "After all, how often do the PPs want to talk directly to us lowly plebs?"

Trying and failing to keep my ego and expectations in

check, I realize that Cole is right. The PPs interact with us as they see fit. There're news stories about their reaching their temporally-displaced arms into our political system, trying to get their research and development centers to be declared tax-free and so on. And yet we have no ready access to them.

"Mr. Velez must be a special individual," the man says. He smiles. "As you say, this is not a frequent occurrence. I myself, for instance, receive all my communiqués as written texts. I've never had the pleasure of a voice message."

"Don't give up hope," Cole says. "If normal people like us can win this lottery, *anything* is possible, right?"

We leave.

We don't speak much on the subway ride home. My mind won't shut up about Shanice.

Sensing this, Cole does his best to distract me with intellectual stimulation. "Did you ever stop to consider this: Folks who run lotteries rely on the addictive properties of the risk-and-reward mechanism hardwired into our heads," he says, "to overcome the inherent irrationality of the premise. They dangle a delicious 'What if?' before prospective players, making us drool in anticipation of pipe dreams. And you know what else does that? Science fiction. In exchange for a small admission fee, it teases us with futures that will likely never come. Seen like this, they're both kind of preposterous, don't you think?"

I ponder his point. "At least science fiction is artistic," I say.

"Sometimes," he chides.

Inside the apartment, I offer Cole beer and he readily accepts one of Leon's "blue bullets," as Leon and his Wisconsinite brethren like to call them. Good thing he's at work.

I'm not a big fan of American-style lager and am sufficiently inebriated on my own emotions so as to render alcohol unnecessary, so I opt for water.

After his first sip, Cole rolls up the right sleeve of his shirt and punches in some commands on his wristplex. His countenance darkens. He messes with the device some more.

"Son of a bitch," he sputters.

I tear my eyes away from my own wristplex, where the blinking red light message indicator does its best to hold me in its hypnotic sway. "What's wrong?"

"Their office must have had some kind of jamming signal," Cole says. "My wristplex didn't record *anything*. Not only that. It looks like it's completely dead. I should sue them."

"Sorry man! Mine looks to be fine. They must somehow target active recorders."

"Get me some paper," Cole says. "Since I don't have audio, I need to write down as much as I can remember right away."

"You got it."

I bring him a pen and a notepad and he scribbles away furiously for five minutes.

During that time I contemplate whether to play Shanice's message, but I can't bring myself to do it. As much as I like and admire Cole, I need to listen to this alone. Who knows what Shanice will say? More significantly, who knows how I'll react?

"You should make notes too," Cole says when he's finished. "It'll be more accurate if it's based on two sets of recollections."

"I…"

"I know you're thinking about that message, but try to focus for a minute." Cole doesn't speak with anger, merely firmness, but all the same I resent the imperiousness a little. Still, we've come this far.

"Okay."

The exercise proves helpful and my irritation at Cole's bossiness passes. Jotting down whatever details I can remember somehow expunges my bad vibes, cleansing me. Stray words lead to a complete phrase, which in turn leads to another, and then—

I stop.

"Oh shit," I whisper, staring at the words before me. "Now I know where I've heard it before. It was bugging me the whole time."

Cole studies my piece of paper. "What are you talking about?"

"'The ultimate invitation to personal freedom.' That's what the guy said."

"You're saying you've heard that before?"

"I think so," I say, doing my damnedest to recollect. "Yes. Very similar. I think the recording said, 'An invitation to personal freedom'."

Cole sets down his beer. "What recording?"

So far I've only told Jill about my contact with Equimedian. Call it paranoia, or perhaps the desire to avoid being judged as pathetically desperate. Cole strikes me as someone I can trust, though sometimes he can be fierce in his judgments of others. But what choice do I really have? If I want his help in trying to get to the bottom of this, I'm going to have to risk it.

"Let me tell you about my weekend…"

SIX

FOR A GOOD portion of Jason Velez's life, science fiction held no special appeal.

Jason wasn't a particularly voracious young reader. Ryan, Jason's younger brother, adored science fiction and horror and insisted that Jason read some of his pulp magazines, but Jason, despite being older, found them unsettling. As a result, Jason gave Ryan the nickname Boglins, which stuck on account of their parents thinking it was cute. In high school Jason tried science fiction again, but the romps he sampled were little more than cowboys and Indians transliterated to Venus, tired Westerns melodramatically writ cosmic, and they soon faded from his memory.

It wasn't until Jason turned twenty-eight that he soared headfirst into the stratosphere of the fantastic. Most people can't reconstruct the exact date a particular hobby or aesthetic affinity is born, but Jason can. It happened on Wednesday the 16th of April 1969.

The previous day, Jason's phone rang a few minutes past seven in the morning.

"Hello?"

"It's time to get ready for school, sleepyhead."

"What?" he said. "Who is this?"

"If you don't get out of bed now you're going to be late, and Mr. Dobs won't tolerate that kind of behavior."

The air in Jason's bedroom stifled him. He took a deep breath and tasted a funny sourness coming up from his throat. "Mom?" he said. "Is that you?"

"Who else, Jason?"

Leaning on his side, his right arm was pins and needles. "Mom, what's going on?"

"You're going to be late, Jason. Your father and I tried so hard to keep you boys punctual. Respectable." A sob. "You don't know what it's like until you have kids of your own. Do you hear me?"

"Mom, what's wrong? Has something happened?" Another sob, and then a click, and then silence.

Jason rubbed his eyes and checked the time to make sure he hadn't misread it. He stood up, too fast, and after the blood rush faded, he dialed his parents' number.

His father, William, picked up. "Son?"

"Dad, what's going on? Mom called."

"Yeah."

"Is she okay?"

Impatiently: "What did she tell you?"

"That I'm going to be late for school."

His father cursed. "She was meant to tell you something else."

"What on earth?"

"We're having a family dinner tonight," he said.

Jason could tell his dad was forcing himself to speak those words as a substitute for a different set of words on his mind. Jason imagined he could hear his dad clenching his jaw muscles and puppeteering rebel vocal cords. "Dinner?"

"*Family* dinner," his dad said, sounding strangled. "That's all. Be here at six sharp. Dress for the occasion."

"I can't at six," Jason says. "I've got work—"

"Listen to me, you ingrate—"

"Fine, whatever, Jesus, I'll figure out a way to make it work. What the hell is all this?"

His dad ended the call.

Should Jason call back? His dad wasn't liable to tell him more than he already had, and Jason had no desire to further provoke the old man's wrath. Mom's incoherence? Jason thought back. And then he realized something. If he didn't selectively ignore certain memories, her symptoms were not completely unfamiliar. She had regressed before: during moments of tough decision-making, she had talked about events that happened years earlier.

Christ.

Jason swallowed.

After all this time, he thought, *are they getting a divorce?*

While he washed his face, while he shaved, while he dressed and combed his hair, while he put an English muffin in the toaster, while he spread butter across it, while he drank his coffee and rinsed the dishes in the sink and brushed his teeth, the idea of divorce, hysterically ballooned at first by newness and shock, deflated and deflated and deflated, becoming less startling and unbelievable by the moment, until it was quieted into a steady hum in his consciousness.

By the time he arrived at his parents' house that evening, half an hour early, he had completely reconciled himself to their divorce, or at least told himself that he had, and his balloon of worry was now filled only with logistical questions. Who would stay in this house? Or were they selling it? Would either of his parents move to a different city, or God forbid, to a different state? Had either of them—he'd have to brave his way through this one—found a new partner? He had a right to know if a stepmom or stepdad were in the cards, didn't he?

When he rang the door, nothing happened for a long time, and then his mom appeared, wearing a yellow shift dress years past its prime. The Florentine wrist tat of a bracelet design reminded Jason of when she'd read to him in bed when he was a child, and how she'd occasionally smoothed over his unruly hair. Presently she lavished him with attention while simultaneously deflecting his questions, a unique mom talent. His dad, meanwhile, was nowhere to be seen.

"I'm home!" Jason yelled when they passed the staircase on their way to the living room.

A door slammed shut upstairs.

At the dining room table, place mats had been set for four, and as he took his seat Jason imagined that his brother Ryan, for whom punctuality was always a challenge, might take a while to show up. Jason made idle chatter with his mom until he couldn't take it anymore.

"Mom, this is ridiculous. I'm going to get Dad," Jason said.

"Stay put," she said. "Your father will be down shortly." Jason sighed. "Will you at least tell me what's for dinner?"

The fullness of her smile erased years and wrinkles alike. "Your favorite."

It had been so long since Jason had come over for dinner that wasn't sure which favorite she had in mind. He thought about the foods of his youth, when his mother was attempting to instill in him a sense of cultural continuity with his two-generation-removed Andalusian lineage. "Gazpacho and fried fish?"

Her florid lips remained trapped in that smile.

He tried again, this time going for something more contemporary. "Hamburger Helper?"

She shook her head.

"Quiche? You know I like quiche."

She shook her head again.

He plopped his arms on the table with too much force, and the silverware rattled. "I give up," he said.

"Pasta primavera, silly, with a side of zucchini bread."

Jason's mouth opened and closed. Pasta primavera was one of his brother's favorite dishes, not his. Clearly the pressures of divorce, or whatever momentous decision his parents had made, were messing up mom's memories.

A loud thumping on the stairs announced his dad's arrival.

Wordlessly, Jason's father sat at the table and began to pray. The muscles of his sizeable arms rippled with tension as he placed his elbows on the table, and the nautical and Japanese tats on his neck and right cheek tautened as he muttered the words.

"Dad?"

Jason hadn't witnessed this particular ritual since he and Ryan were boys. Had his mom's regressive escapism become contagious?

"Dad?"

"Keep your mouth shut while we thank the Lord."

"Bill!" snapped his mom.

Jason recoiled, as though physically stung. He rose, chair teetering but not falling, and marched towards the front door.

"Come back here!" mom screamed.

She started sobbing, which soon turned to wracking spasms.

Jason neither advanced nor retreated. "What the hell is going on?"

He checked the time. Eight minutes past the hour.

His dad finished the prayer and stared at Jason with a face carved into apoplectic rigidity.

"Why won't you talk to me?" Jason said. "Mom? Dad?" He approached the table but didn't sit.

"It was supposed to give him all sorts of advantages in life," his dad said. "Lord knows he needed them. The ability to think more quickly. To focus." His eyes were hollow.

"What?"

"Sit down, son."

Jason did so, limbs numbing.

Dad spoke to the place settings, to the table, to the cutlery, to the walls, to all the un- alive things around them, meticulously avoiding his wife and son. "He signed the paperwork; he knew there were risks. Of course now they say there's no connection between what happened and what they did to the insides of his head." None of the dead things replied; neither did the living. "Your brother Ryan isn't coming home for dinner," Dad said.

"That's why I made you your favorite." Mom sniffled and dabbed at her eyes. The toothy smile peeking out from behind the ruined mascara was a white glimmer under a mud rainbow.

Jason placed his arms on the table, for fear that otherwise they'd fall off his body. "Where is Ryan?"

"He signed up for the program six months ago," his dad

said. "It all happened so fast. One of his friends heard about it and he was so excited. Free room and board for the duration of the program, which was five weeks, and a generous weekly stipend. 'This will be similar to clinical trials,' he told us. 'Except that it'll involve PP technology. I'll be helping them figure out new means of mind-to-mind communication. I'll be making a difference.' We told him to be skeptical, to read the fine print. But he was an adult. He decided. He didn't want you to worry. He made us promise not to tell you. He wanted to let you know when he came back. Wanted to impress you with his new skills. After it was all over, he called us. He didn't sound like himself. He asked if he could come home. We said, 'Of course, son. We're here for you.' He was a shell. He slept most of the day. Wouldn't talk. Wouldn't go outside. No interest in anything. Said they'd robbed him of the ability to dream. We tried to stimulate him, to get him interested in life again. Nothing worked. He wasn't himself anymore. And then… Poor Boglins."

As uttered by his father, Ryan's old nickname, Boglins, became an expressionless linguistic cadaver, a cipher.

"Ryan is…?" Jason couldn't bring himself to speak the word. Later, in the coming decade, he would puzzle about this inability to deploy language at a critical moment, and he would ask himself if it fueled in him the desire to drown himself in words. But right now Jason was stuck in place, at an altitude from everything, separate and above it. He'd become a ceiling-mounted chandelier that wouldn't light up.

"Yes," Dad said.

"Ryan is never this late," his mom said.

Dad directed his still angry gaze at her, and Jason, though it wasn't meant for him, felt himself grazed by its withering intensity. "Stop it, Pat," Dad said. "*Stop, stop, stop.* He's gone. *Our boy is gone.*"

"Ryan is…" Jason repeated, with the same non-ending as before, though this time it wasan assertion rather than a question. His brow, beaded with something clammy-yet-cold, furled up into a mass of wrinkles. He had so many memories of Ryan welling inside him that he felt like his skull was about to burst. "*What happened?*"

"One day after work I came home and found him," his dad said. "He hung himself in our bedroom with one of my belts. I called 911 but there was nothing they could do."

"*Holy fuck.*"

"Jason," Mom admonished.

"We couldn't *prove* it was the PPs' fault, but we knew. Ryan never talked about what happened during the program. The PPs claimed that he fell into a depression because he'd had unrealistic expectations going in, and when the tech they were testing didn't work out, he became disappointed and apathetic. They argued that he had a history of depression. Sons of bitches."

"Ryan must be caught up somewhere," Mom said. "Please make sure his food stays warm." She glided upstairs and a door clicked shut.

"Dad," Jason said. He didn't know how to go on.

"If you want any more details—"

"Not right now."

"Can you believe the gall—someone working for the PPs came by to offer condolences."

"I can't hear anymore," Jason said.

"We have the paperwork he signed. I can show it to you. I can—"

"Fuck the paperwork."

"Ryan's dead. You got that?"

"You can be such a prick," Jason said, because his parents were insane and he had lost his brother. Because a part of him wished that Ryan could be yanked back from the dead so that Jason could ask him how he thought not telling him about this program was a good idea. Because he had memories of happy days together when they were young that would cause him to retch if he confronted them squarely.

"A prick, huh?" Dad had mistaken Jason's ribbing for serious provocation, and Jason could see slaughter dancing in his father's eyes. "Real goddamned shame," he said, "that *Ryan* was the one who had to enroll in that experimental program. That he's the one we lost."

"There's time to remedy that."

On his way out of the house he paused by the stairs. "That was delicious, Mom!" he yelled.

Before he could hear her sobbing again, he slammed the door behind him.

The next day, bored and sleep deprived and hung over and raw after spending the better part of the previous night crying and drinking, wanting to climb up the world's umbilical cord and jam himself back into a warm, safe place, he shuffled over to the corner store to buy more booze. There he saw a trippy-looking paperback, Michael Moorcock's *Behold the Man*, and it reminded him of Boglins, so he picked it up and started reading, opening for himself a host of strange new doors he had never known existed.

SIX AND CHANGE

IT'S PAST MIDNIGHT and I'm having trouble sleeping. I keep thinking about Shanice's message. It was short, frustratingly so: *Jason, Jason. I hope you're well. I wish we could see you. Maybe there's a way. Ask the PPs. And remember, don't let yesterday have undue influence over tomorrow.*

I listen to it several times to make sure I haven't missed anything, but the starting and ending pauses delineate it with irrevocable precision. *I wish we could see you.* What the hell is that supposed to mean? Who's that "we," anyway? And why the "Maybe" in the following sentence? Doesn't Shanice know what's technologically possible and what isn't?

I tell myself that the message is curt because of whatever restrictions the PPs have in place on sending information backwards through time. But that interpretation seems overly benevolent. With equal concision, she could have been more direct and concrete.

In the end, I delete the message. I've no intention of asking the PPs anything.

Of course, the moment I erase Shanice's voice I feel like a fool. What if I change my mind? Have I destroyed the only possible means of theoretically reaching her?

Forget Shanice, I think. *Focus on the realities of your life.*

Immediately my consciousness turns toward my declining eyesight. Why haven't I made the doctor's appointment yet? I'm irritated with myself about that, but smart enough to know that this path will not bring me any closer to sleep. I turn on the night table lamp. Its decadent, disco-inspired, frosted glass globe on a gilt metal base casts exactly the kind of soft, fuzzy light I'm looking for.

With disdainful apathy I rummage through the night table drawer, mentally critiquing everything but telling myself not to be too vicious. These are my belongings, after all, and thus a reflection of my person. Yet there's no denying that these paperbacks form a veritable parade of outrageous covers, incoherent scene excerpts, and hokey taglines. Take this first one at the top, John Boyd's *Sex and the High Command*. Boyd, the author of works such as *The Girl with the Jade Green Eyes*, *The Organ Bank Farm*, and *Barnard's Planet*, which I once enjoyed, is here firing on wobbly cylinders. He posits Vita-Lerp, an orgasm-inducing drug commonly called the V-bomb, which ultimately leads to the eradication of men. I peruse a few chapters and put it back down. There is now little chance that I'll ever want to seek out other Boyd titles long ago committed to memory in case they turned up in a used bookstore, once-dreamed jewels like *The Doomsday Gene*, *The I. Q. Merchant* or *Andromeda Gun*.

That's how much the V-bomb has turned me off. And look at this other paperback, T. L. Sherred's *Alien Island*, the garish, vaguely cubist cover of which proclaims, "A hopeless drunk was the only Earth representative the Regans would accept!" Brian N. Ball's *Timepivot* depicts a naked female body whose head is a giant ear, above which, in the sky, orbits an even more oversized eyeball, and this cover asserts: "Frozen in space, time waited to entrap the lost or strayed…" *What does this even mean?* I think. Hasn't Einstein brought space and time together? How has time detached itself from space and become "frozen" *in* it? Dan Morgan and John Kippax's *The Neutral Stars* declares that "the stars, all space, could be their hunting ground—as it already was for some unknown alien," but surely the alien can't be *that* unknown if it is introduced on the cover. William Rotsler's *Patron of the Arts* "owned the sensatron—and it could kill him!" He better be careful then! The protagonist of Donald J. Pfeil's *Through the Reality Warp* is named Billiard, and surely he will be played by the whimsical gods of the novel's chaotic plot. William D. Blankenship's *The Helix File* is about a disappeared missile dossier and advertises that the protagonist will have to "play decoy in a new and deadly game," which automatically sounds tired and old. In Robert Pohle's *Doom of Three Planets*, a nameless man "was swept off the face of the Earth to become an intergalactic slave on the remote planet, Golcorra." Where are the title's other promised planets, then—or is Earth supposed to be one of them, leaving only one incognito? At least this cover boasts "Editor's S. F. Choice," which I find somewhat amusing, as the editor is choosing to remain anonymous. In John Creasey's *The Insulators*—which is no less than a "Doctor Palfrey Thriller," whatever those are—the cover's face has teeth inside its eye sockets. Zach Hughes' overblown *The Stork Factor* predicts a future in which a "genetic-control system enslaves America—until a freedom-fighter is born with the powers of PSI!" Okay, fine, but the word Stork in the title is less than appealing.

That's it, I think, yawning. *One more ought to put me to sleep.*

Disinterestedly, I snatch one up.

I don't allow myself to judge the book by its cover or blurb. Instead, I dive straight into the story. The first few pages don't hold my attention. But despite my mind drifting every couple of paragraphs, I find myself making soft landings back into the text, not concerned about what I've missed, pleased to be moving forward at all. It's the book's lack of obvious engagement that paradoxically seduces me. If the author is not preoccupied with overt hijinks and immediate stakes, perhaps he has something more subtle up his sleeve.

The plot itself combines many familiar elements from other novels: a Project Genesis, a defense of the now discredited steady-state theory (as manifested through fictional neutrino creation), a messiah leading a new cult (here called the Church of Topological Transformation), the "inversion" of ordinary reality, Mobius loops as rollercoasters (is that a new thing?), hypnosis, psychiatry gone awry, a plethora of hippie drug-isms, fake deaths, quasars, supernovae… and the redefinition of pi. None of it should work, and it certainly shouldn't work together—and perhaps under normal circumstances it doesn't. But my detachment unlocks the book, and once unlocked, the book pushes me into an altered state of mind. The book's tone may be ridiculously New Agey, but I'm agog.

My fingers turn the pages more and more quickly. I'm right there, inhabiting the Inverse Vessel, witnessing the destruction of Pluto, racing along with the scintillations birthed from thundering nonexistence, dialoguing with

Zoroaster's son, following the twisted logic that rewrites probabilistic laws into a flipped bell curve. My heart pounds at an admittedly tacked-on love story involving a secretary. I'm wholly present and involved every step of the cosmic way.

After opening my mind in this manner, at last I reach the explosive finale. The collapsing caves of prose surround me as I race towards the end, stopping just before it's over. I close my eyes and feel myself alive with… color. The color of what? The inside of my mind? No. Not color attached to something, but color in and of itself, as abstract data. *This is what black feels like*, I think, *and this is what blue feels like, and this is what magenta feels like.* I'm somehow *perceiving* color, for the first time, for the fictional, physiochemical interpretation of electromagnetic frequency that it is.

The experience makes me lonely.

Loneliness gives way to a newfound sense of profound vulnerability, and I become fearful of being discovered in this state. I'm in a secret world now. I dawdle here. Before reading the book's final lines I revisit earlier passages, prolonging the experience as much as I can. My mind forms into a new metaphysical organ that presses down upon my consciousness. And at this key moment, as I turn to the last page and take in the final words, I feel convulsions of release deep within.

Coupled with this quaking, the impotence and helplessness of addiction assail me.

My headlong escape into science fiction after Ryan's death ruptured any faith I might have had in the actual world and its putative values. I realize that my obsession is tantamount to an entirely one-sided relationship, a conversation in which I'm talked at by practitioners of the fantastic who have zero interest in listening to me respond. I feel the crushing guilt that comes from having elevated a pastime into a purpose; I'm overcome by the shame and emptiness of having consumed too much candy, of having lost the ability to control my impulses and become dependent on other peoples' imaginations.

My insight rolls on, feeling unstoppable now. Hope is one thing, but the fetishization of belief in technological progress, the belief in the endless perfectibility of the future, is a different proposition. I've spent years in the grip of science fiction's infatuation with other spaces and times, feeling apart from ordinary people. But that's merely another means of wish fulfillment, of self-deception. Surely all addicts consider themselves exempt from consequences at some stage of their self-destructive journeys. Meanwhile, my job facilitates the enslavement of others to the same kind of illusion, albeit through cruder but equally habit-forming means.

I become light-headed.

A gray veil forms around me, and my heart races at the onrush of darkness. I open my mouth and flounder.

The book falls from my hands.

Whatever substrate of reality normally supports us splits open, and I fall through.

II. The Sorrow Makers

SEVEN

I COME TO.

I've no idea what time it is. I look at my wrist, but my wristplex is gone.

The sun is rising. The curtains of my room aren't thick enough to block its rays, which dapple the wall opposite my bed with warm hues.

Feeling the shell of the familiar reforming around me, I hear a knock on the door. "Hey man, are you still up?"

I rub my eyes. What day is this? Why is there a book called *The Infinite Man* lying on the floor?

"Come in." When I speak, I'm surprised by the huskiness of my own voice. "I was reading."

Leon's concern quickly gives way to frustration. "All night?"

I squint. "Looks like it."

"Angela left ten minutes ago. The light's been on in your room since yesterday."

I feel like I'm still operating from somewhere outside myself, trying to find the script that will guide me through this scene, but at the same time I find myself reaching for a greater awareness of what's going on, a greater sensitivity to the circumstances.

"Who's Angela?" I ask, foggy.

"You've met her," Leon says. "I've been dating her for weeks."

"I thought you were talking to someone at work and it didn't pan out?"

Leon sighs. "What are you talking about? I broke up with Lisa so I could get together with Angela. I think you need sleep."

But I'm not tired. I want to resume my contemplation of whatever beguiled me before I passed out, to recapture whatever glimmers of it I can. The sense of falling through… "Sorry if I cramped your style," I say. "I didn't mean to."

Leon's chest inflates and then releases air with deliberation. "Thanks," he says. "But I do worry about you, Jason. Do you really think reading binges are good for your eyes? Shouldn't you be taking better care of yourself?"

"You're probably right," I croak.

"One more thing," he says. "The rent was—"

"I know, I know. Give me two more days. I have most of it. Here, I'll give you what I have so far, and…" I begin rummaging through one of my drawers.

"I'll take the full amount when you have it," he says. "And Jason, if this happens again…" He casts one last glance at the disarray in my room and walks out.

Stillness returns in the wake of his departure, but things feel different now.

❧

What I have to do is clear.

After grinding through a hellish day with Codis—nine installs, three of them in apartments lacking AC, one of them in a hoarder's junior studio—, I remember Ramon's request at the last Custodians gathering, so I meet up with him and give him two boxes of books. His excitement and enthusiasm are all the reward I need. Shortly before parting he cautiously asks what I intend to do with the rest of my collection. I'm blunt and tell him I need to sell it.

Eric Cook is the guy I decide to call. He's a used book dealer, not a particularly high- end one, but he was part of the science fiction circuit long before I knew the difference between Martin Greenberg and Martin H. Greenberg. I've been told that Eric, who always displays an enticing selection of wares, has been a fixture at conventions since they started. Big-name authors tend to sign his stock without much cajoling because they know that those signed copies will travel the nation in good hands and reach readers *somewhere*.

Some of my earliest purchases came from Eric's inventory, and I still remember the first time I met him at his local shop in the city. He has a snub nose, grizzled gray hair and a gray beard that seems disproportionately neater than the rest of his face. He tends to dress in jeans and a black sweater, and his light brown eyes and gentle demeanor confer a sage, professional look. The book-shaped tat on his right cheek was inscribed with ferromagnetic ink that vibrates when his wristplex gets an alert, so his skin literally tingles with industry news. I dial the shop and tell him I've decided to sell off my collection. That gets his interest.

"You sure about this?" he asks.

"Yep. Looking to make a clean break," I say. "Keeping

a few items, but the bulk is yours—for the right price. This has been a long time coming."

"I'm not going to dissuade you," he says. I tell him he'll need to come to the apartment to see what I've got because it's too much for me to carry. He lets me know that he'll swing by tomorrow morning at eight, an hour before his shop opens.

As soon as I hang up, I review the books and magazines I've set aside for safekeeping.

Have I made the right choices? Will I regret splitting up certain series? By keeping to the principle of one short story collection and one novel per author, am I arbitrarily depriving myself of classics?

I spend most of the night skirting the edges of deep sleep, rent by fretting and mounting anxiety. For the last decade these books have seen me through everything. Who or what, when they are gone, will likewise be a witness to my life? At around three in the morning I wake up to pee, and an even more confounding possibility grips me with dread.

What if Eric rejects the majority of what I'm offering? I need the money.

At around seven in the morning I stagger out of bed. I want to send my supervisor a wristplex message letting him know I'm taking a sick day, but I still haven't been able to find my device. So I call and leave him an old-fashioned voicemail instead. Then I review my choices one more time. I regret giving up so many anthologies, but they have to go. Is *Sunflower* the Sydney J. Van Scyoc book I should be holding on to, or is it *Starmother*, or maybe *Cloudcry*? Garry Kilworth's *In Solitary* or *Split Second*? Richard Brautigan's *The Hawkline Monster* or *Sombrero Fallout*?

I make myself coffee and slither back to my room with renewed trepidation. Six minutes past eight I wonder if Eric's been detained, or perhaps gotten cold feet, or—

"No work today?" Leon asks. He usually rolls into his insurance brokerage firm around nine a.m. and he's in the process of getting spruced up.

"Wasn't feeling so hot. Taking the day off." I don't owe him an explanation, but I also have nothing to hide. "Hoping someone will show up shortly to help me clear out some books."

The muscles in Leon's face visibly relax. "Great." Is that genuine optimism in his voice? He lingers for a moment and then he adds "Good luck" before returning to his morning ablutions. I notice he's not wearing his wristplex. Weird. A few minutes later he's gone.

Staring at my selections anew, I decide that my problem is that I haven't been harsh enough. I'm still clinging to too many books and magazines. With both hands, before I have time to doubt myself, I advance upon my "save stacks" and decimate them. In the midst of this bustling reorganization, the doorbell rings, and I'm flooded with relief.

"Good to see you, Eric!" I usher him in, observing that he hasn't aged a day. "Likewise," he says, bobbing his head. Unbidden, he takes off his shoes. "Should we get to it?"

"Let's jump right in," he says.

I lead him to my bedroom and point out the various subcomponents of my collection, making sure to underline anything of a collectible nature as well as items of associational interest. He asks a few questions and then requests permission to inspect certain goods for himself. About thirty hardcovers he studies in detail, removing the dust jackets and remarking on chips, tears and clipped edges, noting any imperfections in the spines and corners of the bindings themselves, searching for discolorations in the pages, any types of blemishes whatsoever. I resist the urge to speak, because nothing gives a buyer the advantage like the seller's stench of desperation.

The paperbacks he gets through more quickly. When he reaches the magazines, he pauses. "I'll need to have one of my specialists confirm my appraisal of these," he says, jotting down some numbers on a notepad. "So keep in mind that whatever I offer will be subject to that validation."

"Got it," I say, unenthused but undeterred.

He spends a few more minutes on his notepad, scribbling comments and numbers. When he raises his head from this busyness and makes eye contact, I start to sweat. "You have an interesting collection," he says. "I'll be honest—a lot of this is pretty obscure stuff, and I should know. For the most part it's in excellent condition, though your newest additions don't live up to that standard. You possess a number of peculiar signed copies and some rare items for which dedicated collectors will pay top dollar. On the flip side, you have no highly sought-after, signed first editions. The magazines are old, which increases their worth, but they're not in very good condition—and again, no first-tier, classic runs. It's almost as though your entire collection is made up of the stuff that usually falls through the cracks of other people's collections."

"I've always marched to the beat of my own drum. Even when it was a harp."

"Keeping in mind my caveat about the mags, here's what I'm willing to offer." He says nothing more, a placid expression on his face, and hands me his notepad. I stare. "Remember, those books over there, I'm keeping."

"Oh," he says, and shakes his head with an air of sadness. "You did mention that. Sorry, forgot. Unfortunately that selection, though small, is where much of the collection's value resides, so if you're adamant about keeping those items for yourself, I'll need to re- evaluate." The book tattoo on his face vibrates. I can see the tiny ripples in the skin. I don't see a wristplex on him, but I notice a small black device attached to his belt. "I'm being paged. Maybe we can reconvene next week?"

I feel the deal slipping through my fingers. "Okay. Let's do this. If I really miss something terribly once it's gone, I can always look for another copy. All-in. I accept your offer."

"Wonderful," he says. Tact restrains his smile. "It sounds like we've got ourselves a deal. Let me go down to my van, where I have some boxes and my check book, and then perhaps you can help me load up the goods?"

"Sure. You don't happen to have cash, do you?"

He frowns. "I'm afraid not. Will that be a problem?"

"A check is fine," I say.

He trots out. I sit in stunned, bittersweet silence while he's gone, trying to etch into my memory what this sea of books looks like. I may never own this many books again. It occurs to me that I should write down as many of the titles I'd initially reserved for myself as I can.

I'm about halfway through when he returns. "Almost done here," I say.

"I understand." He begins folding boxes into shape, and when he's done six, he packs them up expertly in what seems record time. Perhaps on some intuitive level Eric senses my alarm, because he says, "I can tell by how well you've maintained these books that they meant a good deal to you. I'm sure giving them up isn't easy."

"You're right about that."

I finish my list and crouch down before the nearest bookcase, joining in his packing efforts on the next six boxes.

We work in silence broken only by nods and grunts for about an hour. The black device clipped on his belt buzzes a couple more times. He sighs. "Need to get going soon."

He picks up the pace and I have a hard time keeping up. "What is that thing?" I ask, pointing to the source of his alerts. Without pausing he says, "My pager?"

"Yeah," I say. "No wristplex?"

He's distracted, packing the magazines. "No what?"

If I had mine on, I'd simply point to it by way of explanation. "Never mind," I say.

Boxes packed and secured, we make trips to his van until everything's been stashed inside.

He writes me a check.

I accept it and stand there, not knowing what to say. He tries to shake my hand, but my fingers, worn out from all the packing and lifting of boxes, lack the ability to exert any real pressure. Or perhaps it's my psyche betraying me. In a few short seconds the van's engine is going to purr to life, and Mr. Cook is going to drive away with my most intimate history, never to be reconstituted in this exact form again.

He climbs into the driver's seat and rolls down the window. It's a bright morning.

I find myself blinking away tears.

"Should the magazines be worth more than I assessed," he says through the open window, "I'll be sure to call you for an additional payment. Wouldn't want you to think I'm taking advantage of you."

"Eric… did you really forget what I told you about those special books I'd set aside?" I ask. I hope he can't see I'm crying. "Or did you just pretend you did, so you could get a better deal?"

"I'm sorry," he says, an apologetic light in his eyes. His voice, however, is firm. "Trust me, I'm doing you a favor. I've seen collectors like you before. Heck, I used to be one myself. It's a disease. If you hold on to a little, soon that little grows, like a mold, a decade flashes by and you're right back where you started, drowning in the stuff."

"That sounds hyperbolic."

"There wasn't a lot of breathing space in your room, if you don't mind my saying so."

I can't decide if he's my enemy or my friend. That's probably because our transaction has involved lucre, which always complicates things.

His hands grip the steering wheel and he shifts from park into drive. "Look, it's been a pleasure doing business with you. Gotta run."

And the van is away, away, and I'm in the middle of the street.

I rely on purely subconscious processes to make my way back upstairs, where I wash my face.

It's done, I think.

My bedroom's new spaciousness is bewildering.

I feel consumed by it. How can emptiness loom so large? How can an absence be so concrete? My eyes scan the titles I hurriedly jotted down. The words ring hollow, already beginning to lose their evocative power, the weight of a demonstrable presence. Perhaps they only ever existed in my dreams. Is Marge Piercy's *Dance the Eagle to Sleep* a real thing? "At age eighteen, Shawn was officially loved by sixty thousand four hundred and eleven girls registered in his fan clubs," is one of my favorite first lines in all of literature—but am I getting it right? Without any evidence before me, that opening line becomes increasingly improbable, like those times a familiar word suddenly appears to have an unfamiliar spelling. Do the novel's characters—Shawn, Corey, Billy and Joanna—exist any more or less than I do?

Notions of unreality and hyper-reality flow through me. Eventually I find calmness, and after calmness a kind of joy I don't remember having felt in years, maybe ever. A *lightness*. The space around me is no longer a void. It is a blank canvas, waiting for the brush stroke of possibility. I feel physically unencumbered, floating free somewhere in the core of my own body. It's almost like realizing I have a body for the first time. This is *me*. The sensation gives way to giddiness, euphoria.

I've done it. I've managed to say goodbye. To free myself.

And once I cash this check, I'll have the dough to pay this month's overdue rent, and most of next month's.

Do it right away, I think. Before you lose this. Before you backtrack. Before you retreat into the familiar. Before you make new mistakes.

I decide to share the good news with Leon and to thank him for being understanding. Searching for my wristplex again proves futile, so I resort to writing Leon a note with pen and paper.

Then I realize I haven't had breakfast or lunch, and hunger gnaws at me. I find a nearby Ponderosa Steakhouse.

I'm greeted by Tiffany lamps, ceiling fans sadly underpowered, booths with trimmed tops, and brick floors that could use cleaning. My water arrives and I drink half the glass down in one gulp. As I lean back in my seat, I notice a couple in the booth in front of me; both of them are wearing baseball caps, and they've placed a small gray box on their table.

When I look more closely, I see that cables emerging from the backs of their caps meet the device. My server asks the couple what they want, but it takes her three attempts to snap them out of their glassy-eyed stupor. After the server leaves, the man produces a newspaper from the seat and places it on the table. His eyes fixed on his companion, he opens it to a specific page, and she smiles. Not a single word is exchanged. They both begin to read.

When the server stops by to take my order, I say, "Not to be indiscreet… but what's happening between those two?" I point to their booth as nonchalantly as possible.

"Oh." The server smiles. "A telebox."

"Hmmm…" I study the couple. They alternate in turning the newspaper pages, and exchange knowing looks every so often, by turns serious and amused. They never speak.

"Yeah," the waitress says. "They're not super common but we see them once in a while. Mind-to-mind communication."

"Wow," I manage. Not surprising, I suppose, that this is where technology is headed.

I'm sure the justification for this gadget, like with Codis' EmuX, is to bring people closer together, but in reality this couple is more cut-off from the rest of us diners than I would have thought possible, literally plugged into a two-mind realm none of us can access.

"What would you like, sir?"

Despite the tiresome décor and overplayed ad of this place—"It may be a hamburger to you, but it's chopped beef to us"—that's exactly what I end up ordering, a hamburger.

Maybe the advertising works. It's not bad, not great, and I scarf it down.

Next I head to the bank, deposit my check, and get cash.

Back at the apartment, I place the rent cash in an envelope for Leon. Then I revisit my list of life goals. Item 1, selling my collection, was a big one! I've made partial progress on item 2 also, since I now have some money, and on number 5, having recently caught up with Jill. Three out of seven ain't bad. Not bad at all.

Riding the momentum, I decide now is a good time to take the first step towards actually leaving Codis, namely to write a resignation letter. I keep it short and simple, but still end up going through three drafts.

There's an additional item that wasn't on my list originally but should be added because of Jill. Make my eye doctor appointment.

I rustle up the phonebook from the living room coffee table and do a systematic search.

I call a few nearby offices and ask about their terms. After shopping around, I go with one of the costlier places that will accept my insurance through Codis. No point in shortchanging myself on my vision.

Appointment confirmed, I add the item to the list and immediately cross it off. Phone still in hand, I dial a number I should dial more often.

"Hey Mom," I say. "Is Dad around? Can you have him pick up on the other line."

"He'll be right on. How are you, Jason?"

"I'm okay," I say. It's nice not to have to lie.

"Son?" My dad's baritone is strangely calming.

"Hey," I say. "Thanks for jumping on. I wanted to let you guys know that I'm quitting Codis."

After a few beats, my mom asks, "Did something happen?"

"Not really," I say. "I just can't bring myself to work for them anymore."

"It's a good, solid company," my father says.

"I know, Dad. But really, they're furthering the PP's agenda, whatever that may be. I just can't do it anymore." I pause. The memory of Boglins' face, smiling on a long-forgotten weekend afternoon out in the front yard, catches me off guard. "You understand?"

He senses the shift in my voice. I imagine him looking down from the receiver. "I do," he says quietly.

We talk for about fifteen more minutes. They get the gist that I'm making some significant changes in my life and ask me several times if they can help. I let them know I'm coping and I reassure them that I'll be fine. Their offer means a great deal, and I hold on to the sentiment.

Call done, I once again marvel at my room's relative emptiness, which now feels neither oppressive nor liberating. It has become what it was all along, physical space, that's all. Space that needs to be cleaned. There's grime behind the bookcases—which I'm thinking I'll probably donate to the Salvation Army store used by the Custodians—and dust everywhere.

I find cleaning supplies in the kitchen and get to work.

EIGHT

I DECIDE TO sit on my letter to Codis for a few days. I need to make sure my medical benefits cover my forthcoming doctor's appointment, and whatever possible treatment is needed.

My workday is more difficult than usual. I must have missed a tech bulletin update to our install procedures, because on two of the models I set up, I'm unfamiliar with a step that my supervisor has to walk me through. "Make sure that you're up to speed on the latest build release," he says.

On the way home I stop at a local bar to decompress. An orange-and-brown color scheme and dozens of mirrors surround me as I order a chilled twenty-five-cent nip beer in a five-ounce glass.

I'm sitting there minding my own business—in fact daydreaming about one of my favorite D. G. Compton novels, *Twice Ten Thousand Miles*—when I hear a familiar voice placing an order a few stools down.

"Terence?" I ask. "Terence Nylund?"

A smiling head rears up and finds my eyes. "In the flesh," he says.

Terence 'Stretch Armstrong' Nylund. I grab my drink and make my way over to him. His nose remains as sharp and distinguished as the last time I saw him, and on the whole he boasts as much hair, too, though there's been a rearrangement of resources: his thinning scalp has donated follicular goods to the beard covering much of his ruddy complexion. The tats on his arms, hands, neck and forehead, all soft lines making abstract geometric patterns in Waverly ink, distract from but don't hide his weight gain. His blue, wide-set eyes shine as he studies the frays time has wrought on my own visage.

"So good to see you, Jason," he says. "How long has it been?"

I grab the seat beside him. "As a rule, I stop counting after twenty years."

"Good policy," he says. "Live around here?"

"Yeah."

"My firm is on Seventh," he says.

I notice his watch, his shirt. His cufflinks. "Lawyer?"

"I was on the Securities Advisory Committee for the Ontario Securities Commission, then NASD. Focus on civil litigation for Sidley these days. How about you?"

"Congratulations," I say. "Nothing so glamorous. I go into the homes of middle-class folks who like to pretend they're Progress Pilgrims."

His laugh is spiked with curiosity. "Who pays your bills?"

"Codis. You've seen their ads."

He nods. "Never tried simulators. No interest in PP nonsense. The present is all we have."

"The present may be all we have, but it's not evenly distributed," I say. I sip my beer. "Anyway, I'm quitting soon."

"Enticing offer by someone else?"

"Nope."

He examines me. "Well, sometimes a change of pace is what the doctor ordered. Clears out the system."

"That's one thing I'll agree with," I say. "My system could definitely use a good scrub. My bedroom, on the other hand, is spick-and-span."

"You were neat in high school."

"Book hoarding got the better of me after college. But I'm course-correcting. Just did a massive purge, actually."

"You always liked bogarting your books… you were such an intense reader back then. Remember that time you helped me with my book report on *Brave New World*?"

"I do," I say. "But it wasn't *Brave New World*. It was *Fahrenheit 451*."

"I don't think so."

"You're wrong," I say. "I remember it exactly. In fact, I kept a carbon copy."

"Get out."

"Okay, so I couldn't have—it was hand-written. But here's why I'm right: most of what I know about Huxley I learned from my friend Jill. I couldn't have done your assignment for you, I could have barely done mine, if it was Huxley."

He drinks.

I drink.

This may not be merriness, but it's peace of a kind.

I notice he has no wristplex. "You fancy lawyers have some messaging system beyond us mere mortals, huh?"

He shoots me a puzzled look. "Meaning?"

"Never mind." Next, my gaze lands on his ring. "Married?"

"Separated," he says. "Divorce forthcoming. You?"

"Neither."

"Usually one goes before the other."

"I suppose," I say.

"So you got rid of a bunch of books, huh?"

"Exactly."

"Sounds like the right move."

I take a contemplative sip. "Maybe."

"Curious timing, in fact," he says. "Some of my friends are telling me traditional storytelling, using conventional text, is on its way out. Mutational narrative is the next big thing. A whole new art form that will make novels obsolete."

I scoff. "Your friends?" As in: *What would they know about reading novels?*

"I know what you're thinking," he says. "But some of them are smart people. Entrepreneurs and such. I try to listen."

"Have they done any book reports for you?"

He ignores the jab. As he leans forward his rubicund cheeks catch the light. "This new narrative form is about connecting the audience directly with whatever inspired the creator to conceive his or her story. Let me give you an example. Music, let's say. You ever heard an author talking about the music he or she listened to during the writing of a book?"

"I remember an interview with John Brunner in which he talked about electric folk, like Steeleye Span. Noisy stuff like Hawkwind. And revival medieval dance music. Which might explain a few things about Brunner."

"Perfect. Now imagine John Brunner wrote down the specific songs he listened to, in their specific order, while writing his latest novel. He creates a playlist. This is his inspirational art, which, in addition to countless other influences and stimuli, he consumes during the moments of his creative act. His novel is the resultant art that comes out at the end of that creative process and is in turn consumed by the reader. What if you could cut out the middleman, so to speak—the actual text? If you could go straight to the writer's inspirational art, you yourself might generate a variation of the experience intended by the writer in the first place."

"Playing a bunch of Hawkwind tracks and banging my fists on a typewriter doesn't make me John Brunner," I say. "Not even a little bit. Capuchins would have a better chance of pounding out *Stand on Zanzibar* than I would."

"Sure," Terence says. He orders a second Narragansett, seemingly unfazed by my objection. "If you actually wrote down whatever came to you under the influence of his inspirational art, you'd get something unique, filtered by your own particular experiences. You'd get an original Jason Velez novel. But forget the idea of the novel as the end product, and think instead of the end product as the experience you have when reading the novel. What if by listening to the music in the right way you could bypass Brunner's text altogether and go directly to that experience?"

I straighten up. "Trying to imagine how someone might react to some stimulus doesn't get me inside them. There's no way that listening to songs selected by Graham Charnock is ever going to make me experience *The Suicide Machines* or *The Chinese Boxes* or *The Observer*."

"Again, no argument from me. But you could end up having an experience remarkably similar to that created by reading any of the titles you mentioned. If you were in the right frame of mind."

My upper lip presses down hard on my lower one. "I

don't care how you spin it, Terence. Music can't replace words."

"It's all information processed by the brain," he says. "That's not spin. Music creates a brain response; so do words. Only the input channels are different."

"Don't get fancy on me."

He smiles a pained smile. "I'm not—if anything I'm getting neuroscientific. Someone born deaf could experience what we call music if the correct stimulation of the brain was undertaken directly. The ears register air vibrations, and the brain takes the data of those vibrations and calls it 'music.' Same thing with vision. We see the world in color, for example—but that's merely an illusion created by our brain's interpretation of the data generated by specific types of eye receptor cells. Light is electromagnetic radiation and covers a much broader spectrum than the tiny fringe we can 'see.' There's no such thing as 'color' out there! That's a brain construct."

"You're saying it's all brain constructs."

"Exactly," he says. "Which means the signal itself, and not the way you feed the signal in, is the determining factor for the brain's experience."

"So much for the lanky kid who could barely finish his English homework in fifth grade," I say.

"The logic is solid, right?"

"EmuX's work precisely because of what you're saying," I grant. "For argument's sake—not that I buy for a second you could do this in real life, because it would be too complex and subtle a procedure—but for argument's sake let's say that you could stimulate the brain to produce a novel-like experience based on a different sensory input. You'd get a different experience each time you prodded the brain with that signal."

"You have a different experience each time you read the same novel, don't you? In some cases subtle, in others—say, a decade has gone by—maybe more dramatic."

"People will always find pleasure in reading the written word, regardless of what else is on tap."

"People will always find pleasure," he says. "And some may choose to do so through little symbols on a page, but that doesn't mean print will dominate forever."

I throw my hands on the bar. "What is all this, Stretch?"

A few seconds pass. "I've actually tried it," he says.

I study him. "*Christ.*"

"What?"

"Me finding you here wasn't a coincidence, was it?"

"What are you talking about?"

"Don't condescend," I whisper.

He harrumphs, flexes his back on the stool, away from me. "Okay, so maybe I got a call from Leon Sobol."

"What did he say?"

"He told me you got rid of your book collection and might be up for something new. He tried it recently and loved it. He said it's even better than an EmuX."

"And you can hook me up, is that it? For a price, I'm sure. Does he get a referral commission?"

"I'm trying to help."

"Oh, it's worse! *You* called Leon, didn't you? You must be desperate if you went that far back looking for contacts."

"There's not a lot of adventurous folks out there," he says. "People willing to try completely new things."

I blink and slide forward on my stool. His clothes have

gone from glamorous to constricting. I study his watch. Its oversized dark blue strap gives way to an obscenely large textured case display with a blue dial, white markings, and "Pierre Cardin" logo. It's supposed to be mighty impressive, but now I see it for what it really is: a handcuff, shackling Terence to his materialism, to his insatiable need for more.

I measure my tone. "Remember, Terence, it starts with 'turn on,' but it ends with 'drop out.'"

"I'll give you two mutational narrative chips for the price of one," he says. "And a reader. You slot the chip into the reader and connect it with a clip to the sides of your head. Direct dopamine stimulation, like a massage inside your brain. *Bam.*"

I remember the telebox couple at the steakhouse and shudder. This sounds so much worse. I can't bear the thought of anything being in any way connected to my head. "I don't think so," I say.

"You enjoy music don't you?"

"I prefer silence."

He reaches down to grab a briefcase discreetly stacked against the side of the bar. He pops it open and produces a spherical device, two cartridges, and pincered cables.

"Free sample," he says. "Go on. No charge." He licks his lips and repeats, "Free."

"If it takes time," I say, "it isn't free."

"Really, that's it?"

"Good luck to you, old friend."

NINE

"THAT'S IT," DR. MENCHER says. His quick brown eyes, warm with compassion, twinkle behind his large round glasses, an ophthalmological irony not lost on me. "Just like that."

I'm tilting my head back at the angle he's requested. He uncaps a small plastic bottle. "Won't hurt a bit," he says.

He administers two drops in each eye.

I feel them go in, blink a few hot watery blinks, and bring my head forward. Phew—no pain. My shoulders loosen up. "All done?"

"Those were the numbing drops, to take the sting off the next ones."

"Oh."

"Sorry," he says. "I know this is hard for you." I crane my neck again in the indicated fashion.

One more drop per eye. I appreciate the skill of Dr. Mencher's technique, the way he precisely, artfully places the drops in the corner of the eye and lets gravity and geometry do the rest. I blink again.

"Now we wait five minutes." He leaves.

My vision fogs. A moment ago I could read the labels

on his wall chart, which depicts the anatomy of the human eye, and now those legends are blurred.

When he returns, I can only make out a diffuse smear of white—the mass of his hair—and the circular shapes of his spectacles.

He reaches for a familiar object and stops himself. "Did we do the drops already?"

"We sure did," I say. "It's some strong stuff, Doc."

"Okay, good. Needed to get your eyes nice and dilated, Jason. Now let's take a gander."

He grabs a finger-sized flashlight and gently presses my head the way he wants it, starting with the right eye. "Look up." I do my best. "Straight up. That's better." The light whites out everything else. I feel him using his thumb to apply pressure to my eyelid, gently squeezing the eyeball itself. He has me look to the far right, far left, down, and then down right. We follow a similar protocol for the left eye, but it seems to take longer.

Next I slide my chin onto a rest on one of his instruments, and he shines more bright lights in my eyes. "Hold still for this next one." A thermometer-like rod slowly approaches my right eye, until it's pressing right up against it. Rinse and repeat for left. Then more lights. He asks me to read various letters while looking through different combinations of lenses, and to report on the clarity and contrast of the black print against the white background.

"All right," he says. The corners of his smile are pinched.

"As I mentioned before," I say, "I've noticed some poor vision at night. My left eye is my good one, and I'd like to make sure it stays that way."

"About that," he says, smile deepening too much. "Your

prescription in the left eye has changed, which would explain the night vision challenges you've had. You may have also experienced lights as having halos in your right eye?"

"Yes."

He rises from his examining chair. "Jason, it looks like your right eye is developing a cataract."

"A cataract?" I think of Borges and his blindness as an old man. "I'm only thirty-eight."

"Yes," Dr. Mencher says. The compassion in his eyes has grown into tenderness. "Age is not the only determining factor in cataract formation. Though more common in the elderly, some folks get them in their twenties. If you had any surgeries on your eye growing up, this could be a long-term effect."

"I had operations on my right eye, when I was a kid," I say.

"Sometimes patients develop cataracts after that kind of surgery, usually within a year or two. In your case, because you were a child, you may have been more resilient."

"Not that resilient, apparently."

"We can't know for certain what the cause is, but I'm glad you came in so I could diagnose it."

The room seems to have become a lot colder in the last minute. "What's next?"

"The cataract is at a very early stage. It may take years to become problematic, or never do so. If it progresses your prescription may change again. Come in and I'll make sure to update it for you."

"You got drops we can use to dissolve it?"

Dr. Mencher replies firmly. "No."

"So… at some point new glasses won't help."

"I'm afraid not."

"No possible way to cut it out?" I ask.

"That's beyond my ability."

"I can't believe this," I say. "We've sent humans to Mars, but we can't cure a cataract."

He bobs his head in a quizzical fashion. "Humans to Mars," he repeats. "Now that's an idea. You like sci-fi, huh?"

"If you can't fix it, can someone else?"

A pained expression sours his empathetic smile. "I've heard that PPs have more advanced medical techniques than we do."

"Figures," I mutter.

"Forget about it," he says. "It's probably not even true, and nothing I should have mentioned."

"Where does one shop around for a PP medical procedure?"

"You'd have to ask one of them."

"Fat chance," I say. I think about Shanice, my only potential lead. "Could we grow me a new eye in a lab? If they can make clones, why can't they clone eyes?"

"Cloning is a very recent procedure, being performed only on a limited basis and with mixed results. We can't very well grow a clone and then scoop out one of its eyes for you. But that's beside the point. Even if the clone wanted to donate it voluntarily, or we were able to use your genetic material to grow only an eye, like you said, we'd still be left with the problem of connecting it to your optic nerve. That's an obstacle we haven't solved."

I shiver. "How much did the prescription in the left eye change?"

"I'll make sure to write it down for you."

"Besides that, it looks fine, right?"

"Yes." A pause. He's on the verge of saying more. My desire for him to do so is perfectly balanced by dread.

I tip the scale in favor of desire. "Spit it out, Doc."

He performs the unnerving trick of staring straight at me and looking through me at the same time. "In some cases, Jason, folks who get a cataract in one eye get one in the other eye too. It appears to be genetically driven."

Parts of me clench. "Are you seeing any indication of that in the left eye?"

"Not exactly," he says.

"Uh, then what?"

"You've developed a small cluster of blood vessels near the cornea. It shouldn't be impacting your vision, but if it continues to grow it may cause images to waver a little."

"Great. I'm growing my own version of *The Twilight Zone* inside my eyeball."

"Do you have diabetes?"

"No."

"Have you recently had any allergic reactions?"

"Not that I'm aware of."

"Anything that might have triggered your immune system into hyperactivity?"

"I *have* been stressed. Major life changes."

"I haven't seen stress provoke something like this before, but if your hormones and thyroid are being affected, it could be part of a larger response. You should see your regular doctor."

"Right." I have no intention of making such an appointment in the immediate future.

There's only so much good news I can take at once.

"The cluster of blood vessels may be indicative of other changes to come, like an epiretinal membrane, or a cataract, as discussed. I recommend you come in to see me in two months to monitor the cataract on the right eye. We'll set up the appointment before you leave. And of course, don't hesitate to call with any questions, or to come back sooner if anything changes."

"Yeah." I blink a few times, covering up tears I can't even feel because of the numbing drops.

Dr. Mencher scribbles down my new prescription and hands it over to me. Then he opens his file and makes some notes. "What day is today?"

Is he really this absent-minded, or is this an attempt to distract me at the end of my consultation?

"The second worst day of my life," I reply.

TEN

"A GENEROUS OFFER," I say.

On the other end of the line, Jill has asked me if I'd like her to accompany me to Dr. Mencher's office in two months' time. "Which isn't an answer," she remarks.

Astute as always, that's Jill. "I wouldn't want to disrupt your schedule. It's on a Wednesday morning. I assume you'll be teaching."

"I can make the time, Jason. This is important. How are you coping?"

I've prepared for this question. I've told myself there are two extremes: wallowing in self-pity and saying that I'm doing fine. The reality is somewhere in between. Part of the problem of "coping," however, is that I'm not sure I have the words to describe where I am in the process. "Trying to keep a positive attitude," I say.

"That's admirable."

"Don't admire too much. I'm failing often. Case in point, my present disposition isn't particularly cheery."

"How can I help?"

I survey my room. The phone feels cool in my hand. Over the last week, evening temperatures have started to relent, allowing me to open the window as the sun goes down. I didn't realize I'd missed street sounds until a few days ago when, at sunset, I invited them back in. The white noise of the cityscape—it keeps me company. Even if the price is the occasional smell of cabbage from a lower unit. "I wonder if it might have been better not to know," I say. "Since apparently there's no way of treating the cataract anyway."

"I think more information is always better."

"Even when you can't change things?"

"At least now you're in a position to confront reality and plan ahead of it potentially getting worse. And the doctor can keep tabs on the good eye."

"What if it goes bad too?"

"No matter what happens, you're going to get through it."

Again I survey my empty room. "Appreciate the thought," I say. "In the meantime, any practical tips?"

She produces a melodious hum interrupted by lip-smacking. Jill at her idiosyncratically thoughtful best. "Well, one strategy that tends to help me in difficult situations is trying to anticipate worst case scenarios. In your case, knowing how much you enjoy reading, let's think about what we could do… if reading becomes an issue."

"Glad you brought this up," I say. "Remember all the culling we did?"

"How could I forget?"

"Guess what?"

She emits a little gasp. "*All gone?*"

"Yeah," I say. "I gave Ramon two boxes and sold off the rest."

"No way!"

"Jose."

"When?"

"Tuesday."

"But you held on to *something* right?"

"A few items in my night table drawer. Truth be told, I forgot they were there. They're not even my favorites."

She whistles. When she speaks again, her pitch remains high. "How does it feel?" she asks.

"Scary," I say. "Exciting. New."

"Jason. Few people have the courage to follow through on their convictions, particularly when it involves making life changes. I'm really proud of you."

"Thanks. Know any PPs I can call?"

"Hmm. Afraid not."

"It turns out they may have the market cornered in cataract treatments."

"I'll ask around for you. Who knows."

"It's okay. I'm sure I couldn't afford it anyway."

"Didn't Shanice…?"

"She married a PP," I say. "That's all I know."

"Understood. Coming back to the idea of planning. I imagine you'll want to read in the future, even if it's not science fiction."

"Sure."

"It might become a strain on your eyes. Might be hard to read small print."

I shift on my bed, straightening out. I'm sitting against the headboard, made of tile-tufted upholstery, and have been sliding farther and farther down until the angle hurts my neck. "I have to say, I'm not finding this line of thinking particularly uplifting."

"Here's where I'm going: You should consider having someone read out loud to you."

I ponder her suggestion. "Not a bad idea."

"I'm happy to volunteer," she says.

"Jill, you live too far away."

"I'm not that far."

"Besides, I'd probably want a regular schedule, an hour or two a day, which would be too much time to ask you for. And if I should grow nostalgic and want to be read science fiction? You'd be bored out of your mind."

"Hey, I used to like science fiction."

"I remember," I say. "You used to stay up late reading Huxley when you were eleven and then you'd tell me all about it the following morning. What happened to that nerd?"

"That girl went out into the world and discovered all sorts of things. She got a degree in art psychology and became a teacher. Huxley wouldn't have wanted that girl to curb her curiosity, I'm sure. He was a wonderful writer."

"*Was?*"

"Fine—I guess people still enjoy the work he's left us."

"You know," I say, "now that a certain someone was nice enough to give you a bunch of science fiction books, you could sneak some into your curriculum. Your students would thank you."

"I'm not sure the school administration would buy it. But maybe."

"What books are you teaching?"

"*Animal Farm*, *To Kill a Mockingbird* and *Of Mice and Men*," she says. "I've got Eliot and Brontë in there too. My students love all of it. This girl last year, Megan Chimes, told me she read *Anna Karenina* on her own during the summer break. She picked it up because it looked like a fun historical drama. A historical drama! And you know what? She ripped right through it."

"That's what I'm saying. As good as Tolstoy is, he doesn't offer any commentary on the way technology is changing our world."

"You really think there's science fiction up to the level of the writers I just mentioned?"

"The best science fiction is up to it. Try out Thomas M. Disch or Joanna Russ or John Crowley and tell me with a straight face they're not great writers."

"Thomas who?"

"Disch. *334* has a narrative structure to pretzel your mind, and *On Wings of Song* will leave a subcutaneous mark. He's a poet. And essayist. Cole told me Disch is working on a book called *The Folly of Now: The Arts in the Age of Absurdity*. Isn't that a great title?" I should tread carefully here, because the truth is that I haven't read a ton of Disch or Russ myself. And I've actually forgotten the title of Crowley's well-regarded novel—*The Machineries of Summer? Joy Engine?*, something like that—so I hope the focus stays away from him.

"Hmm," Jill says.

"Because this *is* the age of absurdity, no denying it," I press on. "There are clones running around, did you know that?"

"Really? I'd heard some laws were being debated, but that's all…"

"Allegedly, an experimental strategy for empathy development," I say.

"If the template has difficulty with empathy, wouldn't his or her clone have the same issue?"

This is one of many reasons I like talking to Jill. "I didn't even think about that," I say. "Maybe the clone's empathy problem is somehow edited out, or environmentally adjusted? Anyway, I don't see this taking off. The one I met—the two I met?—, they were really out there."

"And you've been around some very, uh, *creative* people."

"Yes I have! Anyway, it's an example of what I was saying. Science changes the world, and science fiction records those changes."

"I admire your passion," she says. "Clearly your relationship with sci-fi is deeper than mine. Which leads me back to my original point. You're going to continue enjoying the stuff in the future. Maybe Leon could be a reader for you? He's right there."

Though the gesture is lost on her, I shake my head. "He's got his own job to worry about. And his dating life seems to have kicked into high gear recently. Also, have you heard his voice? A tortured cat would sound more soothing."

"You're awful."

"And yet you tolerate me."

"More than that. I want to help you. You could place an ad."

"Not a bad idea," I say.

"By the way, are we on for next week?"

I have no recollection of any plans with Jill. The length of the ensuing silence must make this clear to her. "I—"

"Dinner Thursday night, remember? You'll finally get to meet Tommy."

Now I'm utterly baffled. "Tommy?"

I hear her take a long sip of what I assume is chamomile tea. "Tommy." After repeating the name, I imagine her bobbing her head in the way I know she does. "Tommy Kappel. I've told you about him. We've been going out for about a month."

"Nu-uh," I say. "First I'm hearing of this."

"Are you messing with me right now?"

"I swear. I've never heard of Tommy—"

"Kappel. Yes you have. I know I've told you about him." Tenderness infuses her voice. I hear her put down her cup. "Jason, are you feeling okay? This is weird."

"I tend to have a good memory," I point out. "But lately I've felt a bit…off."

"Anything come to mind?"

I ponder a while. "Well, I stayed up all night reading last week and since then things have felt…off somehow. I goofed up at work, missed some kind of update. Didn't realize Leon was dating again. I don't know, maybe I need to catch up on sleep. Oh, and I haven't been able to find my wristplex since that night. Happen to have a spare?"

"Huh?"

"My wristplex. I've looked everywhere."

"Is that some kind of wrist phone or something?"

If Jill were standing in front of me, I'd place my hands on her shoulders and stare at her with disbelief. "You're kidding?"

"I haven't heard that term before. But sometimes you talk about geeky Codis tech stuff I don't know."

"Jill—this isn't funny. I've seen you wear a wristplex."

"Are you talking about that bracelet I have with the intricate design?"

"No," I say. "This has electronics in it."

"I'm one hundred percent sure I'm not wrong about this, Jason."

"I didn't dream the darned thing up," I say, shifting from puzzlement to frustration. "So now we have two mysteries on our hands. Go on, tell me about Tommy."

"What's there to tell?" she says. "I like him. He's an engineer. Well-traveled. Well-read. Loves jazz. Gentle guy. You would get along. I've suggested the three of us get together before, but both times you were conveniently busy."

I'm really starting to worry now. "What was my excuse?"

"You were working."

At least that part sounds plausible. "When was this?"

"The last time was when I came over and helped you cull the collection."

I concentrate on my memories of that morning. Nothing about Tommy. "If you say so. I swear, I can't remember it."

"You're sure you're feeling fine?"

"Yeah."

"Did the eye doctor give you any medicine with side-effects?"

"No. He just dilated my eyes."

"I think you should see a doctor tomorrow. Just have someone check you out. To be on the safe side."

"Okay."

"Tell me how it goes. And please make a note of our dinner plans."

"I will." I yawn. "I really am beat. Maybe sleep will magically reset my noggin."

"I hope so," she says. "Have a good night, Jason."

"You too."

I put down the phone, turn off the lights, and welcome oblivion.

ELEVEN

I DO AS Jill suggested and visit a doctor. He runs some tests and tells me he can't find anything wrong. He says maybe when I stayed up all night, I became dehydrated, which can lead to temporary confusion and even memory lapses. Yeah, right. So much for that.

At work the next day I screw up again. Mr. Wirt schedules a one-on-one with me in his office. I arrive five minutes early, wondering if what he's about to tell me will make my resignation letter obsolete.

"Thanks for making the time to see me," he says when I'm seated. He reviews some notes on a screen facing opposite me. His watermelon-red, narrow-spread-collar dress shirt does little to set me at ease.

"Of course," I say. "I'm sorry about the last few days. Truth is, I haven't exactly been feeling like myself."

"That's what I wanted to discuss," he says. His age-spotted face is calm, his voice serene. "What are your career goals with Codis, Jason? Where do you see yourself next year, the year after that?"

"Honestly, sir, I've been feeling like Codis and I may not be the best fit."

If he's surprised by this revelation, he doesn't show it. "Lack of motivation affects performance, but it can also affect one's outlook. If you have things going on in your personal life, I want you to know that I'm here, and that we have resources to help with a variety of situations."

"I appreciate that, but my personal life is fine."

"Then perhaps I haven't been doing my job helping you feel valued here at work."

This is the moment, I think. *I should resign right now.* But with my upcoming cataract follow-up appointment, would that be wise? What if my eyesight takes a turn for the worse?

"Nothing like that," I say. "I think it's just lack of sleep. I'll do better."

His eyes probe me. "If there's anything I can help with, you'll let me know?"

"You bet."

"This company is going places," he says. "There're some exciting things right around the corner. I want you to be part of our future. You've contributed to our success and deserve to be in on the rewards."

"Yes, sir."

"Please take the rest of the day off," he says. "Paid time. I'll approve the timesheet."

"Thank you."

I push this exchange out of my mind, and on my way home I decide to revisit a book I read a few months ago: John Morressy's *Frostworld and Dreamfire*. The protagonist is a humanoid called Hult on the alien planet Hraggellon. He undergoes several stages of transformation. Lest his race become extinct, he must make his way to another world in which the only other remnants of his kind, the majestic Onhla, are said to exist. Morressy does a nice job with the time dilation of space travel, and his descriptions of the alien worlds are compelling, particularly when he covers cold and wind and loneliness. That aesthetic speaks to me, with summer coming to a close. Thinking about it now, Hult's three stages of metamorphosis may also resonate because they evoke the three freaky trapdoor dreams I had. And there're these beasts called gorwols. I like gorwols. Tonight, I decide, I will re-read Hult's adventurous quest—except I won't be reading it for myself.

Following Jill's sage advice, I placed an ad for a reader on several bulletin boards in my neighborhood, and this evening I'll be meeting Andre Cantor, a young man who replied on the same bulletin board. Despite the low pay, he "sounded" enthusiastic. He's a high school senior who's looking to make a little extra dough on the side, and he says he's a voracious reader with a strong reading voice.

If our interview—which at this point I'm thinking is a mere formality—goes well I'll ask him if he's willing to start right away, and we'll get into Morressy's book. Who knows, I may even want to revisit some of Morressy's other entries in this same "Del Whitby" series, romps like *Nail Down the Stars* or *Under a Calculating Star*. Maybe we'll go right back to the beginning with *Starbrat*. I know I'm supposed to give up this kind of reading, but I figure a couple of novels for old-time's sake are okay.

I march into our apartment with zest, only to discover when I reach my bedroom that Morressy was one of the many casualties of Eric Cook's visit. For some reason, during the afternoon's final installation I had assumed Morressy lingered in my nightstand drawer. No such luck. Reviewing the titles I did hold onto, I'm tempted to toss them in the garbage. I would, too, if it weren't for *The Infinite Man*, whose embers warm my memory.

In the living room I find Leon, who has gotten off the phone after making plans for a dinner rendezvous.

"Hey Leon," I say, "I have a favor to ask."

"Thanks for your note, and for the cash," he says.

"My pleasure."

"What's up?"

"A young kid named Andre is supposed to be here around seven," I say, "but I need to pop out for a few minutes. I'll be back by seven, but in case he shows up early, would you mind asking him to wait?"

He looks at me with thinly veiled alarm. "Where are you off to?"

"I need to pick something up for the interview. There was a mix-up with one of the titles I sold recently. I thought I'd kept it but evidently I was wrong. I just need to buy back that one book."

"Are you sure this is a good idea?"

"It was a mistake, and I need to fix it," I say with audible determination.

He sighs. "Okay."

As soon as I'm down the stairs I realize my time estimate may have been optimistic, but I don't want to further delay my return by turning around, going back up, and telling Leon I might be a bit late.

The subway has an unexpected delay about five blocks from the shop, and rather than risk further lags, I get out and walk the rest of the way.

At the shop I spot Eric behind the counter, but he's busy

with customers. I decide to amble and browse rather than continuing to hover.

At last the buyers grab their large bags and vacate the shop. "Eric, it's good to see you," I say.

He glances up from his inventory logbook. "Hey, Jason." A moment later his eyes are back on the logbook.

"Looks like you're doing good business."

He runs a hand down his gray beard, as tidy as ever. "I'm getting by," he says. "Long day. How can I help you?"

"Listen, that collection you purchased from me recently, I hope it's going to good people. You know, knowledgeable readers who appreciate the stuff. Anyway, I made a small error. There was this novel by—"

Eric raises his hand. For the first time I notice how smudged with dirt his skin is, how black his fingernails. Toiling in the used book biz apparently leaves its marks.

"They're gone," he says.

"Wait, you didn't even let me tell you which book I'm talking about. I made an honest mistake."

"The whole lot is gone."

"Really? That fast?"

He doesn't look amused. "I'm sorry. Like I said, it's been a long day. Collector came in three days ago and snapped up all the boxes from your place. We hadn't even had time to catalog or shelf the items. He didn't care. He went through the first few boxes and made us a great offer. Have to think of the business side of things—you understand."

"Ah," I say, placing both hands on the counter. "Quite the reader, I'll bet."

Eric's eyes refuse to shake hands with mine. I feel like a

fool, with my gaze extended and unreciprocated. "Maybe," he says, and it sounds to me like *Maybe not*.

"I mean, to buy all those boxes. Did he happen to mention what he does?"

"Think he said he's a realtor."

"A realtor."

"Yep."

"Any way I could get his number? Maybe he wouldn't mind returning that one paperback, if he knew, if he understood—"

"There's nothing to understand," Eric says, and his mouth sets. His body becomes more imposing. "You sold me the books, Jason. I paid you. End of story."

My gaze lingers on his dirty hands, on the shadows pooling beneath his eyes. "I should have never given up that book. So I made an error—I'm not perfect. Let me call this realtor of yours."

"I don't give out customer information."

"What does a realtor want with boxes of sf anyway?"

"He didn't care that they were science fiction."

"Didn't care? What, he buys books by the metric ton?"

"That's right," Eric says, crossing his arms. "It's for staging purposes. He uses them to dress up shelves and take pictures of homes. He doesn't read them. That's why he buys in bulk. Romances, thrillers, science fiction, Westerns, whatever he can get his hands on for a decent per-unit price. He prefers hardcovers, but paperbacks create a nice ambiance too. He liked your mix. Said it would come in handy. Might be back for more. I don't want anyone bothering him."

Units. This word echoes in my mind, a solemn repeating chime that sets off other adjacent bells like *functional* and *commodity* and *profit* and *appearances* and *photographs* and finally *shallow* and *loneliness* and *wasteful* and *regret*. The bells toll and toll, until the severity of Eric's stern silence interrupts them.

"Fine," I say.

"You're welcome to check our stock. Keep in mind, we close in twenty minutes."

I locate the appropriate section and inspect the shelf, but my eyes can't parse the titles on the spines. This produces a hammering inside my ribcage, a rush of adrenaline with nowhere to go.

I lean forward and down, knees groaning. Still a jumble of squiggly lines.

I glance around. Other customers seem to be having no problem locating books, so it's not faulty lighting.

I try one eye, then the other. The left, mercifully, is better than the right, but still not quite good enough.

I leave the store, saying "No luck" when I pass by Eric, who nods and proceeds to ring up another customer.

The ride back home takes longer than expected due to another subway problem. I sit there, helpless, time seemingly distended. I close my eyes until motion resumes.

By the time I'm home my body feels like it's past midnight. My watch says seven thirty-five.

"That kid came around," Leon says.

I kick off my shoes as soon as I've crossed the threshold into our apartment. "I'm sorry I'm late. What happened?"

"He waited for half an hour and then I asked him to leave. You just missed him."

"What did you end up telling him?"

"We didn't speak much."

"Oh."

"Sorry. I didn't want to try and make arrangements on your behalf."

"Sure. Did he leave a message for me?"

"Afraid not." Leon checks himself out in the hallway mirror and makes a few adjustments. "Hope it still works out though."

I remember his plans. "Thanks. Your date?"

"Just a cocktail," he says.

Back inside my room, I simmer for a while but hold myself in check. This is really all my fault. I obsessed with having that particular book on hand for Andre. But blaming myself now won't accomplish anything. What I should do is redirect that energy constructively.

I pick up the phone and dial the Equimedian number. The call connects, a click follows, and then it rings some more, with a different tone.

The person who greets me is as composed and charming as Quiana was, but it's not her. "Let me cut to the chase," I interrupt. "I know you offer meditation services, and so on. But I'm calling about a specific medical condition affecting my eye. I want to know if you have any means of dealing with this."

I proceed to give her the details, and after a long disclaimer about Equimedian not being associated with any board of physicians, and so on and so forth, she puts me on hold. When she returns to the line, her voice is assured and soothing. "We may have the ability to help you," she says. "But we would need a specialist to examine your eye. Here are some available appointment slots." She reads me days and times.

"Thank you," I say, taking note. At least, as far-fetched as it might be, this is a possibility. I'm still not sure this isn't a cultish group using self-help as a front, but I haven't completely written them off yet either. "I'll call you back to confirm within the next few days."

TWELVE

ONE EVENING, WHEN Jason was fourteen years old, he and his brother Ryan, then eleven, showed up at the house two hours later than expected.

Their mom gave them one look, said, "Oh my Lord! Thank God you're okay!" and pulled them inside.

Okay was a relative term. In the bathroom, she reached for her first aid kit.

Ryan was the center of attention. "This is going to sting," she whispered, disinfecting cuts and scrapes. "And that eye is going to look terrible tomorrow." She applied ice on Ryan's swollen eyelid, salve when the puffiness started to come down, and threw in a few prayers for good measure.

"My wrist," Ryan moaned.

"Dear me," Patricia said after examining it. "Could be fractured. We'll have the doctor look at it tomorrow. I'm going to bandage it for now."

Their father, while apparently stoic, demanded an account of what had happened.

Jason began his story by explaining that Ryan had asked if they could stop at a local store on the way home so that Ryan could pick up the latest issue of one of a dozen science fiction magazines he read with religious fervor. Jason related to his concerned parents that he had bargained with his younger brother and convinced him to go to the Schenectady Avenue branch of the city's Public Library instead. It was considerably farther away, and in the opposite direction, but Jason was willing to endure the trip if it meant Ryan would check out real books for free rather than squandering his allowance on that pulpy crap for which he had developed such an appetite. Everything went fine until they arrived at the library. Partway up the stairs, before they could make their way inside, they were spotted by a band of three older kids from their same school, none of whom cared for Ryan, who had a reputation for being a geek. Jason did his best to defend Ryan, but it was three against one. While Jason fended off the worst of it, one unfortunate shove caused Ryan to lose his balance and tumble down the steps. Hence the black eye and the injured wrist.

Their parents were understandably angry. Jason was told in no uncertain terms that from now on he was to come straight home from school with his brother every evening, no detours, no exceptions. Both boys were asked to name their assailants, but neither of them did. Ryan was showered with affection by their mother. They were fed and sent off to bed.

The following morning their father gave Jason a sternly-worded letter to deliver to the school's headmaster. The letter never reached its intended recipient. More significantly, the incident was not brought up again, and Jason's story was never revisited. No further details were requested and none were provided. In this regard, Jason's story was a success.

Countless times, he wished it hadn't been. Parts of Jason's story were true.

Small parts.

The real story began six months earlier, with a kid named Dustin Shea.

Dustin was a new arrival at Jason and Ryan's school. Heavily freckled, several inches taller and more gangly than Jason, Dustin took an avid interest in his new classmates, specially Jason.

One day he stopped Jason after class and started talking to him about his collection of World War II model plane kits. Jason couldn't follow the technical details, but it was easy to get swept up in the storm of Dustin's enthusiasm as he rambled on about the Curtiss P-40 Warhawk or the Bell P-39 Airacobra or the North American Aviation P-51 Mustang. The strange boy simulated the noises of the plane's engines by sticking out his tongue, pressing it down and blowing hard. Many years later Jason would still remember that sound, somewhere between a hum, a low-pitched trill and a lisp. Few words of significance were traded. That first encounter ended with Jason telling Dustin that he had to walk Ryan home. Ryan, waiting for Jason and Dustin to wrap up, had extracted one of his science fiction magazines from his bag and was reading it in front of them. Dustin made a disparaging face. "I know," Jason said.

During the next few weeks Dustin continued to talk to Jason about his model airplanes, and some days he didn't wait until school was done but sought him out during their breaks. His energy seemed endless, and occasionally it got him in trouble with the teachers.

This wasn't something that Jason witnessed directly, but he soon became Dustin's confidante regarding such incidents. The news would often be delivered by Dustin in hushed tones and words that started with, "You won't believe what they did to me this time…"

As time passed, Dustin made several remarks conveying less than enthusiasm for Ryan. "You always have to rush off right after class," he said one day, "so you can get him home on time. What a bother that must be."

"I can walk myself home," Ryan replied indignantly.

"Mom would be mad," Jason replied. He didn't, however, expressly disagree with Dustin's sentiment.

Over the course of the next month Jason noticed Dustin becoming friendly with some of their other classmates, and something unpleasant stirred within as he observed his own star wane and theirs rise. Reversing the previous dynamic, he made it a point to seek Dustin out. The results were not as desired. In fact, the more Jason made himself available to Dustin, the less interested in him Dustin seemed to be. In time Jason learned that Dustin and four or five other kids had formed some kind of group. He heard this secondhand, which almost pained him more than his actual exclusion from said group. After tormenting himself about it for three days, Jason finally approached Dustin and asked him about it outright.

"Do you guys have a name or anything?"

Dustin smiled in an unpleasant way. "What's it to you?"

"I thought that maybe I…"

"We'll see," Dustin said.

Soon after this, Jason heard another rumor, this time about Dustin's mom. Apparently she was afflicted by some kind of malady, and Dustin helped to take care of her. Her symptoms, it was said, included a mercurial temper, slurred speech, terrible headaches, cold sweats and a pallid complexion during her periods of "remission." Jason didn't know the name of the disease but he realized it was serious. And he knew it must be vexing for Dustin, because his mom often failed to complete her house chores, was late picking up Dustin after school, and had at times been too ill to show up altogether. She was generally not, from what Jason gathered, of a sunny disposition.

Soon after learning this, moved by compassion, Jason approached Dustin and asked if there was anything he could do to help.

Dustin wrapped his hand into a fist, and something cold inside his eyes pierced through the rest of his face like a blade parting putty. He stepped closer to Jason, so close that Jason could smell his breath, which held a strong, pungent aroma Jason didn't associate with boys their age. "My mom's a lazy tramp and don't you ever feel sorry for her or I'll slug you, understand?"

Jason quivered in place. "Don't snap your cap."

"You think this is something?" Dustin's face was less than an inch from Jason's now, close enough for Jason to see the network of veins in the other boy's bloodshot eyes.

Jason's shoulders sagged. "I… I didn't…"

"I…I…I," Dustin mocked. He began to rock his body back and forth in concert with the repeated syllables and droning sounds.

"Please stop," Jason whispered.

Dustin grabbed him by his school uniform's collar. "How's this for flipping my wig, huh?"

"Let go!"

"Tell me what my mom is, and I might."

The pressure made it hard to breathe. And again, that stench of intoxication. "Lazy?"

"A tramp. *Say it.*"

Breathe, Jason thought. "Lazy." *Breathe*. "Tramp."

Dustin let go. "See, that wasn't so hard now, was it?"

Jason reeled back and gasped.

Dustin let out an explosive laugh. "Don't be such a percy pants."

"I'm sorry," Jason said, face burning. His arms were shaking. "I'm sorry," he said again, not sure what he was apologizing for, but sure that he should.

Dustin patted him on the shoulder and straightened out his ruffled collar. "It's okay," he said. He slipped a torn shirt button into Jason's chest pocket. "You did fine. Maybe you should be in our little club after all. I'll consider it."

That evening, Jason found himself alternating between extreme sullenness and exhilaration at the dinner table. Anger at the way he'd been treated dripped inside him and turned into the desperate hope that he'd be let into Dustin's group. While Jason was in this state, Mom asked Ryan to pass over a plate of Brussels sprouts, but he was reading one of his science fiction magazines and didn't hear her.

"Put that away," Dad told him. "From now on, no reading at the dinner table."

"But why?" Ryan moaned.

"Don't be such a whiny baby," Jason said. He snatched the magazine and threw it on the floor. "Stupid crap."

Mom said, "Jason, don't pick on your brother!"

Jason pulled out his chair and went to their shared bedroom. He was sick and tired of having to inhabit the same space as Ryan, who had smelly feet, never combed his hair, was always late, and couldn't for the life of him be pulled away from his dumb rags and comics. Life had been so perfect before Ryan had arrived… Jason's sleep that night was troubled.

The next day at school, Dustin approached him. Again, his breath smelled foul. "You need to do one thing to prove yourself to us."

Jason said, "What?"

Dustin explained.

And in the space of less than a second, Jason agreed.

The plan came to fruition the following afternoon. During math class it was brought to the teacher's attention that Ryan was reading a comic book at his desk instead of working on the assigned problem. When the teacher saw this was true, she asked Ryan for the comic book and confiscated it from him. "Hand me any others you have in your bag," she said.

As Ryan did so, deep silence draped the classroom, and Jason observed a sense of mortification befall his younger brother. "My God," said the teacher, as quickly as possible grabbing the magazines Ryan had produced and concealing them from the other students' inquisitive eyes. "Where did you even find this filth?" she said. "Your parents are going to be hearing about this, young man."

That evening their parents did indeed receive a phone call from Miss Soto, who warned about the corrupting influence of "girlie" magazines and pinups, and advised that they take serious measures to prevent Ryan from tumbling down a path of moral corruption.

Ryan claimed innocence, exclaiming that he had been set up, that someone at school had played a trick on him, but his parents didn't care. His father spanked him, his science fiction reading privileges were revoked for the rest of the semester, and he was sent to bed without dinner.

When word of what had happened in class reached Dustin, he tapped Jason on the shoulder and said, "Good job. Meet us here today an hour after school. There's something I want to show you." He slipped Jason a piece of paper on which barely legible writing indicated where to meet and smiled in an enigmatic way.

Jason debated whether to attend or not. On the one hand, this was exactly what he'd been dreaming of for the better part of a month. To finally be permitted to enter this elite, hidden society, to become privy to its secrets and enjoy its benefits! On the other, the sound of Ryan wailing while he was being spanked echoed in Jason's mind, and an uncomfortable tension settled somewhere between his chest and his stomach, and nothing that he did shook it off. In the end temptation and curiosity won the day.

Jason showed up at the rendezvous early, sure that this would give him some kind of tactical advantage. It was particularly disappointing, therefore, to arrive with the gathering of five kids in the alley already in full swing. At first Jason was ignored, but after finishing a little speech, the gist of which seemed to be on how to improve various techniques of deception, Dustin pointed him out to the small band. "And now," he said, "let's welcome a new addition to our group."

All eyes fell on Jason.

"You're the boy with the retard brother," one of Dustin's lackies said.

Jason felt that tension in his torso harden and become brittle, but he forced himself to hold it in.

"Ryan's been taught a lesson," Dustin said.

The same kid who had made the comment spit out. "Good. Don't want to be associated with no geeks."

Dustin produced an oily grin similar to the way he'd smiled when giving Jason the paper with the directions to the alley earlier that day. Jason couldn't say why, but he found the smile repugnant.

"What's so funny?" Jason asked.

"Just happy that you're here," Dustin said, and did it again.

A cold wind blew through the alley. Jason felt chills everywhere. "Okay, so I'm here. What's the big stink about?"

"If you're cold," Dustin said, "we've got something that'll help you keep warm." Dustin reached into his bag and pulled out a flask.

Jason frowned.

"Hot milk," Dustin said, and one of the boys snickered. "Try it."

Jason scoffed. "Uh, no thanks."

Dustin leered. He brought the uncapped flask up to Jason and held it near his face. A disagreeable smell wafted up, as of molasses, oak and rubbing alcohol.

"Yuk."

"Don't be stupid. Drink some. Otherwise you can't be in the club."

Jason's face twisted. "Fine."

Dustin moved the flask to Jason's lips and tilted it, so that a jet of whatever it contained spurted out. As it entered Jason's mouth, his eyes and throat burned and he spat it out. The kids laughed.

"Another gulp, this time down the hatch."

Jason turned his head sideways, but Dustin's hands were on his chin, straightening it, pushing his mouth open. Jason gagged but forced himself through it.

"Much better," Dustin exclaimed, releasing him.

An evening gust blew through the alley. For the first time since getting here Jason realized it smelled like garbage.

"I think I'm about done here," he mumbled. Dustin stood in front of him, blocking the way out.

He reached into his pocket and a moment later something flashed in his hand. "This is what I wanted to show you," he said. Dustin's white knuckles gripped a Swiss Army knife by its reddish handle, the large blade extended. He held his left hand closed.

Jason retreated. The boys hissed and booed and cackled.

Dustin opened his left hand to reveal another Swiss Army Knife. "Yours," he said.

"I… I don't want it."

"Yes you do. Here." Dustin let the knife fall.

Jason studied Dustin's eyes, but it was like looking into infinity. There was no bottom. The boys pressed in from all sides. Jason felt himself shunted towards Dustin.

He reached out, shuddering.

For an instant he was convinced that Dustin was going to slice the palm of his hand. But then the moment passed, and he felt the handle of the army knife pressed upon his skin instead.

Dustin produced the odious flask once more, guzzled from it, burped.

"My dad's an Army man," Dustin said, marveling at his knife, "and he told me this model is rare. I got one for each of us. We always carry them with us. It's part of the deal. Don't you dare ding it or scratch it up."

"I'll take care of it," Jason said meekly.

"Good," Dustin said.

After that Dustin told him about the purpose of the group, the rules they followed, and above all how it must remain secret. Jason barely heard a word. His mouth still stung from the giggle water in Dustin's flash, which made the rounds with the other boys, and his mind kept replaying the sound of Ryan crying during his spanking. That sound wouldn't let up and it drowned out everything else.

That night Jason waited until the lights were out in their room and almost confessed to Ryan about his role in the girlie magazine incident, and about this new club, but at the last moment his throat clamped up and the words wouldn't come.

He tried again the following night, and again he failed.

Ryan had stopped speaking to him, or speaking much in general, since the cataclysmic ban of his science fiction reading privileges, which made it that much harder for Jason to break through his own shame and sense of culpability. In fact, as the days wore on, Ryan seemed to disappear ever farther into himself, perhaps retreating into a secret realm of make-believe to take the place of the narrative realms that had been snatched away from him.

The following week Jason didn't attend one of the group's gatherings in the smelly alley, and the next day Dustin expressed his displeasure to him about it. He smiled in his gross manner and patted his pocket, where Jason knew Dustin's knife lay snug against his leg. "Don't let us down again."

That night the dam finally broke with Ryan and in the darkness of their room everything came spilling out of Jason. He omitted nothing. Ryan didn't reply. "Please, say something," Jason whispered. "Please."

After a pause so long that it made Jason wonder whether Ryan had fallen asleep, Ryan said, "I forgive you. But I won't stop reading my magazines. I don't care what the other kids think."

"I'll get you new ones," Jason said. "I promise." Sleep came easily after that.

He missed another group meeting, and the day after that he decided to make things up to Ryan. First, he took his brother to a candy store and purchased his favorite sweets and all the science fiction magazines that were on the rack. Then they set out for the library, where Jason would check out as many science fiction books for Ryan as was permitted.

Throughout the long walk from the candy store to the library, Jason wondered several times whether he and Ryan were being followed, and by the time they arrived at the front landing he had his answer.

Dustin and the other five boys advanced quickly.

"Run!" Jason said, but Ryan was holding two magazines in his hand and had a hard time keeping his balance while negotiating the upward steps.

The boys extended their blades, and Dustin said, "You filthy little snitch. You told him about us, didn't you? And you're buying him more of this crap. You're embarrassing all of us."

No one was moving now. Ryan gripped the magazines against his chest. "Leave him out of this," Jason said. "He's suffered enough."

"Awww, poor infant," Dustin said, "needs to suck his thumb to feel better."

One of the boys shoved Ryan sideways and another boy thrust him back on the rebound.

Ryan's magazines fell. Dustin kicked them away.

Another boy swung a punch at Ryan and the blow struck right above his eye. He yelled out.

Jason lunged towards Dustin, who clearly wasn't expecting it, and the surprise momentum allowed him to take him down. In retaliation two of the other boys pushed Ryan forward, and he fell headfirst. His arms came up to protect his face as he fell, and he landed on his wrist, hollering in pain.

Meanwhile Dustin scrambled to retrieve his knife, which he'd lost during his own fall, and this gave Jason his chance. He extended the blade of his knife and held it near Dustin's face. Dustin's skin, already pale, turned gray and sickly.

"Leave him alone," Jason said. "I mean it."

The scuffle had drawn attention. A tall man in a smart, blue wool suit and a striped, burgundy tie who had just exited the library paused at the top of the stairs and peered down at them.

"What's the trouble here?" he asked.

Dustin's cronies crowded around Dustin, waiting for direction.

Jason managed to put away his knife without turning around, so that the man wouldn't see it.

"Just a little horseplay," Dustin called out to the observer.

"I see," the man said. He straightened his tie and frowned. "This isn't the place for roughhousing. *This is a library.*"

"Yes sir," Jason said. In one swift and continuous movement he gathered up the fallen magazines and helped Ryan stand upright. "Sorry for the disturbance. We're on our way."

He grabbed Ryan and they marched off.

On the walk home, Jason said, "I'll hide the magazines.

And I'll make up a story. Don't say anything and you'll be fine. Trust me, okay? You were brave today." Ryan nodded.

As they walked on in silence, Jason's mind wouldn't stop replaying the events of the afternoon. He found his gaze wandering upwards, towards the sky. For years he would remember precisely how it looked: pale gray rimmed by a blue-violet haze on the horizon, empty and wide and heavy under the autumnal dusk, with only a few bright, small stars beginning to show. The indifference and vastness of that sky chilled and awed him. It reached deep inside him and settled, hard and true.

THIRTEEN

I BRUSH MY teeth, tidying loose strands of unruly hair, pick out a fresh pair of jeans and an orange t-shirt from a clothes-dune on a chair, and tip-toe out of my room. As I walk down the stairwell, I hear the door to the apartment open and Leon call my name, but I don't stop.

I hit the sun-warmed sidewalk with zeal, clop down the escalator to the subway, take it to my designated station and eat the upward escalator stairs two by two, excited to see Cole. I can't wait to bring him up to speed on recent events, including my disbursed collection, my doctor's visit, my encounter with Terence Nylund, my follow-up call with Equimedian and the glimmer of hope it offers. It feels like I haven't talked to Cole in forever.

Flustered, face prickling with itchy pores on the verge of sweat, I trot down the street looking for the coffee shop, convinced I'll somehow get lost or walk right by it. My left eyelid twitches and I feel my forehead palpitate, so I slow down. By the time I enter the coffee shop my floaters have thankfully sunk away from my field of vision. At last I allow myself a moment of composure in which to take in the locale and check the time. Good—twenty minutes early.

Plenty of time to study the menu and be prepared to order when Cole arrives. I walk toward the main counter but find the print on the wall menu too small to read.

"Excuse me," I say, trying to get the attention of one of the order takers behind the counter, but there are two couples ahead of me, who look unkindly upon my breach of protocol. The order taker ignores me, so I scoot back.

The sound of a Space Invaders arcade game on the opposite wall intrudes on my thoughts every few seconds until Cole shows up, clad in an olive-colored, button-down shirt and a black tie. Cole lingers by the counter for a moment, wholly observant of the world around him, spots me and approaches. There's pep in his step and style in his smile.

"Hey!" he says. "Anything look good?"

"You tell me," I reply. "I can't read the menu from here."

"No worries," Cole says. We make some quick decisions, order, and seek out an empty booth.

As soon as we ease into conversation, I feel confidence envelop me like a favorite blanket, perhaps pilly and stretched, but snug. Cole's mere presence is so stilling. We recall several jokes from Custodians and Mayflies meetings, talk about our current and forthcoming reads. Then I bring Cole up to speed on the significant developments in my life. I speak without shame, without dramatizing but also not glossing over painful moments. *This*, I think, *is what friendship looks like.*

When I'm done, Cole says, "Amigo. You've had quite the last couple of weeks. Yet you seem to be taking it all in stride."

"'Seem' may be the operative word."

"If it helps, money stuff is a concern for most people.

Life in the commune was dirt cheap and I managed to save up some, but that's rare."

"Yeah. As a last resort, I suppose, I have my parents. I could move back in with them."

"You're always welcome wherever I'm staying, but I'd be hard-pressed to tell you where my travels will take me a month from now."

"I admire that about you."

"Bah," Cole says, shrugging self-effacingly. "Just indecision."

"Trying to get close to my folks, after everything, is challenging."

"Were you guys tight before?"

"In a way." I give him a condensed version of my youth and adolescence, of how Ryan seemed to have had difficulties adjusting to life as an adult. I end up telling him, though it wasn't my plan, about how Ryan's enrollment in the experimental PP program ended in tragedy. While I talk Cole's weathered face radiates warmth, and his heavily lidded, dark brown eyes are startlingly clear.

"The past touches our futures in ways we can't understand." Cole rolls up the sleeves of his shirt, revealing intricate sleeve tats that stop shy of the wrists. I've never seen tats like these: their henna-like hues appear somehow to be reforming into new designs before my very eyes. He blinks. "Got these in Korea," Cole says. "I saw a lot of strange things over there. Great beauty—and great horrors. My spirit took a beating on an expedition to the countryside just a week before I flew back here. I saw a soldier shoot a man in the head three times for a minor offense. I'll never forget it."

I can't help but picture an officer firing three shots into

the head of a man I've never met and now never will, bang bang bang, three explosions that obliterate this imaginary face, reducing it to a blood-spattered, caved-in cranium dripping with gristle. I feel myself grow pale. Was Cole close enough to have blood from the inside of this man's head splash onto his face? Brain bits and bone fragments? What was the smell like? How long did the man's body stay upright before collapsing: a fraction of a second, half a second, more? How long did that parody of verticality continue even as the brain ceased operation? I decide not to ask.

Our server brings us tea. The pot's rising steam for an instant transforms Cole into a primeval fog figure. Then Cole is back to himself, urbane and polished.

"I was lucky as hell," he continues. "I was traveling with a group of locals, and later on the same day that the man was shot, the military came to the place we were staying and woke us up. They barged in, shouting. I remember bright lights. They took three others outside the front of the house. More gunshots. I broke down and started crying. The following morning one of the people in the group told me those three had been suspected of political dissidence, maybe smuggling. After they were shot they were cut into pieces with machetes. The group survivors asked me if I wanted to join them on a trip to a nearby river, to see if they could find any of their friends' pieces in the water. I felt so sick. I brought the trip to an end soon after that. I've never seen death at close quarters like that, Jason. My dad suffered a stroke some years back, when I was abroad. I didn't get to say goodbye to him. When you were talking about your brother... this all came back. An editor I knew once told me he believed in the interconnectedness of all things, that if you could truly perceive the hidden relationships of things, you'd realize there's no end and no beginning to anything, it's all one massive, ongoing, always-happening event, an infinity of complex, interdependent cycles. I don't think I really understood what he was talking about until right now. I'm going to include this in my short commune memoir, which is halfway done."

I'm stunned. I've always suspected depths to Cole that I'm only now learning about.

Bang bang bang. All of it can end, like *that*, with the squeeze of a dumb trigger by a miserable finger. A finger! It's probably ending like that for someone somewhere right *now*, right this instant, all possibilities collapsing down to the size of a bullet-hole for some cursed soul, perhaps with no one to witness the flame-snuffing. I try to reach out mentally across the twists and braids of space and time, to make contact with that poor anonymous death-in-the-making. *You are not alone*. Despite everything, despite the woes I've shared with Cole, I feel immeasurably lucky—for I'm alive. *Alive*. Perhaps it's selfish to use Cole's experiences like this, to appropriate violence and familial loss and apply them towards the betterment of my personal perspective. But how else ought these things to serve us? Should the deaths Cole described fade into obscurity? If so, why then did he share them with me? Surely, he would approve of any fortifying liquor that can be distilled from these tragedies. Selfish, maybe, but not pointless. Not at all.

"I had no idea," I say finally. "Kinda puts things into perspective."

Cole rolls his sleeves back down. "Those markings help me remember," he says. "I got them on the last day of my trip, hours before my flight back home."

"When did all this happen?"

"End of last year," Cole says.

I frown. "What month?"

He reflects. "Right before Christmas."

"Interesting," I say. "I remember you at the Mayflies meeting where Toby Fux got hammered and we had to put him to bed. Wasn't that around Christmas?"

"I don't remember that," Cole states.

"I know you were there. You got a stern talking to from Toby when you showed up, because he felt you'd been over-fraternizing with the Custodians. You and Pam Santos were the ones who helped me put him to bed later."

"Really?"

"Toby had just gotten his new H. R. Giger inks, and he was a little too zealous in his celebration. There's no way you'd forget this."

"I'm telling you, I wasn't stateside at the time," Cole says. He sits back. "What's more, I kept my plane tickets as an emotional souvenir of my experiences. Trade secret: I keep all my travel documents in case I ever want to write about my trips, so I'll have exact dates and times."

I cock my head. Sun cascades in through the booth windows. There's one more sip of tea left in my mug. I down it. "Any plans for the rest of the day?"

"It's Sunday. I haven't thought that far ahead." Cole's eyes narrow. "I think I know what's on your mind."

"Let's go to your place and find those tickets," I say. "I know I'm not misremembering. There were plenty of other people at the party that would corroborate your presence there."

"Are you sure it wasn't a different year?"

"I'm sure," I say.

"Okay. You're on."

Cole settles our bill and we head towards the subway. The conversation shoots off in new directions, starting with the recent fallout from the Three Mile Island radioactive gas leak, and then moving on to ongoing concerns about Skylab's longevity. Next Cole talks to me about economic philosophy. He wears his learning lightly, and I take plenty of mental notes, finding Cole's enthusiasm contagious.

As we board the subway, I say, "Sometimes I'm jealous of your reading."

"Come on, Simone de Beauvoir's *The Second Sex* is pretty famous."

"Sure, but Alfred North Whitehead's *Process and Reality: An Essay in Cosmology* isn't," I counter. "And you've actually read both, not just heard other people talk about them."

"You're an incredible reader, Jason."

"I'm an inveterate consumer of Belmont paperbacks and Pyramid Books and Leisure Books," I say. "I've read *both* of Dave Van Arnam's Star Barbarian novels, which I think disqualifies me of any meaningful literary opinions right there."

"Don't be so hard on yourself."

"I chose to give up my time to read Barrington J. Bayley's *The Garments of Caean* and Del DowDell's *Spearmen of Arn*; Robert E. Vardeman's *The Sandcats of Rhyl* and Clay Grant's *The Demon Samurai*; Steve Vance's *Planet of the Gawfs* and William Doxey's *ESPionage*. Who does that?"

A pall falls on my recollection of conversations I've had with other readers throughout the years, with enthusiasts whose only crime was to have tastes divergent from mine.

Realizing that I've been judgmental shakes a part of me,

compounding the sense of otherness caused by my recent discrepant memories. So much so that by the time we reach the final stop Cole detects the change in my demeanor.

"You okay?" he asks.

"Just a lot of stuff for me to process," I say. "I think the news about my eye has caused me to be in a particularly introspective mood lately. Feeling less certain about who I am. I never in a hundred years thought I would get rid of my books, but here we are. And you're not the only person I've had memory mismatches with."

We climb the stairs and walk towards Cole's street. "Oh?"

"Jill told me she's been dating this guy called Tommy, which struck me as news. Terence told me I did a book report for him on Aldous Huxley—no way. Now you're saying you were in Korea last December when I know full well you were at the Mayflies party. One of these I could accept, maybe two, but it's really starting to bother me. Has my head somehow gotten attached to someone else's neck? Did I suddenly turn into Jennifer Bowman in Sue Payer's *Second Body* or something?"

As we cross to the sidewalk of Cole's apartment, I'm momentarily blinded by the midday sun. For a second, I perceive a jagged flash inside my right eye, as though roots comprised of light had sprung up within the lens of my eye and were sprouting in a chaotic network of outward-reaching tendrils and vines.

Dazed, I stop. "Jason?"

A garbage truck drives by, momentarily eclipsing us and providing welcome shade.

"Sorry," I say. "My eye's acting up. Tell me something:

when was the last time you remember me wearing my wrist-plex?"

Cole's confusion is evident in his half-smile. "Is that one of your Codis gizmos?"

I open my mouth, close it, re-open it and say, "See, that's another thing that's messed up. We all used to wear these watches around our wrists that were linked to a central grid and could transmit messages. *And nobody seems to remember them.*"

Cole's eyebrows crimp. "This is starting to become concerning. Maybe we should call an ambulance?"

"I feel fine," I say. "I went to the doctor last week and he couldn't find anything wrong with me."

Cole considers. "There's no elevator and my apartment is on the fifth floor. I think you could do without additional exertion right now. Wait for me here. I'll go up and get the tickets."

I lean against the wall. "Okey dokey. I'll be right here."

Cole scuttles down the block and disappears into his building.

Time passes in a kind of reverie. I can't remember what I've been thinking about when Cole resurfaces.

"Here you go," he says, handing me two clipped boarding passes.

I can't read the print. In a silly gesture I raise them up towards the light. Still no luck. I hold them close to my face, then far away, but no amount of distance helps the focus crystallize.

"I can't..." I begin.

Cole places his hands on my shoulders and speaks. The words sound faraway to me, as though they were being uttered from the other side of a creek. The creek floods into a stream, its torrential flow ever louder, and the stream swells into a river, pushing Cole, on the opposite shore, off into the distance, and the river balloons and engorges until it transforms into an ocean.

I try to seek safety in this new place onto which I've been swept. I'm on a piece of land two feet by two feet, and that's all the space I need. An eternal, indefatigable force holds the ocean at bay from my tiny, neat parcel of land, this territory that is truly, inviolably my own. All is quiet. All is peace. Surrounded by water on my tiny islet, isolated from any possibility of threats or demands or expectations, wellness washes over me, an ocean of calm atop the ocean of water. Time passes, or it doesn't. I crane my neck forward and try to make out a wavering image on the ocean surface. It's not a mirrored face, for there is no one besides me in this secret place, nor visible anywhere on the horizon, and yet the quivering form is *someone's*. I study it further. Leon. Those are Leon's features. The face dances in the water. I lose myself in its contemplative gaze. It speaks to me. I understand. In that moment, sunlight dissolves the image, whose particles drift off into the recirculating system from which they emerged, forever bound to complete a cycle of division and reunion. But I don't need to follow their paths, to trace their arcane journeys. For I see how these same particles can combine to form a different face, the face of someone long dead: Boglins. Ryan is not inside Leon, now or ever, but for a moment it appears that way. From a distance one could make that mistake. And it's an error, I realize, that I've been making since I moved in with him. Unconsciously, I've expected Leon to assume the form, the manner, the behavior of Ryan. I've expected Leon to intuitively understand my needs, like Boglins would have done, and I've expected him to be centered and bright and quirky and eccentric, rather than ordinary and self-involved. I know without a doubt that I hurt Boglins with my actions when we were growing up, and I know without a doubt that part of Boglins' eventual suicide is on my shoulders. It's obvious now. The mistake with Leon was entirely on my part. My vision has been defective, subject to a distorting illusion that attempted to resurrect Ryan. Fascinated by this discovery, I wait for another image to form on the surface, confident that it will. Nothing comes. Nothing. Only still, clear waters. My piece of land shrinks. I'm down to one foot by one foot. Barely enough room to turn around.

Patience, I tell myself. A new vision will coalesce. And it does. This time the face is Jill's. And the uncanny resemblance, when seen from a certain point of view, of this shimmering face is to my mom, Patricia. Another unconscious projection, then. I've been burdening Jill with the filter of my mother. Why? At first blush, they couldn't be more different. Jill is determined, no-nonsense, a strong, independent, self-realized woman who does something she believes in. My mom was… not that. She was caring and protective, in her own way, but also weak. Submissive to the demands of others, to the demands of her husband. Shattered by Ryan's suicide, unable to do much at all after that. My mom has always been unreasonably afraid of confrontation, and when life confronted her with tragedy she was destined to lose. Jill, on the other hand, is a fighter. So why the overlay? Because they both care about me, maybe. Because they're invested in my wellbeing, in the outcome of my struggles, in my visual disability. Perhaps. Perhaps. But this is so unfair to Jill. As with Ryan and Leon, I watch the image fragment into a million particles, each of them absorbed into the planetary system, a billion individual journeys. Let them go, I think. Let the false pictures go. Leon is Leon. Jill is Jill. They are only themselves. Cleanse and purify your vision. Make it pristine, make it true. Give each of them the opportunity to be who they are. Give them permission to exist as independent entities, beings separate from you. Don't reframe them. Don't condemn them to your refractions and projections. Accept their gifts. Accept Jill's generosity of spirit and don't confuse it for anything else but kindness. Don't be afraid of her. Be open. The surface of the ocean calms. Endless quietude. But the force holding the ocean in place advances towards me, presses in against me, so that the only dry land now is the exact shape of my body. I'm engulfed, but dry. A paradox: space, but no room. I consume all the available dryness, all the resources. Is it enough for me to survive? Light from everywhere pierces the water.

A new image.

I know at once that this will be the final one. The particles rush in. The image shapes into a face. It's me. And inside my face there's someone else. I need a little more light to make it out. The face softens and liquefies.

No.

It's—who's inside me?—did I see?—melting away—thawing into everywhere—who—who—who—

"Jason, have you heard a single word I've said?" Cole says.

My vision flashes and darkness takes me.

III. We Can Build Everyone

FOURTEEN

COLD. SO COLD. Forehead chilled and damp.

I open my eyes. I remember whole days working for Codis that now feel less of an achievement than this single determined movement. A gray skein blurs my field of vision when I close my left eye, diffusing light. Everything out of focus. An array of black floaters settles at the bottom of my vision. I tilt my head. The floaters swim back up to the top, then drift down again. With both eyes open my depth perception is off, and the edges of whatever I focus on are smeared, their contours warped. Slowly I recognize my environment. I'm on the living room couch. A hand is pressing an icepack against my forehead.

"You may have a concussion," a familiar voice says.

"Jill?"

She pulls the icepack away and feels my head.

"You fainted on the street," she says. "You were with Cole, who called 911, then looked me up and called me. By the time medics arrived you were in and out. They said you were probably dehydrated, but they wanted to take you to the hospital for tests. Cole said no. I said no as well. We know how you hate those places. So we had them bring you home, and Leon helped settle you in. You've been asleep for about four hours. You were running hot but seem better now. Would you like water?"

I nod. The movement, though gentle, causes floaters to re-disperse and then re-settle at the bottom of my visual field, like a snow globe, only this snow is black and the globe is my eye's vitreous. "Thanks for taking care of me," I manage.

She places the icepack in the freezer and brings me a glass of water. It's not refreshing at all. Makes me queasy. I sink back into the couch.

"Drink some more."

"In a bit."

"Okay."

"Is Leon here?"

"He went out to buy groceries. Apparently it was your turn to do so last week. He wasn't upset about it, considering the circumstances."

"You waited here the whole time? What have you been doing for four hours?"

"This and that," she says. "Mostly making sure your breathing was regular. You spoke a few times, but I couldn't make sense of it."

"I wonder what Cole thinks of me," I muse, and sigh.

"He stayed here for a bit, so we had a chance to talk," she says. "We're both worried about you."

"No need," I say.

"Apparently you guys had a real heart-to-heart. Intense stuff."

"That's an understatement."

"Equimedian says they might be able to fix your eye?"

"Perhaps. But I'm not getting my hopes up."

"That's the Jason I know," she says and smiles. "You sound like you're starting to feel better."

"Yes," I say. "You can definitely go home now."

She rises from the chair positioned by the couch and gathers her things. "Help me up before you leave."

As she stuffs pillows behind my back, blood rushes to my head. I see myself on the sidewalk, under the blazing sun. I see Cole talking to me, but I can't hear what he's saying. And I see water. An ocean encircles me. Faces dance on the water. I see through the mirrored surface.

I study Jill. "I…"

I reach out my hand. Her fingers brush up against my wrist as she turns my hand palm up and places hers atop it, in a firm but friendly fashion. Then her hand releases mine as she re-arranges her position on the chair.

Accept her generosity of spirit. The words bubble up from that water-enclosed experience. *Be open.*

She looks at me for a long time. There are flecks of color I've never noticed in her eyes before—shades of chestnut and cedar that give way to gold and amber as her face relaxes. Then it hits me. The delicate strands of her spider-web-patterned ink are all missing.

"Your tats?" I say.

"What about them?"

"They're gone."

She leans forward towards me, then leans right back, flush against the back of the chair. "Jason, this is the kind of stuff that was getting Cole and me concerned. What on earth are you talking about?" She shows me her ankle and then raises the sleeve on her blouse. I see spider-web ink in both places.

"No," I say. "That's not right. You had those… on your face."

"On my face."

"Yes." I use my fingers to trace out on my own face the exact pattern I remember on hers.

"You're putting me on," she says.

"Actually," I say, "I'm not. I'm as serious as a First Folio. Everybody has face tats."

"Well, your face looks pretty un-tatted to me."

"Okay, not everybody. *Most* people. I was an exception to the rule."

She flattens the frills on her blouse and tidies her hair, then shakes her head. "You dreamed that up. Maybe we were wrong to have the medics leave you here."

"Ask Leon," I say. "Or Cole. Or anyone. I swear to God I'm not making this up."

"This is nuts, Jason. *I know what my own face looks like.*"

She rises from the chair, takes my glass, tops it off with water from the kitchen sink and slides it back onto the coffee table. "Here. Drink up." She bobs her chin. "Why don't I have Tommy come over and he can tell you you're hallucinating."

"Tommy," I repeat. "He's the guy you've been seeing for a month, right? I'm glad I still remember some things."

"*Six* months," she corrects. "He's seen my face a lot during that time. I think he's a credible witness."

"Every time you talk about him, I find out you've been dating him longer than the time before."

"You think I'm making up dates? Why would I do that?"

"I don't know," I confess. "It's frankly out of character."

"Then maybe I'm not doing anything of the kind, and you're the one who's out of character."

I drink half the glass of water in one chug and come to a determination. Whatever's going on with me it's no use having Jill obsess about it, and there's certainly no need for her to disturb Tommy. Since I seem to have other memories that don't line up with her and Cole, I need to find evidence that supports my version—or hers, or Cole's, or whoever's. It's no use arguing without proof. "Okay. Tommy—six months. Face markings—you never had them. Got it."

She blinks slowly, in that weird way cats sometimes do. "You sure you're okay?"

"Yeah."

She grabs her purse. "You'll ring me if you need anything?"

"I will."

"And you'll get plenty of rest? Leon should be back soon. Call 911 if anything feels off. It's been a bad enough summer."

I wonder if she's talking about the decline of my eyesight or if it's even about me. I decide I'm not sure I want to find out. "Will do."

I walk her to the front door and she leans in for a hug, which proves awkward, I'm sure my fault.

Back inside, I re-apply the icepack Jill used on my forehead. My neck stiffens. I stand in the kitchen, unsure what to do next.

In time bags rustle, the front door lock turns and Leon comes in.

"Hey man," he says, plopping the groceries on the counter. "Glad to see you're up and about."

I immediately sense that there's something different about him. I study his face. *I'll be damned.* "Not you as well," I mumble.

"Me as well what?"

I'm not ready for a repeat of the absurd conversation I had with Jill regarding her face tats, not so soon. My eyes skim the paper bag surfaces. "Jill said you were buying food."

"And… you're surprised she wasn't lying?"

"I guess."

He chuckles, stocks the fridge with the new purchases, and heats a pan with olive oil. "Why would she?"

I think of Leon's behavior of late. I make a concerted effort to recall what I learned from my transcendent water-encompassing vision. I need to give him space to be himself. He's not my brother; never was. He's his own person. "I dunno," I say. "Maybe to cover for the fact you were on another date? I've given you crap about your girlfriends. It's none of my business. I'm sorry."

He chops vegetables and slides them into the pan with an efficiency derived from practice. "Don't be dramatic," he says. "I told you about Cory in confidence and I appreciate you keeping it on the down low."

"Cory?"

"Jason, come on."

"Last thing I remember you were dating Angela—what happened to her?"

"What?"

"And before that it was Lisa. Yes. Lisa. You remember Lisa?"

"Jason—I'm really not following."

"I don't know why you'd deny any of this."

Leon dedicates himself to the next steps in the elaboration of his dish. I determine he's cooking for at least two people, and there may be leftovers.

"Ah," I say. "Angela's coming over for dinner. Is that it?"

He stirs the fry pan a few times and then places the utensil down on the counter with what I can only describe as definitiveness. "So there is absolutely no chance of miscommunication let me be clear," Leon says. "I have no idea who Lisa or Angela are. Last year I realized some things about myself… stuff I hadn't been dealing with for a long time. I gave myself permission to be, well, really me. A short time after that I met Cory. He's been incredibly understanding, having only recently come out himself. Only three people know about us so far. We're doing this very gradually, Jason. You know it's a sensitive subject for me, so let's move on. I know you've been through a lot, but enough's enough."

The vegetables sizzle away, my confidence close behind. I add this to the list of items requiring investigation. "I'm tired. I need some shuteye."

"Now? You don't want any of this? I cooked some for you."

Common sense tells me to go to bed, but my stomach has opinions. "It does smell good."

"You'll sleep better."

He's right.

I eat a bit, then a bit more. "Nice job," I say.

After we're done, I clear away our plates. "Can I ask you something?" He says, "Sure."

"Do you know what a wristplex is?"

"I think so," he says. "They're these devices. You wear them on your wrist, obviously, and they relay some kind of messages."

"Yes!" I exclaim. "*Hallelujah*. Finally. I knew I wasn't nuts."

"I only know because you told me about them that night you stayed up," he says. "I think you got high on that book you were reading or something. I mean, who ever heard of such a thing? I guess they'd be handy, I'll give you that."

As quickly as my hope had soared, it plummets. Okay, let's leave the wristplex thing to the side. Let's imagine for a moment there's a perfectly rational explanation for that. What about face ink? My memories of Leon's own markings, starting on the sides of his face and trailing down his neck in helical, snake-like fashion, are crisp and vivid. I can't have dreamt he had those markings. I live with him. Day in and day out, I *saw* them. I massage my eyelids. I try to think of nothing. What if, I consider, my eye has been playing tricks on me all along? Hallucinations? Can my distorted lens have been causing me to imagine shadows on people's faces all these years? Has my brain tried to parse those nebulous textures as best it could and imagined order where no order existed? If so, why the change now? Wouldn't that suggest my vision has suddenly cleared up and improved? Yet I know this is not the case. My acuity, if anything, has worsened over the last weeks.

As evening falls, a sense of wrongness looms within.

FIFTEEN

"IT MIGHT BE good for you," Leon says. "You're welcome to stay home, of course, but I thought I'd give you some warning. To be honest, I'm a little nervous about tonight—it's the first time we're eating in. So there's that."

Given Leon's perennial slick looks and aura of confidence, it takes me a moment to appreciate that yes, this same man that I thought I knew so well for the last half-dozen years is an individual far more sensitive than I had imagined. He's plagued by the same insecurities and fears we all have. As recently as last month, I remember him trying to reinvent himself as a player—but he insists that wasn't the case. I feel like I've broken through the persona now, to the real Leon within. He has more in common with my own book-besotted past than he'd probably like to admit.

At his beseeching look, I can't help but laugh. "Give me five."

"Thanks for being a sport."

True to my word, I'm out the door in that time. As I walk down our street, I realize it's the third Friday of the month, and so why the hell not, I make my way to the bar that holds readings on East 4th Street. Not having attended one in forever, I'd forgotten that these days they do two read-ings instead of one. I enter the literary watering hole when the first reading wraps up.

The room is packed, but not to the point of discomfort. As Kathleen Correa, an author with whom I'm not familiar, begins to read, the background din of voices and clinking glasses quiets down.

The venue's light showcases the author on a stage while plunging the rest of us in darkness. At first, I'm too far away to see her in detail, my poor eyesight relaying to me only the figure of a woman of average build and long brown hair. Her voice conveys a dark, captivating energy. Kathleen Correa is an earnest reader, bringing her text to life with a mysterious vibrancy that suggests both remarkable youthfulness and a kind of aching maturity. Her voice rises and falls in unusual rhythms, following the subtle contours of her writing's emo-tional sinews.

After ten minutes I'm closer to the stage. I see that Kath-leen Correa has large eyes, orbs that appear to be peering into this world from some other. Her broad forehead and long face are graced by an elegant, patrician nose and a small mouth. In accordance with what I'm coming to accept as the new norm, no special art decorates her face, though I do spy a mauve-toned fleur-de-lis inked on her forearm. A mordant passage in her story leads to the revelation of dimples, and a shift to surreal horror deepens her voice with dread while a flush blossoms in her cheeks.

Reading concluded, the lights go up and we applaud. She says thanks and comes down to our level. We make eye contact. I approach and proffer my hand. "Quite a story. Where can I read the rest of it?"

"Thanks," she says, tentative. "Not sure yet."

I smile, nervous but hopeful. "Oh?"

"It hasn't been published," she says. "Work in progress. My first novel." She studies me with a curious intensity, looking for what? Honesty? Traces of negative judgment? Signs of potential psychopathy?

"Impressive," I say, and mean it. "I'm sure you won't have trouble getting it published. Honestly, if the rest is like what you shared, it's better than anything I've read this year."

Her eyes soften and she holds herself less stiffly. "I've been writing it for six years. Tonight was my first public reading. Glad you enjoyed it."

"Congratulations."

A friend comes by with a vodka-and-cranberry juice drink for Kathleen. Introductions are made all round, and a few others join us to festoon Kathleen with plaudits, which she accepts with palpable relief. We drink and share anecdotes. At one point she excuses herself to smoke outside. Through our start-and-stop conversation, I learn her biographical basics. She was born in Madison, Wisconsin, moved to Denver, Colorado, where she earned a PhD in English from the University of Denver, and now she's hoping to land a teaching gig at a city college, while on the hunt for an agent to represent her novel to one of the major publishers.

Eventually the bar begins to clear out. As our group disperses, I say, "You know, I've been thinking about your novel excerpt. Something about it has gotten under my skin. It was very evocative." I don't want to sound creepy, a stalker declaring himself to the cause of his latest infatuation, but I have to make it clear there's something at stake for me here beyond socializing. This is honesty, not adulation.

She studies me. "How so?"

"Again, great reading," interjects a man, while the woman by his side adds, "Yes, lovely. We're going to call it a night. Pleasure meeting you!"

"You were saying?" Kathleen asks.

"This is probably not going to make much sense, but it made me think of a triangle."

Eyebrows raised, she says, "A triangle?"

"It wasn't anywhere in the actual words. But… the narrative structure. The secondary character from the first scene is the protagonist of the second scene, the secondary character from the second scene is the protagonist in the third scene, and *that* scene's secondary character turns out to be the protagonist from the first scene. Three interlocking sides. Symmetrical. Besides the implied murder, it's charming and clever."

"I was thinking about my family's garden in Madison when I wrote that chapter," she says. "They have a triangular-shaped sunshade for those two weeks of the year when they need protection from the sun. Who knows, maybe that was in my subconscious…"

"So I picked up on something?"

"I think so," she says, eyes closed for a moment. "I didn't do that deliberately. But does it matter that the narrative shape is somehow triangular?"

I feel myself losing my nerve. "I'm not sure how to explain…"

"Would coffee help?"

"Coffee," I say. "Okay. Yeah, let's. I know a place nearby. Open all night."

"But it won't take you that long to explain the significance of triangles."

"Hopefully not." I point to Kathleen's friend, settling her bill at the bar.

"I'll ask if she wants to join us."

"Sure."

They exchange a few words, both of them smile, and then Kathleen returns to where I'm standing. "Jo and her hubby are walking home. What did you say your job was again?" She checks the time.

"Cog in the machine—I work for Codis."

"Nice. I have a few meetings tomorrow, but nothing early."

On our walk to the diner, she asks if I have any lights, which I don't, so we stop at a convenience store where she buys some cigs.

A few minutes later we run into a familiar figure. I reach forward for an effusive hug. "Jason!" he says. "I'm so glad to see you out and about."

"Yeah," I say, not wanting to get into the details about my little episode in front of Kathleen.

"This is Kathleen Correa," I say. "Spectacular writer."

"Enchanté," Cole says.

"Likewise," says Kathleen.

Cole lets us know he's on his way to the bar we left, a common haunt for both of us over the years, and I tell him it was emptying out when we departed. "Perfect," he says. "Nothing I hate more than socializing in public. Intercourse is for private quarters, and solitude for public spaces." He winks. "So Jason, I have a proposition for you. There's a fanzine I'd like you to write for. I know the editor—great guy. He's looking for some fresh perspectives from long-time fans for the debut issue. Your name instantly came to mind. You can do an essay, a book review, whatever you want."

"Wow, thanks," I say.

"My pleasure. And guess what? I've finished my manuscript of the commune memoir. It's titled *My Pillars*. Our chat at the diner helped me come up with the finishing touches."

"Congratulations." I beam. "You know I want to read it."

"People are reacting in interesting ways when I tell them I wrote it. The other day I mentioned it to one of my commune pals. We're standing on the corner of Sixth Street, in Alphabet City, and she says, 'I hope you didn't change the names. I want to be able to show people what we did.' Can you believe it? 'Of course I changed the names,' I said. 'The book's mostly about drug sales and polymorphous sex. I'd like the people involved not to go to jail.' She was clearly disappointed, but them's the breaks. By the way, a friend of mine invited me to Paris, and I thought, 'Why the hell not?' So I'll be embracing life as a soixante-huitard, though I hear I'm a decade behind on that score. It was lovely meeting you Kathleen. Jason—we'll be in touch."

He makes his exit. "Nice guy," observes Kathleen as we resume our walk.

"He's the best," I concur.

Settled into a booth at the diner, we talk for a few minutes before returning to the subject of triangles.

"On second thought," she says, "I'm not sure I buy your analysis of who's the lead and who's the secondary character in each of the three scenes. Which causes your theory to collapse, doesn't it?"

"I guess that's fair," I say. "You do give each character almost equal weight. Maybe it was a stretch."

"So how did you decide which was secondary?"

"Honestly?" I say. "Whoever was mentioned in the very first line of the scene, I defined him or her as that scene's main character. Since each scene only had two characters, by elimination the remaining character would be the secondary one."

"Talk about arbitrary! You might as well have decided to go by who had the longest name, or who was mentioned last rather than first! Why should an ending be less important than a beginning?"

The coffee has revitalized her, and she's tapping into a little combative streak that I find stimulating. "You have a point. Let's say we use the last referenced name instead of the first. That reverses all three relationships—but still preserves my idea of three interlocking sides."

She smiles with her dimples, rolls her eyes in mock disapproval. "Coincidence."

"Or maybe that garden sunshade of yours is really in there."

"Tell me about the triangle you were envisioning," she says.

"I'm hungry."

"So order food."

I do. Kathleen declines the opportunity when the waitress asks her, but then asks if I would be okay with sharing some of my order. Of course, I say. I've asked for their 2+2+2 special, which consists of two pancakes with cream chipped beef, bacon and sausage, plus a side of Disco fries, which is fries with mozza and gravy. It's a ridiculous quantity of food and I'm vaguely embarrassed to have ordered it.

A few bites in, I say, "An equilateral triangle. At least, on a basic level."

"And on a not-so-basic level?"

First pancake consumed, I dig into the fries. "It's going to sound weird."

"Try me."

"A Penrose triangle."

"What's that?"

I explain it to her. She's familiar with M. C. Escher, which makes it easy. "You got all that from my fifteen-minute reading?"

The second pancake summons me, and I answer the call, despite a rival invitation from the bacon. "There's more," I mumble.

"Uh oh." She attacks the fries. "Now you're going to get all metaphysical on me."

I smile, set down my fork, sip water, wipe my lips. "Based on your description of the novel, I feel like it's related to a series of three interconnected dreams I had."

She stops eating. "How so?"

"The way your characters have these breakthroughs about the meaning of their lives. The disorientation they experience. I think that's what my three dreams were about. I have an extremely intense memory of having been in free fall."

"Free fall?"

"Yes," I say, and pause.

"Wait, this gets worse?"

"Your book isn't the kind of thing I normally go for. Though my 'normal' may be about to change."

"What are you talking about?"

"I tend—well, tended—to stick to science fiction."

"You sound apologetic."

"I've read a lot of trashy books. I do admit to loving some of them."

"I see nothing wrong with that."

"Guilty pleasure," I say.

"I don't believe in such a thing."

The second pancake dies a delicious death. "Really?"

"If you enjoy something, no need to apologize to anyone for it—least of all yourself."

"You're telling me there aren't things you do which you know don't represent the best use of your time, and which you wish you hadn't done, or maybe done less of, after the fact?"

"I don't want to waste time regretting my choices. If I feel dissatisfied, I try to make a better choice next time. But I don't let myself feel guilty about what I did. It was the best I could do—at that time."

"You're saying you always do your best?" I ask.

"Don't we all?"

"Seriously?"

"It's tautological," she insists. "If you could do better at any given moment, then that's what you would be doing. The fact that you aren't means that you aren't capable of it."

"I don't always do my best," I protest. "I would argue few people consistently do."

"It's not about doing your best, in some abstract, theoretical sense. It's about doing your *possible* best under the precise circumstances you're in. Your realistic, achievable, practical best. Not some best you've imagined that doesn't account for real-life situations."

"Wait a minute," I say. "If you actually believe this, then

what about wickedness in the world? The best that the murderer was capable of was killing? He had no choice but to kill? Doesn't this absolve everyone of moral responsibility? 'Your Honor, bashing my neighbor's head in with an aluminum baseball bat and setting his house on fire was simply the best I was capable of at the time.'"

"You're confusing things. In terms of the killer's actions, I would say yes, that was the best he could have done at the time. He abysmally failed to uphold the standards of social behavior we believe in, as codified by law, but there's never a guarantee that a person's best will exceed those standards. In fact, I'd say it's pretty sure someone is always bound to have a personal best that falls short of them—which is why they exist in the first place."

"You're saying our hypothetical killer is innocent?" I ask, perplexed. "It sounds like that's what you're suggesting."

"He's guilty of murder and arson," she says. Her tone is firm, but not abrasive. "I made that clear."

"But not guilty of…?"

"Of having been capable of doing better than he did."

I get a flashback to a conversation I had with Cole years ago, and I think I've uncovered the flaw in Kathleen's argument. "We're entering *Candide* territory here. This is the best of all possible worlds, and so on."

"I never made that claim," she says. "Imagine there are countless worlds. What I'm saying is that each of them is the best it can be, in exactly whatever form it is. Our world is the best *it* can be right now, but there could be other worlds out there that are better than ours. And so on, up and down an infinite regress. Our own world's best may change in time, too, maybe reaching a higher level than its current one, or falling to a lower level. Also, Voltaire was ridiculing Leibniz, so if we're going to quote that line, let's credit the right thinker."

I'm out of my depth. I should have probably made that concession ten minutes ago. But Kathleen seems to be enjoying the little joust as much as I am. "More coffee?" I ask.

"Sure."

I get the waitress' attention. She clears our plates and refills our cups. I glance at my watch and barely register that it's one in the morning. "Your talk of all these worlds has just made me think of something. I wonder if there's a world where their history is different from ours, but their literature is exactly the same."

"If we can imagine it, it exists."

My mind boggles. "That world would have every science fiction book I've ever read."

"But they'd probably interpret them differently," she says. "Since text is a function of context."

"I guess you're right," I say, mulling it over. "I wonder if something like *The Andromeda Strain* would have made a blip on anyone's radar if it weren't for the discovery of extrasolar germ fossils in our Moon rocks. Maybe that book flopped in their world. Perhaps *Mission of Gravity* was considered far-fetched because they hadn't discovered super-oblate planets beyond the Kuiper belt. Maybe their rash of 1970s time travel novels was inspired by something *other* than Progress Pilgrim fever. And their Moon base fiction…"

"A Moon base," she echoes. I see her eyes assessing me.

Is this her version of the strange look I got from my eye doctor when I brought up our having landed on Mars? I'm afraid to probe, so I redirect us back to our previous current. "You said Voltaire was riffing on Leibniz. So walk me through Leibniz, if you'd be so kind."

"I'm self-taught in all this," she says. "To be fair to good old Gottfried, his ideas were often misunderstood by those mocking him. He wasn't saying that there's no evil or suffering in the world, but rather that if the world existed in any other configuration but its actual one, there would be *more* evil than there is. He believed that reason takes precedence over other means of acquiring knowledge, and that was how he built his argument, through reason."

"I find it hard to believe that something like the PPs is the best this world can come up with," I say.

"What do you have against the PPs?"

"Oooh, long story," I say. "Let's stick with Leibniz for a second. I bet God plays a part in his argument. That hardly seems *reasonable* to me."

She grins. "God chooses to create the world. God is morally perfect and all-powerful, and thus will necessarily create the most moral world possible. If God did anything less, it would be immoral on God's part, and God's not limited in his world-making ability, because it's God we're talking about. Technically part of this argument relies on 'the principle of sufficient reason,' but I've given you the gist."

"Your position isn't far from Leibniz's."

"Sure. But that doesn't mean it coincides with Voltaire's inaccurate reformulation."

I raise my hands in surrender. "Point taken." My coffee refill is too hot, but I grasp the steaming cup anyway. Irrational on my part, maybe, because nothing is gained by it since I can't drink until it cools down. And yet it's my choice—which leads me to my next contention. "If all this is as you say, what about free will? We're always doing our best, so choice goes out the window."

She sips her coffee and throws her head back a little, coquettish yet defiant. "You really want to get into free will?"

"Only in the context of what we're talking about. It's the word *best* that's bugging me. If what I do is the best I'm capable of, then that means I could have done something worse. Best only makes sense when there are alternatives. It's a comparative term. If only one outcome is possible, it's both best and worst simultaneously. So what I'm saying is, if I have free will, the freedom to act as I choose, then there are alternatives, which means I might not always do my best. And if I'm always doing my best, then my actions are somehow predetermined and we're throwing free will out the window, so my best is nothing to get giddy about."

I blow on my coffee, drink once, tentatively, then again, triumphantly.

"What if," she says, "you have free will, and your exercise of that free will leads you to always do your best? See, we're getting caught up in semantics."

"How so?"

"It's a question of temporality," she declares. "We agree that *before* you decide to do something, you have alternatives."

"Yes. Yes. That's what I'm saying."

"You can choose to behave however you want. If you assign value judgment to one path over another, and then don't elect that path, by your definition you'd be not doing your best."

"Finally! Progress. Thank God."

"Let's leave God out of it."

"Not if you agree with Leibniz."

"Shush. I understand your perspective, Jason. I completely get it. Now try to understand mine. What I'm saying is, before I do something, I don't assign values to the alternatives. I may examine pros and cons, and so on, but I don't say that one course of action is objectively better than another. After the fact, my choice is gone—I've already acted. And I say, looking in that rearview mirror, that whatever I chose was by definition the best I could have done."

"Ah," I say. "So I'm using 'best' in a forward-looking way, and you're using it in a backward-looking way. That's the divide."

"Yup. The reason I think this way is not to torture myself with regret. Which is another way of looking forward."

"You've rewritten the rulebook to encourage a more positive outlook."

"That's what the rulebook is there for. If it isn't helping me be happy, why *wouldn't* I rewrite it?"

We both laugh.

I look at her eyes, those large orbs that suggest a distant presence peering in at this mundane world from some remote realm. "I like the way you think," I say.

"It beats the alternative."

"This whole thing got started because I admitted to a guilty pleasure. Which in your estimation shouldn't be guilty."

"Bravo."

"Have you read any science fiction?"

"Not a ton. Tell me how you got into it."

I explain to her that I was twenty-eight years old, and I confide in her about the Family Tragedy, and what it did to me. I tell her I started with Moorcock, and then discovered an old anthology titled *My Best Science Fiction Story*, which cast roots in soils fecund and diverse, and I tell her about Wells' *The Time Machine* and Heinlein's *The Door Into Summer* and Bester's *The Stars My Destination* and Sturgeon's *More than Human* and Vance's *The Dying Earth* and Zelazny's *Lord of Light* and Joanna Russ' *Picnic on Paradise.* Then I put the kibosh on my rhapsodic list-making and start asking her questions about her early reading, and what led to her becoming a writer.

We talk about our favorite books, and our lives—are they separate topics?—for maybe an hour more, and somewhere on the outer edge of that free-flowing exchange she asks me what I meant earlier with my comment about the PPs.

"Because of what ended up happening to Ryan," I say, "I could never look kindly on them."

"To be honest," she says, "I'm fascinated by them. I wouldn't mind learning about micro-temporal displacement."

"You play their lottery?"

"Nah."

"So maybe you're not that curious."

"Or maybe I think lotteries have terrible odds, and I don't want to be a sucker."

"I'm with you," I say. "Someone gave me free tickets, though, so I decided to sacrifice my principles for the slim chance of material gain."

She looks amused. "You played?"

"I played," I say. "Seemed silly to throw the tickets away. Another thing that I don't like about the PPs is the division they represent," I say. "It's them versus us. Because of them we're living through a period of deep schism. *Bruised armistice* is how Cole described it to me a few months ago."

"There's definitely something in the air. You can tell things are on the verge of changing. I like that phrase, bruised armistice. If that's true, then maybe it's time for us to heal. There're groups out there, you know. New philosophies that might point the way to a better future."

"The Hippies wanted to change the world and look how that worked out."

"So cynical. Does that mean we should stop wanting to change it, or that we should figure out a better approach?"

"I'm open to new ideas. By which I don't mean navel-gazing."

"We have a lot of belief systems to choose from these days. Some of the groups I've heard about are big on the idea of transcendence, stuff like that. The brain is fascinating. Everything we think of as real doesn't exist, not in a true sense—it's merely all information processed by the brain. It's the input signal itself, and not how our senses feed it to us, that matters. That's what I've been told, anyway."

"When you say 'groups' and 'transcendence,' I think cults."

"Maybe," she says. "Lots of rumors at the University of Denver."

"What kind of rumors?"

"There's supposed to be this one group called Equi-something. Like your equilateral triangle, only that wasn't the word. Neat coincidence I suppose."

I put the coffee cup down very slowly and stare. "Equi-median?"

"That's it. How on Earth did you know?"

This is the first time I've seen Kathleen express unadulterated surprise. "Not only do I know about them," I say, lowering my voice, "I happen to have talked to them. They've offered to help me with a medical issue. They invited me to come to their office."

"No kidding."

"And," I say, "I'm allowed a plus one."

"Holy cow. Did you make an appointment?"

"Not yet." Another pause for maximum dramatic effect.

"Are you in town for a while?"

"I am."

"Interested in going?"

"Maybe," she says. "Yeah, you know what? Yes. I am."

We figure out a date and time that work for both us. "They might be obnoxious salespeople," I say. "It's probably going to be boring."

"Those rumors I heard said that they select their candidates. That means you were picked," she says.

"Exclusivity makes it interesting?"

"It raises questions."

"The foremost being, *how broken is their selection process that they invited me?* You know, that Groucho Marx chestnut about clubs that'll have you."

"Who's talking about joining anything?" she says. "I was only thinking about snooping around."

"Ha."

We decide it's time to call it quits and shuffle out.

I walk Kathleen to the front of her building, an indeterminate number of blocks away that feels like seven but could be sixteen.

It dawns on me that during the hours we've spent together not once have I spied her staring at my droopy eyelid, and this fills me with a warm feeling. I ask her for her phone number and she provides it.

A few steps from the building entrance, Kathleen stops and looks up at the sky. She says, "I call you / as in years past, one friend to another / in little songs / afraid of the sunrise."

I nod, soaking in the moment.

"A poet named Pizarnik," she says. "Sad bird."

"In little songs," I repeat, "afraid of the sunrise. Yes—that's the way it is, isn't it?"

SIXTEEN

"MAYBE THIS WASN'T a great first choice," I say, not hiding my frustration.

Andre, seventeen years old, five feet four, unshaven, sporting a ponytail, in scraggy denims and a t-shirt that says THE WINTER OF LOVE, rolls his eyes. "I didn't know we were going to be reading something this wacky."

He lets the October 1979 issue of *Fantasy & Science Fiction* fall on the coffee table with a loud plop. "I'll have you know," I say, grabbing the magazine, "that this single issue you've so dismissively tossed aside contains a lot of great writing. It's a special thirtieth-anniversary-issue—which means it's celebrating something that's been around a decade longer than you."

"I get it. It's old. Where did you find it, anyway?"

"It was in my closet," I say, matter-of-factly. "One of my last remaining treasures…"

He huffs and scratches at the scruffy brown fringes of hair on his gaunt cheeks. "All I'm saying is, I didn't realize you wanted me to read you, like, experimental stuff. I'm doing my best here, but you gotta work with me. I'm trying.

I even came by that one time when you said you'd be here, and you weren't, and I didn't give up, right?"

"I appreciate that you left me that mailbox note and came back," I say. I'm a little bleary-eyed from my all-night adventure with Kathleen and do my best to hide it. "Sorry about that mix-up. Look, you want this job, right?"

"Yeah, sure, man. Wouldn't be here if I didn't."

"Then let's get past everything that's happened and focus on what still needs to happen. Which is you reading to me so I can follow along."

"Yeah."

"So we're going to try again."

"Fine by me."

"But it won't be 'Selectra Six-Ten' this time."

"Man, that's a messed-up story. It's like it was confusing *on purpose*," Andre says.

"Maybe so. Read some of the other titles again."

Dejectedly, he flips the magazine to the table of contents, and after some hums and whistles says, "'Jeffy Is Five,' how about that one? Who's Jeffy anyway? Is that short for, like, Jeffrey?"

I frown. "You mean '*Jeffty* Is Five'?"

"Oh, yeah."

"Please focus when you're reading. If you mispronounce words, it makes it hard for me to follow."

"What kind of a name is Jeffty? And he's five years old? Maybe let's try another one."

I need coffee, desperately, or water, or patience plunged straight into my temples. "Pick a different one then."

"Chill."

"Tell me the names of some of the other authors."

"Bud-rys, Disch, Davidson, Bou-cher, Tiptree, Jackson, Keyes, Knight, Sturgeon. Can I ask you something? Why are you into this stuff so much? These guys sound like weirdos."

"Don't judge people by their names."

"Do you have, like, a real job?"

"I work for a company called Codis."

"I heard of them," he says. "My friend's mom hooked him up with one of their machines. He loves that thing almost as much as you do this magazine."

"That's wonderful," I say, my voice indicating the opposite. "Back to our reading. Let's go with the Tiptree, Jr."

"'The Women Men Don't See'," he says. "That's it."

"Who would that even be? Men see women, like all the time."

"Please read."

Andre begins. Now as before, he's awful. He stammers and stumbles and hems and haws and starts sentences over in the middle and skips some words and mispronounces others to such an extent that I wonder if he's putting on an act. I've never heard someone read so poorly in my life. There's no way I'm going to be paying him five bucks an hour for what amounts to auditory torture. He was clearly lying when he said he was an avid reader and boasted about winning local spelling bees. But I need to pretend I'm giving him a chance. If I dismiss him now, after only a few minutes, he could become belligerent. And without Leon around, for once, I don't want to set myself up for any kind of confrontation. My reflexes feel like they're operating ten times more slowly than usual, and they're usually not so great to begin with.

So he drones on, no intonation, no sense of rhythm or

pacing or even basic enunciation, and I sink deeper into my chair.

After about five minutes he stops. I know the story well enough to realize we haven't reached the end, though I so wish we had. "What's wrong?" I ask.

"I'm thirsty. All this reading."

"Get yourself some water. Glasses are in the cabinet to the right of the stove."

Andre calls back, "No glasses here."

"Right cabinet!"

"I looked there!"

I roll my eyes, rise, and march to the cabinet, which I swing open in the way only someone making a point would.

But there are no glasses there. Only plates and bowls. Puzzled, I try the cabinet to the left of the sink.

There they are. Hmm. Leon must have moved stuff around recently and failed to tell me.

"Sorry," I say. "I didn't mean to snap." I sit back down.

"Want some?" Andre asks.

My chapped lips reply on my behalf. "Yes."

Andre returns with two tall glasses. I ease back into the chair and sip along while he resumes his stilted, halting read-ing.

The world dims and I find myself returning to last night's events. I'm walking down the street with Kathleen, captivated by her aura, by the magic of the moment, and she makes a joke about something, and her smile is so…

The world goes away.

When it comes back, my head is pounding, neck barely moving.

My lips are chapped at the corners of my mouth. My

eyelids feel crusted shut, receiving light and pain in equal measure.

I moan and wrench my shoulders sideways, trying to get my body to face up rather than down. My arms cooperate only after strenuous exertion. I'm heaving but can barely hear my own breath. I try to make a sound, to call for help, but all I manage to produce is a strangled grunt. I try again and this time croak. My elbows sting as I rotate my neck, and my arms fall at my sides, hitting something hard. What is this, wood?

I'm on the floor.

I stare at the ceiling.

Familiar.

Living room.

Yes.

I'm on the living room floor.

My head begins to clear, making space for the perception of my body's immobility, an impossible gravitational burden. I focus on my breathing until it becomes more regular and tell myself my body weighs the same as always, it's my inner sense of it that's off-kilter.

Stable breathing helps. Bit by bit the fog lifts and my eyes widen, and it all starts to come together.

I'm not far from where Andre and I were reading. I can see the foot of the couch from here. Which means the armchair must be behind me. So I must have fallen forward and hit my head. Pain stems from the back of my skull. I'm sharp enough to trace it now, to run my fingers up my nape to the knot of soreness. Ouch. Jesus.

How did this happen? How did I bang the back of my

head and land face down? With stronger lungs and vocal cords that semi-work, I try again, more loudly. "Andre?"

Then: "Leon? Anyone?"

Stillness pervades the apartment. I shift, testing whether I can lie on my side. My next step is to curl up into a ball and press my hands against my belly. I hold myself like this until my limbs ask for relief. Then I unfurl and force myself up to my knees. Verticality greets me with nausea. I clear my throat, grunt again. "Hello?" I manage, and this time the words sound like real words as opposed to gurgles. "Anybody home?"

I hear a sound from somewhere inside the apartment, like a door opening.

I drag my feet to the kitchen and hug the counter. The throbbing in my head is worse than the most clanging passage by R. L. Fanthorpe. I turn on the faucet and let it run, splash some water on my face. Better. Droplets run down my skin in rivulets of wakefulness.

Again, a sound.

"Hey! I'm in the kitchen! Whoever you are, I can hear you!" The creaking stops.

"Goddamnit," I mutter, drying my face.

I make it to the front door and find it locked.

I backtrack down the corridor, down to the bedrooms. I spot the door to our laundry closet—ajar.

I pull it open.

Body and face half-buried in jackets, Andre is cowering against the right-hand side. "What the hell?" I snap.

His face peeks out, pale and sweat-sheened. "Are they gone?"

"Who?"

"Who??" His loudness grates on me. "The guys who broke in here, man! The dudes that hit your noggin."

I stare and blink. "Hold on."

I walk to my room. Then I check Leon's room, the bathrooms, the living room. "No one is here but us, so you can come out," I yell.

Andre slinks to the living room.

I sit down, and the head-pounding recedes to a dull bleating. "Tell me what happened, exactly."

"I was reading the magazine you gave me. The Tiptree, Jr. story, remember that?"

"Yes, go on."

"You fell asleep. I only noticed when I was done. I went to the bathroom. While I was in there I heard steps and then voices, kind of frantic. I made out two guys rummaging around. Hid in the laundry closet without them seeing me. Heard them crack a joke about taking out your lights. I waited it out, man. Waited out the storm."

As I try to picture what he's described, a novel I haven't thought about in years, J. T. McIntosh's *The Suiciders*, comes to mind. An occult group has learned how to duplicate human beings and wishes to use them as pawns in an operatic—but, as is so often the case, half-baked and ill-defined—plan to take over space. Right now I feel like I've been duplicated, like this has happened to some other hapless Jason. Maybe I was duplicated a while back, when wristplexes and face tats and history started changing. Perhaps one of McIntosh's psychic witches cast a spell on me. Rey Cottrell, the book's fearless protagonist, would know how to right things. Unfortunately, I am not Rey Cottrell.

"What did the two guys say they were looking for?" I ask.

"I couldn't hear much."

"But you heard them joke about knocking me out?"

"That was before I hid."

"They went through my stuff?"

"I guess."

"Did you call the police?"

He sneers. "You got a phone in the closet?"

"Understood," I say.

I walk to the phone and pick up the receiver.

Hunched over, hands in his pockets, he looks at the door. "Peace out."

"I need you to stay here. You're the only witness. The police are going to have questions."

He taps his foot. "Man, I'm not talking to the police."

"You have to. You're the only one who saw the perps. Andre, they broke into my apartment and assaulted me. How would you feel if someone did that to you?"

"Every day is worse than this where I live," he says, and shrugs.

"That's very unfortunate," I say. "But just hang on for a second."

I dial information and am connected to a nearby station. While I report the incident I glance in his direction, making sure that he understands I'm watching him, and he replies with a put-out look, letting me know he sees me watching him and wants *me* to understand that he doesn't like it.

"They're sending someone over," I say, putting down the phone. He taps his foot. "This is where I wish you luck."

"They'll want to talk to you."

"I got places to be."

"On a Saturday afternoon? School's out."

"I didn't agree to any of this shit," he says. "I was supposed to read for an hour. That's it."

"I'll triple your pay."

"Ain't about the money, man."

I can't keep him here against his will, and based on his reticence to talk even to me, I'm starting to doubt whether his account would be helpful to the police anyway. "Okay."

"My cash?"

I go to my room, fish out five bucks, and give it to him.

Before opening the front door, he says, "I'm sorry about your head and all. I don't think this reading plan is gonna work out. That magazine—what a fry."

"You're probably right," I say. "Take care of yourself."

A ghost of a smile visits his face, wan and quick to dissolve back into the ether. "You too."

The door closes and I head to my bedroom. Examining the space next to the wardrobe, I realize that one of the half-height shelving units was moved—I can see little marks on the floor—and then dragged back to its original position. I spot no other obvious traces of the intruders. The desk near the window and the chair on which I pile dirty clothes look untouched, as does my unmade bed. I open my night table drawer and find it still jammed with two rows of paperbacks. Have they been moved around? Hard to tell.

On a whim, I walk over to the window. Leaning close to the frame, so I can see the edge of the street corner, I make out a white van. Its left door slides open and a young man of slight frame and long hair climbs in. With the glare of the mid-day sun, my limited angle and poor vision, I can't make out his face. Seconds later the door closes and the van pulls out, engine revving hard.

Was that Andre?

Acting purely on gut instinct, I scuttle to the dresser. I open the second drawer and go straight for the gray metal tin stashed behind sock-balls and an array of diaries containing embarrassments that go back two decades.

I open the tin.

The Equimedian flyer is gone.

SEVENTEEN

THE REST OF the day drags, an accretion of formless, depthless experiences. I press an icepack on my head until my fingers numb. I doze in the living room, though not on the recliner where I allegedly fell asleep before the break-in. Too tired to forage for food, I make myself a meager sandwich with lettuce, mealy bread, and turkey slices, slathering everything in spicy mustard. After a few desultory bites I toss the rest. In a fit of distraction-seeking diligence, I work through the dirty dishes in the sink and clean the countertop. The mindlessness of tidying up is soothing. The police never show up. I call the station again, and am told, with the same professionalism as the initial assurance that they would be here this afternoon, that they were needed elsewhere and will come by tomorrow. I scoff and request to speak to a supervisor and am turned down. I give up.

Evening falls. I try to read, but it's not working. Even the special anniversary *F&SF* issue fails to thrill. The fiction is beyond my current emotional stamina. Gahan Wilson's cartoons appear distorted, flat and un-amusing, while the nonfiction induces yawns. And yet before setting it down I do find brief solace in the following lines of John Ciardi's poem

"Love Letter from Mars": "(Can we shut out what we shut in?) … 'A lot of extra-sensory fuss,' / I tell myself, but can't command / the balance of my mood." The balance of my mood—is what, exactly? Rattled. Thirsty. I pour myself a beer and watch the foam froth away into nothingness. I nurse it as I nurse my disconsolation. *Can we shut out what we shut in?*

The headache returns with a vengeance and I apply the icepack again. Eventually a key turns in the front door and Leon marches in, whistling a tune.

"Hey." He inspects the living room. "Wow, this place looks clean. Thanks." Then he looks at me. "You, on the other hand, don't look great."

"That's putting it mildly," I say, placing the toweled icepack on the couch. "There was…"

He rummages through the fridge and pops open a can of Olympia Gold. "There was a what?"

"To the best of my knowledge, I think someone broke in and knocked me out."

Leon scrunches up his face and sets down the beer. "Oh my God. Are you okay?"

"I'm exhausted." I place my hands on my lap. "I was with Andre. He read to me.

Then, as his story goes, I fell asleep. Andre hid in the closet during the break-in. That's his account, anyway."

"What were they after?"

I cross my arms. "They stole a small item from my room."

"And you're saying this kid hid in the closet."

"That's where I found him."

"I dunno," he says.

"Don't know what?"

"It seems… convenient."

"I can't argue with you."

"What if Andre…?"

"I know." I look down. "I've been thinking the same thing."

"I mean, who else could have set it up?"

"Only thing is, how would he have known I'd drift off?" Leon cocks his head. "Did he offer you anything to drink?"

My stomach launches into a process of inversion and gyration I don't recommend unless you're a trained astronaut. I take a breath I hope will be forceful enough to hold down its churning contents. For an instant I feel like I'm locked inside one of my trapdoor dreams, plunging into nothingness. I stare at my beer-foam-lined glass. I pick it up and examine the bottom with the same intentness as if it were a microscope opening up vistas on new realities.

"I'm such a moron." I blink. My cheeks burn up. "He asked if he could have water. I told him to get it himself. And then he brought me some too. Next thing you know, I wake up with a splitting headache."

Leon's voice becomes meek. He holds his arms at his sides. "No sense beating yourself up," he says. "There's no way you could have known. In a way I feel responsible. I met Andre the evening you went out and I didn't suspect anything. Maybe this wouldn't have happened if I'd been around. But I was with Cory and… Anyway. Just tell me: what can I do to help?"

"Honestly," I say, eyes warming with tears, "I think you deserve a better roommate. Someone who's got their shit together. Someone who doesn't invite disaster and get the apartment vandalized."

"Oh Jason," he says. "You're a fine roommate. I've no

desire to see you leave. And I know you've had a lot going on. I mean, clearly, something's happening with you. I didn't want to bring it up, but maybe now's as good a time as any. I noticed that recently you started putting things in the wrong place in the kitchen. You keep shifting that chair by the wall near the window. It's a tiny thing, it's so weird. And wrist-plexes and these other things you've been telling me about... Do you think something's wrong?"

It's pointless to deny it, but I'm self-conscious and embarrassed enough as it is and want the attention off me. "You should check your stuff, just in case."

"Okay."

He disappears into his bedroom, and I listen to dark thoughts within my mind, trying to reshape them into something lighter.

"Nothing missing," he says a short while later.

"Leon, I've decided I'm going to move out," I say. "I'm going to call my parents—"

"Jason, stop. Seriously, there's no need for this kind of talk. I wasn't trying to make you feel uncomfortable. I'm sorry if anything I said upset you. But I do think—"

"No, it's fine. Everything you said is logical and true. Which is why I think it'll be helpful to be around family, to deal with... whatever the fuck's happening to me."

"I get that," he says. He adopts a pained expression. "But is now the best time to make such a serious decision? It's been an insane day. Maybe tomorrow we can revisit this?" He pauses. "Plus, I really don't want to have to look for someone else with whom to split the rent!"

I half-smile. "That's nice of you to say. But it's for the best."

His chin protrudes. "You positive?"

"Yes. It feels right." I take a few steps towards my bedroom. "You should probably change the locks."

"Good point."

The reality of what I'm setting in motion starts to sink in, and I don't want to break down into a full paroxysm of emotion in front of Leon, so I excuse myself.

I strip to my undies, letting my clothes fall on the floor, and get into bed.

I'm afraid I might fall into one of my trapdoor dreams, or worse, wake up to find people are subtly different again, but the world grows heavy around me and sleep whisks me away.

I wake up soon after dawn, heart on overdrive.

What...?

Awareness dispels sleep, bringing back last night's conversation. I'm moving out, that's what. I get up and shave, welcoming the dull, repetitive movements.

I open my closet and begin removing its contents, dumping everything on the bed.

When the bed is full, I push things into piles, more or less randomly. The clothes mounds are soon joined by a pocket transistor radio, notebooks, pens, pencils, legal documents, sepia- tinged pictures, a cased guitar, a record player in need of repair, a dozen LPs, my desk lamp, a camera, some pet rocks I bought in 1976, a cork pop gun I haven't fired in seventeen years, a set of three matching red-and-white Wizzzers my dad gave me, four metal cups that have been gathering dust in the bathroom, two bottle-shaped drip candles, a foldable Papasan chair, a box containing the Test Match game—only played once—, a broken Simon electronic memory board, a handful of Beton World War II toy-soldiers my parents gave me as a kid, an incomplete set of Funk & Wagnalls I've been meaning to give away, and non-sequential Captain Marvel comics my parents urged me to keep after Ryan killed himself.

Besides two spider plants near the window and the rest of the furniture in the room, including one chair, my dresser, my bed, and a few other items, this represents the sum total of my possessions.

I survey this material summation of me-ness, this amalgam of curios and artifacts and stupidly bright clothes.

I need to start anew.

I sob.

Energy seeps out of my body, and I find myself sliding against the bed frame down to the floor.

How did you let it come to this, Jason?

What would Boglins think of your life if he was still around?

I'm overcome by an urge to reach out and hug my parents, to ask them out to lunch. I picture myself sitting at a restaurant table with them, laughing and nodding and then delighting in the delicious, buttery warmth and flaky crust of a freshly made quiche. I do the next best thing to this fantasy, which is calling them.

"Hey bud," Dad says. "Hey Dad. I…"

"Let me get your mother on."

"Okay." I hear fumbling.

Mom's voice, impossibly chipper: "Hi Jason!"

"Morning. Am I interrupting breakfast?"

"I had my toast two hours ago," Mom says. "You know your dad likes to sleep in when he can. William, have you eaten?"

"What're you talking about, I had scrambled eggs before you went out for your morning walk."

"Oh, that's right, dear. So Jason, how are things?"

"I… I wanted to say…" I can't do this over the phone, not all of it, but maybe I can do enough to get into a position where I can do the rest. *Swallow your pride, Jason.* "I wanted to ask… if by any chance I could… well, stay with you guys for a while. I'm thinking of looking for a new job, and…"

"Of course," Mom says. "Stay here as long as you want."

"Thank you, Mom. It won't be for long, I promise."

Dad says, "You're always welcome, son."

"Thanks. I hope this isn't too sudden, but I was thinking next week. I'm paid up here through the rest of the month, but I want to move sooner than that. I figure you guys probably need a few days to—"

"Nonsense," Dad says. His gruffness has never been this welcome. "Your old room is waiting for you. We'll freshen things up. Come home whenever you want."

"Dad…."

"We'll see you soon," he says.

"This is going to be so lovely," Mom adds.

"I'll call to confirm the time and date over the next few days."

"Who's going to move your furniture?" Dad asks.

"Leon can probably help with that," I say. "Or I may sell it. Not sure yet."

"Whatever you need," Mom says.

"Thank you, guys," I say. "I love you."

"Love you too," she says, and I hear Dad add, "Take care of yourself."

As though sliding down some invisible line of force, I reach for my wallet. I take out a crumpled napkin, pick up the phone again, and while it rings, I try to get my heartbeat under control.

"Hello?"

Adrenaline quavers my voice. "Kathleen?"

"Yeah," she says. "Who is this?"

"It's Jason. From your reading."

"Hey, Jason." There's a bubbly lightness to her voice, a peppy morning froth. "How's it going?"

"Hope this isn't a bad time," I say hurriedly. "I really enjoyed our conversation Friday night. And…"

"And?"

"I wanted to ask if you'd like to get breakfast."

"Today?"

"Sure." Pause. "Or whenever you're available. I'm flexible. But I'm kind of hungry."

"You're funny," she says. "I know a great spot." She gives me the details. "See you there in… forty-five?"

"I'll be there."

It's a fun morning. The banter flows freely, and at the end of our rendezvous we confirm the date and time of our forthcoming visit to the Equimedian office. Good thing I called and scheduled it before the flyer was taken, or I'd really be screwed.

When I'm back home, I re-evaluate my disheveled belongings. After talking to my parents and sharing the morning with Kathleen, my life doesn't feel quite so empty.

EIGHTEEN

A Review of Doris Piserchia's <u>Spaceling</u>
and Some Inferences about its Author
by Jason Velez

When my friend Cole Wellmann asked me
to contribute to a new magazine called
<u>Aura</u>, being launched by his friend and
publisher Jose Alcarez, I agreed with a
fair amount of trepidation. This nervous-
ness had nothing to do with the purview
of this new publishing venture, which as
the editor's remit will surely make clear
is to give a voice to gay sf and fantasy
writers who wish to speak openly about
certain issues of the day. Indeed, when
Cole shared with me that <u>Aura</u>'s editor,
Margot Chernus, was to include in the
debut issue an article by David Gerrold
that originally appeared in the November 1978 issue of <u>Future Life</u>, a piece
in which Mr. Gerrold makes logical and
brave statements about the implications
of a certain California senator's wish

to ban the employment of gays as teachers, I knew I wanted to be a part of this outfit. Mr. Gerrold, though he may barely recall me from a brief conversation we had at a recent convention, is a luminary of the field and a valuable social activist, furthering the causes of equal rights and inclusiveness at a time when they are sorely needed. Then too, Cole is my friend and I couldn't turn down his invitation. My hesitation arose not from concerns about the quality or contents of <u>Aura</u>, but entirely from the realization that I myself have recently experienced what we might term a sense of estrangement from the sf field. I therefore wasn't sure I could genuinely commit myself to the task at hand, as I wouldn't want my honesty compromised, yet feared lapsing into vituperation. Too many times I have looked forward to reading reviews in allegedly fan-friendly zines such as <u>Sky Hook</u>, <u>Warhoon</u>, <u>Axe</u>, <u>Xero</u>, <u>Fantasy Commentator</u> and <u>Inside</u> only to find thinly disguised screeds and rants by posturing pseudonymous authors instead of fair assessments of the works under consideration. Thusly I bring this self-indulgent preamble to a close. I wish merely to communicate to the readers that I approach Doris Piserchia's latest novel <u>Spaceling</u> from the point of view of someone who no longer identifies with the sf clan, but who nevertheless wishes to honor it and feels a sense of gratitude for all the comforts it has offered him through the years.

To the book, then—though, in fact, we probably ought to acknowledge one final complication before launching into the review proper. I am, at the time of this writing, aware of one previous review of _Spaceling_, by Martin Wooster, which appeared in the Fall issue of the venerated journal _Thrust_. I know this because _Aura_'s editor kindly informed me of it. However, I was not provided with a copy of said issue of _Thrust_ and have not located one in time for this deadline. I have therefore not read Wooster's analysis. Thus, should I duplicate anything Mr. Wooster says, please be assured that this is merely the result of two minds following parallel tracks, rather than one chugging along in pursuit of another. I should also disclose that I have read no previous novels by Doris Piserchia, though I have it on good authority that _Star Rider_ (1974) is vivid and rousing, with splashes of van Vogtian panache. This review, therefore, doubles as a case study in whether _Spaceling_ provides a suitable entry point into the author's oeuvre.

The story: A precocious but amnesiac girl by the name of Daryl, we learn, is a "muter," that is to say, she possesses the ability to traverse other dimensions by means of floating rings. Daryl, while attempting to reconstruct her past or at least understand why she can't remember it, becomes embroiled, as one might expect, in a complicated plot whose outcome could not only upset her society but wreak havoc across these other ring-accessible dimensions.

The action begins at once: "It wasn't the thrill of the chase that caused me to step out ambitiously but the fact that Gorwyn had sent his two best runners after me."

As I hope this opening exemplifies, Piserchia excels at inventiveness and at conveying the strangeness of her imagined world as a given, rather than pausing to deliberate on its various functions. She also compellingly evokes for the reader, by means of highly immersive sensory descriptions, what it might be like to physically transform in order to acclimatize to another dimension. These passages may demand more than a single reading for full appreciation.

The novel's plot is an entangled affair, perhaps more baroque than required for the philosophical musings Piserchia has in mind. It may or may not all make sense in the end, but at the very least, it's a fun ride. More importantly, Daryl is a complex character, and we are readily drawn into her imperiled situation. She is a first-person narrator, admittedly unreliable, and perhaps we can attribute lack of clarity regarding certain plot developments to the imperfections of her apprehending consciousness.

Beyond these generalities, I would like to focus now on the author's penchant for two particular themes that may plausibly help to explain her novel's provocative combination of headlong pacing and oneiric weirdness. Indeed, the first is velocity—or rather, speed—itself, which the author frequently invokes. Consider, for example, the following: "For thirty minutes I ran at top speed through a deep labyrinth without coming across a single obstacle or impediment." Later: "I hurtled and continued to hurtle with the mass of spewing liquid until finally I was washed into a labyrinth and carried through it all at breakneck speed." Later still: "Having twenty-five greyhounds on one's trail made for good speed but I wasn't that good and they began making headway toward my heels." (Readers will also note the repetition of "labyrinth," another word that appears often, and is suggestive of the novel's plot).

So things are moving quickly. Which brings me to the second notion: the subconscious. During these events that unfold with haste, Daryl references the subconscious explicitly a number of times to explain either her own, sometimes quite unexpected, actions, or those of her co-adventurers. Herewith three representative examples:

1. "Specters haunted their dreams

while sinister sounds reverberated
against the walls of their subconscious."

2. "Subconsciously you're searching
for a family."

3. "I think I subconsciously hoped
to find a friend during my aimless
wanderings for I remained essentially human with my former needs
and desires constantly surfacing
to plague me."

Often, the ascribing of subconscious
motivations occurs only after the fact,
as in 3). The novel contains many other
instances of the subconscious beyond those
quoted. Furthermore, there are <u>indirect</u>
allusions to the subconscious as well,
and some of Piserchia's imagery seems to
have been plucked directly, if you will
pardon the momentary Freudian allusion,
from the id.

We see then how the combination of the
above pressures—an insistence on rapid-
ity, and the repeated visitations of
subconscious processes—lead not only to
the novel's unsettling effect, but help
explain why other reviewers have thought
of van Vogt in connection with Piserchia's work. ~~Lewis Carroll also springs
to mind.~~ [Margot: Please strike. I'm
reaching too far with that comparison.]

As I confessed at the outset, I find
myself in a time of transition. Science

fiction perhaps no longer holds for me the golden promise that it once did, and yet I have not abandoned my admiration for the genre, particularly for the relationships it has helped to foster—as with the aforementioned Mr.

Wellmann, prompter of this piece. I cannot help but read _Spaceling_ through this fractured lens, and I'll admit freely that I chose 1) through 3) above because they can be interpreted by me in a very personal light. What if Piserchia is using the idea of the subconscious as a stand-in for science fiction itself or, perhaps even more broadly, for storytelling? Her novel takes on a new meaning in this view. In the passage from which 1) is lifted, the "specters" and "sinister sounds" may be metaphors for unexplored possibilities of being. In fact, the very alternate dimensions to which Daryl jaunts may represent the alternate perspectives often encouraged by science fiction. Beyond its mere textual value, science fiction is community—the very "family" mentioned in 2). Indeed, Daryl is an orphaned girl, and many readers of our genre have experienced feelings of alienation from parents, siblings, and conventional social structures with such intensity that such readers will well understand "orphanhood" in a generalized sense. Yet, even in the most satisfying of communal relations, the fundamental needs of the individual cannot be ignored or suppressed—as is made clear by 3).

Daryl's journey is one of adolescent self-discovery, and in this way corresponds to well-established "coming-of-age" tropes. The means by which she learns her lessons and evolves are highly unconventional and peculiar, mirroring the trajectory followed by many of us who have spent years dreaming of faraway spaces and times. Books are the dimensional "rings" we use to transit to these distant lands, and in these voyages we ourselves, like Daryl, are rendered "muters." We can then reasonably assert that there's a little bit of her in all of us. <u>Spaceling</u> taps into this wisdom in odd yet satisfying ways.

Where the dream of the novel's text ends, we begin.

NINETEEN

IN BETWEEN MY second and third installs of the day I receive a call from Mr. Wirt through the video phone in the Codis vehicle I use for service appointments. I look for a residential street and pull over.

"Mr. Wirt—how can I help?"

"I'd like to talk off the clock for a minute," he says. "I know you value good efficiency metrics."

Off the clock? That can't be a good thing. "Yes, sir."

"How are you doing?" Mr. Wirt says. "The last time we met, you were dealing with some personal issues, and since then I note that you've taken a number of sick days."

"About that," I say. "I appreciate the chat we had. I didn't want to bug you. But I may as well tell you, there was a break-in at my apartment."

"Holy cow," he says. "That kind of thing can be pretty traumatic."

"I've also been dealing with some medical issues involving my vision."

"Not to pry into your personal affairs, but are you okay?"

Something about the expression on his face—empathy that's been somehow rehearsed—makes me guarded.

"I'm hanging in there," I say stiffly.

"Understood," he says. "The timing on this stinks, but listen, human resources has brought to my attention that you've exceeded your allowance of paid sick time for the year."

"I'm sorry," I reply. "I don't expect to use any more going forward."

"It's alright," he says. "Now that I have some idea of what you're dealing with, I'll authorize unpaid sick time if you need it."

"I don't expect to."

"Listen, all of this may be taking more of a toll than you realize, Jason. There's a second reason I wanted to talk to you. I received a complaint from one of your recent customers, and as a result I need to put you on a warning. I've researched the situation, and there's evidence to back up the customer."

I frown. "What did I do?"

"You arrived late, and you were verbally confrontational."

I think back to recent installs and none of this sounds familiar. "According to the customer, that is. Don't I get the chance to present my side of the story?"

"He has home surveillance to prove it."

"Someone recorded me without permission?" I say. "That's bogus."

"It was inside his home. He had the right to record the incident. And we—meaning you—signed a form acknowledging that you might be recorded during your installs when you completed your orientation package."

"I've never seen that."

"It's in the small print, along with other disclosures. Anyway, the point is that the video doesn't lie, Jason. You were less than professional."

I know I've been distracted lately, and I've suffered from knowledge gaps, but this sounds much more egregious. "What's the customer's name? Let me at least check my records."

"There's no need for that," Mr. Wirt says. "Like I said, I've already done the research, and the customer is telling the truth."

"I'd like to see it with my own eyes, thank you very much. When did it happen?"

"Friday."

"Time of day?"

"Afternoon. Around two."

"I'm sorry if I was late," I begin, but I have nowhere else to go from here, because I honestly don't remember any problems on Friday afternoon installs.

"Did something happen on the way?" Mr. Wirt asks.

"Like what?"

"Not sure, something that might have upset you. You seemed really irritated."

"I was probably mad at myself for not knowing something. I take pride in my work."

"I know you do," Mr. Wirt says. "You used to earn a fair share of customer commendations."

I'm not aware of ever receiving customer compliments, but it seems unwise to contest anything in my favor, especially in the present context.

"Yeah, it's a shame," I say, hoping that my agreement will help end the conversation.

"Now that you're on a warning, it's imperative that you behave respectfully towards every customer. It's always imperative, naturally, but any more incidents like this would push you from a warning status to termination."

"Termination?"

"I don't like it any more than you do, but those are the rules."

Mr. Wirt must have missed the almost wishful note in my voice as I echoed the word. "Okay," I say. "Thanks for letting me know. Can I get a copy of the footage? I want to review it and make sure I don't repeat that type of behavior again."

"You'll get it. You should know that the customer made an additional claim, one not backed up by surveillance, because the alleged event took place in the bathroom, which isn't monitored by his equipment. So I'm not accusing you of anything. I'm simply relaying what the customer is claiming. He says that you stole something."

"Stole something?" All things considered, I feel like I've been dealing with this pretty well.

Until now.

"Respectfully, sir, that's bullshit."

"Jason, I understand that you—"

"I don't steal. I'm not a thief. And it's not an accusation I take lightly." I feel myself gaining in anger, like a plane on a runway prepping for takeoff.

"I didn't say—"

This is going to be a bumpy ride. "Right, sure. You're telling me what someone else said. But if you didn't believe it was at least *possible*, why bother? You must have some doubt."

"It's standard procedure for me to relay this, that's all.

Perception can sometimes be as important as facts," he says. "So you need to be aware of what the customer perceived."

"Here's my perception: this customer fabricated the whole thing. The surveillance is fake. The incident never happened. I haven't had any bad 2-pm installs, period."

It takes him a moment to bounce back from this. "Uh, Jason, I hope you're not the one calling *me* a liar."

I enunciate my words with extra clarity. "I didn't do whatever the surveillance purportedly shows. You're going to have to believe either me or the doctored footage."

"Claiming it's doctored strikes me as a bit paranoid," he says. "Look, if it makes you any happier, I'll play the recording right now. You'll hear it's you."

I wait as he queues it up. Then I listen. I hear someone who sounds exactly like me saying things I have no memory of ever having said, in a manner befitting precisely how I would have said them if I had.

"Extremely convincing," I say. "But it's not me. Never happened."

"Jason, let's think about this logically for a second. Why would a customer go to all this trouble to make an accusation against one of our employees if there wasn't some truth to it?"

"The customer could have a number of reasons," I say. "Maybe he wants free service. Maybe he has a grudge against Codis, or wants to set up a lawsuit. What I can tell you in no uncertain terms is that I really don't appreciate having my integrity questioned. How am I supposed to feel working for a company that takes the word of a stranger over one of their employees?"

"There's *evidence*," he says. "There's simply no reason to

think it's fake. What do you want me to do, hire the FBI to prove to you that it's authentic? All this hostility, Jason—it's truly misdirected. If you're this angry with me, how unlikely is it that you would have had an outburst with a client? You're not helping your case with your behavior."

"*Screw* my case," I say through gnashed teeth. "I won't be accused of something I didn't do. If the customer didn't create that recording, then maybe *Codis* did. How do you like my paranoia now? It's very neat. This way you get to put me on a warning and work me out of the business, so I get no severance pay. Create false evidence to justify firing me. Except *it never happened*."

"I urge you to think very carefully about your tone."

"Mr. Wirt, you can't fire me because I quit."

I disconnect the call before he can reply.

He calls back but I don't pick up. He tries again, and again I decline to answer.

I sit in the driver's seat of a vehicle that doesn't belong to me, sweating, trying to breathe. I rock back and forth. When the white-hot flash of anger passes and the rocking subsides, I sit some more.

What now?

I start the car and drive, no direction in mind. I use the act of driving to enter a kind of trance the only purpose of which is not to think. The longer I drive, the more I can disappear out of myself. I lower the windows and keep the engine going. After an hour the fuel gauge indicator snatches me back to reality. I find a gas station, fuel up and resume driving. A while later I'm back in familiar surroundings, a neighborhood in which I performed an installation last month.

I'm also, I realize, not too far from Kathleen's place. I circle the block six times and eventually find a spot.

The car phone is supposed to be used strictly for Codis business. "Too bad so sad," I mutter, and dial Kathleen's number.

"Hello?"

"Hey," I say. "I know I'm early. We're not supposed to meet for another hour. But I have some exciting news to share, so I figured I'd call. Do you have a second?"

"I do," she says. "I just finished revising a chapter of my novel. Talked to one of the agents I met at the reading and she had some great suggestions. I think she's going to be a match."

"That's wonderful. Congratulations."

"So what's your news?"

"To put it bluntly, I'm no longer on Codis' payroll," I say.

"Your choice?"

"Well," I say, "I suppose. It was inevitable, sooner or later."

"Then I guess I'm happy for you," she says. "Though I understand it probably feels stressful."

"You're right about that," I reply.

"Are you still up for our visit to the Equimedian office this evening?"

"Yes," I say. "Any distraction right now is a good thing."

"Okay," she says. "You're free to change your mind, you know. I'd totally get it."

"No, it'll be fun."

"Okay."

"I need to run an errand before then, or I'd invite you over now. Do you mind?"

"Not at all."

"Great," Kathleen says. "By the way, I enjoyed our breakfast the other day."

I smile. "Me too."

"See you soon."

"I'm looking forward to it."

I sit and wait, wondering what to do with the hour I have to kill. I decide that hearing Cole's voice is sure to improve my mood. Alas, he doesn't answer.

I try Jill next. She picks up right away. I fill her in on my exchange with Mr. Wirt. She expresses her support for me and asks if there's anything she can do to help. "I don't think so," I say. "All this time, Jill, I kept finding ways to justify my paycheck. No longer. I'm kind of glad it's over."

She replies in measured tones. "I think it's probably for the best." Long pause. "You won't have to make those mental gymnastics regarding their involvement with Equimedian anymore."

Though the sun is still out, I feel shadows deepen around the vehicle, as though sunset has been triggered by Jill's words. A soft white spans the horizon for a few moments before it bleeds into lavender and deep Prussian blue. I listen to myself breathe because it convinces me that I am, in fact, breathing. "What does Equimedian have to do with anything?"

"Oh, you know," Jill says. "Remember that *New York Times* front-page piece about the alleged ties between Equimedian and Codis and three other major entertainment providers?"

"What? When was this?"

"About three weeks ago. Jason, I know you saw it because *you're the one that told me about it.*"

My insides curdle. "It's my memory again," I say. Though now is far from an appropriate time, Michael G. Coney's novel *Mirror Image* pops into my head. On the planet Marilyn, Alex Stordahl discovers life-forms with a defensive trait that allows them to be physically and mentally indistinguishable from humans. In time these "amorphs" become convinced that they are in fact human. Is there an amorph of me running around the city, doing the things people tell me I've done, saying the things people tell me I've said?

"Maybe I've been cloned," I say.

"Cut it out," Jill says.

"No, I'm serious."

"Cloned—Jason, really?"

"What if there's more than one of me? That might explain some of the memory issues I seem to be experiencing."

"There's no such thing as cloning, outside of science fiction that is."

"Jill, give me a break. I told you about the empathy therapy. That guy I did an install for?"

"I've never heard a word of this. But it's starting to make me nervous. Maybe it's time to get you to the emergency ward. Next thing I know, you'll be talking about androids as housekeepers."

So it's even worse than I suspected. Now clones have disappeared from the world, along with face tats and wristplexes and presumably our Moon base and Mars landing. "Jill, I went to the doctor after the last time this happened,"

I say. "He couldn't find anything wrong beyond mild dehydration. Let me ask you something. It concerns Leon. Who is he dating?"

"I believe the guy's named Cory. Or maybe Cody? Casey?"

"Cory, right. Except it was news to me after I fainted on the street. It's the second time this has happened. I noticed some changes the first time after I stayed up all night and passed out. Some kind of shift. For instance, Leon was single, and then Leon was dating. And then after the second blackout, Leon went from dating women to men. You—you were single. Then suddenly you had started dating Tommy. And then you'd been dating him for six months. Things like that. I don't know what any of this means, or why it's happening. But I trust you, Jill. I need you to understand that this is what I'm experiencing. I don't have memory gaps. I just remember things *differently*. Other versions."

"If your memories are changing after losing consciousness each time, maybe—and I hate to even say this—you're suffering some kind of brain damage. Why are you passing out in the first place? I think you need to get to the root cause of this before it gets worse."

"Believe me, I intend to. I'm wondering if the most recent thing you told me is a clue somehow. I have no difficulty believing that Equimedian is dicey."

"Here's a thought. The break-in happened shortly after you made that call."

"How would they—"

"If they're in league with Codis, they could have access to all kinds of information and technology."

"Possibly," I say. "But the only thing that was missing

from my room was the Equimedian flyer. Why would they steal their own flyer?"

"Hmmm. You're sure that was the only thing?"

"Yeah. Positivo."

"Then I don't know," she admits.

"I'm not saying Equimedian isn't up to something, but it just seems like it may be more complicated. Which makes the timing of our conversation perfect, since I'm going to visit their office in about thirty minutes."

"Say what?"

"Eye consultation," I explain. "Remember I told you they might be able to help? They offered to do a preliminary consult and tell me my options. See, I suspected that they might be in league with the PPs, which would account for their advanced technology. Plus, something Cole and I heard at the PP lottery office was similar to something the Equimedian gal told me over the phone."

Concern elevates the pitch of Jill's voice. "You're going alone?"

"No. I told you about Kathleen, the writer? She was curious about their outfit and she's coming with."

"Where are you right now?"

I give her the street name. "I'm sitting in the Codis car, waiting to pick up Kathleen in a bit. I'll return the vehicle to the office tomorrow."

"Please be extra careful."

"I will."

"Get out of there if anything feels off."

"You bet," I assure her. "And I'll call you when I get back home tonight."

"Please do. Tommy's coming over for dinner, but I'll make sure to answer."

"Enjoy your date."

"You too," she says, "if that's what it is."

"Maybe."

"Talk soon."

"Bye."

After I hang up, a peculiar lethargy washes over me. I let out a long sigh and close my eyes. I feel my body growing heavy, sinking into the car seat. Then all of the pressure disappears. I weigh nothing. In this new, free-floating state, fragments of my conversation with Jill play back in my head. *Codis. Equimedian. Mental gymnastics. Ways to justify my paycheck.* I watch myself perform installation after installation, week after week, month after month, year after year. I remember apartments, faces, smells, fragments of conversations. I remember a customer who offered me dope. I remember a woman who tried to sell me her religion. I remember the sounds of a couple having sex in a bedroom while I set up shop for their roommate in the living room. I think back on the most gorgeous homes and the most squalid interiors. I see all of this work unspool in slow-motion freeze-frames and in continuous, smooth fast-forward simultaneously, from my first day with the company through today. And then my view splits off into individual channels of experience, every pathway of every single customer putting on an EmuX and plugging into the system. I inhabit thousands and thousands of minds, see the world—real and simulated—through their eyes, feel their emotions, hear their thoughts. All of this is my doing. There's a trace of me, a spark of whatever makes me who I am, trapped in every interface, lingering in every connection. I have deployed nodes for Codis to colonize not only the residences, but the private mental spaces, of countless individuals. *I* have facilitated this. *Me.* I have helped to entrap people, to lull them into an endless, decadent fantasy, always on the cusp of an imagined moment that will not and cannot, by its very design, ever arrive. I have helped them to get on their knees and drink from a trough whose brew can only make them thirstier. I have led them to a libation that withers instead of nourishing.

Seducing them with the promise of hyper-reality, I have put them to sleep. I see it.

And then I see nothing at all.

IV. THE COMPOSERS OF TIME

TWENTY

MY CONSCIOUSNESS IS prodded by the sound of flugelhorns, cornets, marimbas, a saxello, clavinet, electric bass and thumping drums. Before I know where I am, I groan and say, "For God's sakes, the racket…"

"That racket is Eddie Henderson's *Sunburst*," a man answers. "'Explodition' is probably my favorite cut. Truly stellar. Thought it might be a nice way to wake up."

My face is slack. Is this what death feels like? Just in case it isn't, I massage the skin to stimulate blood-flow, and soon sensation returns.

I open my eyes and the light raining in through a living room window nicks a thousand little jagged cuts into my awareness. "Ouch," I moan. My eyes take a minute or two to adjust to the initially excruciating mid-afternoon brightness, and then rove over my surroundings.

The man who just talked to me is sitting in a recliner. I myself, I realize, am strewn indecorously on a couch.

I sit up. I point to the window. "Fresh air, please." The man complies and pulls it open a few inches. The swoosh of outside air and the sounds of light traffic somewhere below, audible under the loud music, act like reality-rails along which the train of my cognition can chugga-chugga forward.

The song ends and another begins. "Yep," the man says. "This is great. Check it out. Herbie Hancock's 'You'll Know When You Get There,' from his masterpiece *Mwandishi*." The mellower vibe makes me hopeful we can have a conversation.

"Who are you?" I say. "And where am I?"

"Name's Tommy," he says. "I'm Jill's boyfriend. This is our apartment."

Ah yes. Tommy, the well-travelled, well-read engineer. "Where's Jill? And how did I end up in your living room?"

"She's at work," Tommy says. "She didn't get much sleep last night. When I got home, she told me you had talked to her, had told her you'd call her after going someplace, and then you didn't. She asked me to join her, and we went to the street she'd written down, looked for Codis vehicles and found you. You were out of it. Completely zonked. The inside of the car was broiling and you were covered in sweat. We brought you here and set you up on the couch."

The sax is starting to pick up now—I can't tell if it's the same track or a new one—and I'm not sure I've heard him correctly.

I stare in disbelief. "You found me in the Codis car?"

"Yeah. Good thing she was looking out for you."

"How were you able to get in?"

"Fortunately for us you left it unlocked."

"Hmm." I pull down the orange-brown floral and paisley-patterned blanket covering me and confirm that I never made it out of my clothes, which in light of Tommy's story feel sticky and gross. Following my coma-like sleep, I can barely move. I long to pull the blanket back up and tell Tommy to go away. But I'm a guest here. I should attempt to act moderately housebroken.

"Can I ask something stupid?" I say.

"Shoot."

"You live here?"

He smiles. "Yes sir."

"If you don't mind my being nosy, how long?"

"Jill and I have been living together for almost a year. Only two months to the big day."

"You're… engaged?"

"We sure are." He looks at the door, as though evoking Jill's presence, and then flashes his ring. "I'm glad Jill warned me that you might have some questions after waking up. Otherwise, I'd be pretty worried right about now."

"I appreciate your patience, believe me."

"How did you sleep?" he asks.

My back aches. My neck aches. My mouth smells like a skunk climbed into it and decomposed while I slept.

I realize I need to answer Tommy's question. "Your couch is comfy."

He says, "I'm glad. It's going to be your bed for a while."

"But—"

"We insist. Jill called Leon last night after finding you in the car, went over—Leon hopes you feel better, by the way—and picked up some of your belongings. He said that even though you were about to move out, you're welcome back anytime if you change your mind; he's hardly ever home because of all the time he spends at the local chapter, so you'd have plenty of peace and quiet. Over there in those bags, that's yours." He points. Then he focuses on the music.

"And now Sam Rivers' *Streams*? This station is knocking it out of the park."

Somewhere in the new sonic jungle of sax, piano and gongs a flute emerges, like a reed peeking out from the undergrowth. I sit up straighter. "Did you say the local chapter?"

"Right."

"As in, of a religious community?"

"As in, the United Presbyterian Church. You know, Leon being a minister and all."

Oh shit. It must have happened again.

"Leon is a minister. Did I hear you correctly?" Tommy turns down the music.

"That's right."

I decide to give myself a moment before asking him more questions. I need it to preserve what tatters of my sanity remain. He uses this time to remark on the next musical selection, a track from Miroslav Vitous' *Purple*, and the one after that, from Lonnie Liston Smith & the Cosmic Echoes' *Expansions*. The latter has a more straightforward beat. Thank the heavens.

"Electric jazz is really your thing," I observe.

He nods. "As long as it's spacey, you know."

"Believe me, I know all about spacey."

Next up is a live album called *Listen to the Silence* by someone named George Russell. The shifting timpani, organs, and Fender bass act as a spunky soundtrack to the uncertainties brewing in my mind.

"Jill says you like to read," I comment. "For sure."

"Favorite genres?"

"I'm a history buff. Some science. And biographies. I'm addicted to other people's life stories."

"Interesting." I pause. "Science fiction?"

"Sorry," he says. "Not my cup of tea. I tried a couple of books, like *Dune*, back in college, but I bounced off them. Later this friend of mine insisted I read something called *Ringplanet* or *Rinkworld* or something like that, and I couldn't grok it at all."

I've no desire to press him on this subject, nor to point out the irony of his using a word popularized by Robert Heinlein's work. *De gustibus non est disputandum* and what have you.

Tommy must notice I'm perking up. "Can I get you something to eat?" he asks.

"Coffee please," I say. "Toast if you have some. And if it's not too rude, could I shower?"

"By all means."

"By the way, what time is it?"

"About 3 pm. I took the day off to look after you until Jill gets back."

"That's very kind of you."

I focus on the last things I remember from the previous night.

"Can I use your phone?"

"Sure. What's up?"

"I completely stood someone up," I say.

"Oh, that writer. Jill mentioned her name."

"Right."

In my wallet I find the wrinkled napkin with Kathleen's number. Three rings later her voicemail kicks in. I leave a somewhat incoherent message, which I nevertheless hope will convey my apology.

After the coffee and toast, I steal away into the bathroom with a change of clothes from one of my bags.

The jet of cool water, the scrubbing and soaping, bring alertness and an inkling of hope. All I know so far from my exchange with Tommy is that in this version of reality he and Jill have been cohabiting for longer than I remember them dating, and that this Leon is, to put it mildly, different from the one I know—*knew*. Based on these two pieces of information alone I can surmise there will be plenty of other changes awaiting my discovery.

To this end, I should focus on practicalities.

I brush my teeth and slip into clean clothes.

When I emerge, I see Jill in the kitchen talking with Tommy in a low voice. "Jason." Relief kindles her eyes. "How do you feel?"

"I'm… figuring things out," I say. "Getting into the swing of being back amongst the living. Tommy had me groovin' out."

"I'm glad he's let his hair down around you." She pinches Tommy's cheek and kisses his shoulder.

"So…" I begin.

"So…" she continues.

As I approach, she and Tommy exchange glances.

"I know this is a tough situation," she says. "But whatever you need, please ask us. We've been talking. Here's something to help you get back on your feet." She hands me an envelope.

"I can't," I say.

"Please," Tommy says.

"It's too much," I say without opening it.

"If you feel strongly about it, you can always pay us back later. Though we're not asking you to."

I reach forward to hug her, and then I shake his hand.

"I'm only taking this because you're agreeing to let me pay it back."

I get a refill on the coffee and put together a rough plan for the rest of the day. It's not too soon, I figure, to begin thinking about new employment. I have tech skills and experience, but at this point I'm willing to take whatever I can find. I need to call my parents soon to talk about the move. I make a note to return the Codis vehicle, too, which is now one day late.

Then I swing by the bank and ask for my balance. I'm expecting bad news: the account should be depleted, maybe overdrawn.

It isn't. Far from it.

I'm convinced there's been a mistake, but the teller triple-checks the number.

Apparently, along with my final Codis paycheck, a sizable transfer was made to me today. The description is vaguely similar to Codis. I don't like it. I don't want to be financially beholden to anyone connected with Codis or Equimedian. "I need that transfer undone," I advise the teller. "I wasn't supposed to receive that money. It's not mine."

"But sir—"

"Do whatever you have to to reverse it."

"I'll make a note for my manager to look into it. Do you have a phone number where we can reach you?"

"Not at the moment," I say.

It takes me about half an hour to calm down. When I return to Jill and Tommy's apartment, he's out doing some shopping while she prepares dinner. I check for messages but Kathleen hasn't called back.

"Tommy seems like a sweet guy," I say to Jill. "I'm glad to see that things have… progressed."

"How so?"

"Jill, do you remember the phone conversation we had yesterday before I passed out in the Codis car?"

There's a look that deer get in headlights, and then there's the look that the humans who are driving the car to which the headlights are attached get when they see the deer's fright. Jill's face contorts into that second expression. "Are you telling me it's happened again? Things have changed from what you remember?"

"I'm afraid so."

"Me and Tommy?"

"As of yesterday, I have no memory of you guys living together—or being engaged."

"Get real."

"Jill, I'm as serious as a first edition of *1984*."

"Jason," she says. To the best of my recollection, my name has never sounded like a warning before.

"I know what you're going to say," I reply. "You're going to cite all the reasons why you're right and I'm wrong. I don't want to argue about it. In fact, I'll grant you that you and Tommy both remember it the same way, so clearly I'm the outlier here. And you're going to tell me to have my head examined—which I've already done, and they haven't found anything wrong."

I think about Bob Shaw's novel *Who Goes Here?*, in which memory engram erasure is one of the benefits of joining the Space Legion. Has someone messed with my memory? If so, they could have removed my memories of their memory tampering. But I don't have gaps, rather alternate memories.

What's the end game here? Memory recordings are standard fare in John Varley's Eight Worlds stories. Maybe Codis has already developed something along these lines and I'm their unwitting guinea pig? Can they remember things for me wholesale, to paraphrase that mainstay of reality-implosion, Phil Dick? Or maybe my memories, rather than being created, have been transferred to me from another person, like in van Vogt's *Tyranopolis*? But then why are so many things still right? *Get a grip, Jason. This is your life, not a tawdry paperback.*

The next question seems natural in light of my disconnect from Jill. Have I read too much science fiction? Has it left me permanently unhinged from the real world?

"Maybe you're somehow generating the version of events you prefer to remember," Jill says, "and as that narrative takes root in your mind, it supplants what's really happened. Maybe you've suffered some kind of head trauma."

"Maybe," I say. "I wonder how far back the discrepancies go. How long have you been teaching at Brentwood High?"

"Nine years," she says.

"Okay, good. Right. Nine years. Have you ever been married?"

"You know I have."

"Mark Levine. Not a good guy. Correct?"

"Correct."

"What do you think of Aldous Huxley's work?"

"What?"

"You heard me."

"I'm not sure," she says. "I liked his stuff when I was a teen."

"How old?"

"Thirteen," she says. "Maybe fourteen."

"Did you have any favorites besides *Brave New World*?"

"*After Many a Summer* was pretty good."

"Have you ever taught science fiction?"

"No."

"Everything you're saying is consistent with what I remember. Let's try something more recent. Shanice Vega."

"We sort of got along."

"Yes, I remember that. You used to tease me with this word, I don't recall what it was. You'd say to me after hanging out with her that you two had had a… Beckett conversation? A Becker interaction?"

"A Bechdel interaction," Jill says, and laughs.

"You never explained to me what that meant."

"That we weren't talking about you," she teases.

"Fine," I say. "How long were Shanice and I together?"

"I think some three years."

"Right."

"And then," she starts.

"Go on."

"Well, after the breakup," Jill says, "you were in a dark place. You withdrew. I didn't take it personally. When you were ready to get back into the world, you did."

"I stopped talking to you?"

"Not just me."

"That I have no memory of."

"Maybe you blocked it out."

"Let me ask you one more. When did I start reading science fiction?"

She sounds surprised. "You? Gosh. You've always loved it."

"Try again. This is important."

"You told me you read it in school. Your brother was into the stuff and he turned you on to it."

"That's not what happened," I say. "I thought it was junk at the time. Gave Ryan a hard time for it. Made his life hell."

"You could have fooled me."

"Jill, listen to me. I don't want to get into the whole sordid saga, but it was only after Boglins died that I really fell hard for the stuff. That was ten years ago."

"Boglins?"

"Ryan. My brother."

"Jason, you're testing me again, right?" I can see it, banshee panic trapped in her mouth, waiting to explode into being, a hardening of her face and a closing of her pupils. "You're trying to trip me up?"

I speak slowly, full of conviction. "Absolutely not."

She looks at me as though from a vast distance. "Your brother died over twenty years ago. When he tried to protect you from that bully at school. One of the bully's gang pulled a knife, he rushed him, and it ended up stabbing him in the chest."

"Come again?"

"You remember that bully. Dustin something?"

"*Shea*?"

"Yes."

Now I can't help but think of Jack Williamson's *The Legion of Time*—published in magazine form in 1938, three years before I was born—and its famous John Barr scenario, the fulcrum moment where John Barr's interest in a magnet leads to one world and his distraction with a pebble to another very different world, both of them identical prior to that moment.

Philosophers, armed with quantum mechanics, have argued that every instant of our lives is like a John Barr choice, an infinity of unfolding, reduplicating possibilities leading to uncountable realities. I know without a doubt that I was the one involved with Dustin Shea and his ignoble ilk, and that my brother died after enrolling in an experimental PP program.

Despite my imaginative prowess, I can't seriously entertain Jill's version. Me the victim, Ryan my protector? But we might be getting somewhere. The year of Ryan's death isn't a matter of subjective recall. I make a note to look up his obit in the library.

"Jason, maybe we should get the police involved."

"I agree that something isn't right," I say, "but the cops won't be able to do anything about it. How long would you say we've been friends, Jill?"

"About fifteen years."

"So according to you, we weren't friends in school?"

"We didn't even go to the same school."

"Then how did we meet?"

"At that demonstration, in December '64. We both marched. I was part of the Student Peace Union. There were over a thousand protesters."

"The way I remember things, I was never there."

"The you *I* know has always been politically active."

"I think Church is doing okay."

"Who?"

"The President."

She shakes her head. "Jason, it's President Carter. What are we going to do about this?"

I give her question serious thought. "I'm not in pain," I

say. "I seem to be functioning fine cognitively, except for my memories. I'm not sure why, but I think it's somehow connected with Equimedian, maybe Codis. Ever since I found that flyer, things have become messed up."

She gives me the patented Jill Hann look of concern. At least that's one variable that doesn't appear to have changed between shifts.

"How can I help you?"

"I don't want to get you further involved," I say. "I'm going to call Cole. Maybe he and I can figure a plan of attack."

"Okay," she says.

When Tommy gets home from his shopping the three of us have dinner. The conversation is uneasy. I try to shift us away from my current predicament, though it seems to seep into everything. In the living room there's a bookcase full of history books, and I ask Tommy for some recommendations. Figure it might be good to familiarize myself with this reality's past. He picks out four or five volumes and offers a few words of praise for each. "Let me know if this stuff's too dry," he says. "I tend to favor an unsentimental approach. Modern writers are good at sticking to the facts. The history books from ten or twenty years ago can be overly romantic. I don't believe in idealizing the past."

"Got it, thanks," I say.

Books set aside, I decide it's only proper that Tommy and Jill should get some alone time. I phone up Cole and he agrees to meet me downstairs in half an hour. Jill and Tommy give me a key, and I ask them not to wait up for me. I pass the time by going for a walk. This neighborhood is charming but some of the smaller, cramped streets smell like burning rubber mixed with a dank aroma of roadkill, fried rice and motor oil. The smell seems to settle in the edges of my nostrils and I can't vacate it. My eyesight, too, appears to degrade, and I decide to wait out the last five minutes standing in place.

"Good to see you," I say when Cole shows up.

"Likewise," he says, jovially. He pauses to study me. "My friend, you look a tad distressed."

"Things have been, uh, interesting. I'll fill you in on the way."

"Very well. Where are we going?"

"Good question," I say glumly.

"Actually, there's a party that was advertised in one of the fanzines recently," he says. "It's only five stops from here. I know an editor who'll likely be there that I'd like to talk to, if you're feeling up to it."

I take my emotional temperature. As in other moments of uncertainty in my life, I look up at the sky. It feels cavernous and vast in the gathering twilight, with barely a handful of stars on display. Memories of a similar sky long ago make me tremulous. A chill reaches deep inside me, and I don't fight it. After it's passed through, I feel better.

"Let's do it," I say.

TWENTY-ONE

BY THE TIME Cole and I arrive at the shindig, I'm starting to have second thoughts about venturing out into the world. A fan is hosting the event to honor the fact that his wife, a prolific semi-professional illustrator, has been active in the field for forty years. Thank goodness, Cole expects mostly fans of visual art forms to be present, so I needn't worry about bumping into many Custodians or Mayflies I know.

The apartment is a small one-bedroom crammed with bookshelves and paintings and sketches, some of them presumably by the artist, Carol. Someone offers me a soft drink made on a SodaStream—"get busy with the fizzy"—and I accept, much to my rapid regret. The folk music being played on the turntable and the ambient conversational chatter make it hard to hear oneself think, which I sort of welcome. Eventually Cole and I find a corner where two men and a woman seem to be conversing quite intently. I locate the kitchen and come back with two beers.

"If you're looking for invisible enemies, look no farther than *Jaws*," one of the men is saying. "It doesn't get more obvious than that. A hidden uncontrollable force, right in

241

the water. It's out of sight but plainly in nature. *It's the force of nature itself.*"

"Sure. But check out what that director—Spielberg? Spielbender?—did in his earlier flick, *Duel*. Same thing. An uncontrollable force, in the form of a truck, obsessively and relentlessly pursuing its victim. It's not about the truck driver's face or identity. The driver is hidden. Is the truck supposed to be a force of nature? I doubt it. I think the notion of a hidden force is something specific to this director, rather than a general trend as you're claiming. It's not about nature. It's about invisibility on an abstract level."

The woman notices Cole first, then me. She smiles knowingly, as though she's been watching this ping pong match for a while with little stake in the outcome. I observe the irony of the man who animatedly said the word "invisibility" not having noticed Cole and me as we approached.

"If you're saying it's about Spielberg, then how do you explain *The Towering Inferno*? Another uncontrollable force at work."

"Limit your selection to films about nature gone wrong and of course you're going to find a common theme of nature going wrong. That's called circular reasoning."

"Let's do horror then. *The Exorcist*. Uncontrollable hidden force."

This is as good a moment as any to jump in. "In a way, one could view *The Godfather* through the same lens. The Sicilian mafia—organized crime in general—is a hidden and far- reaching force within our cityscape." I'm taking a chance, assuming that *The Godfather* is a thing folks will recognize in this version of the world, but I've been lucky in that books and films appear to have remained constant through my shifts so far.

"Yes!" The first man, whose brown eyes cast a glaucous, perhaps alcohol-induced, sheen, lurches forward towards me, and I humor him with a half-embrace. He's six four, maybe six five, barrel-shaped, with long curly hair and the kind of beard resulting from four late nights rather than forethought and a trimming razor. "He's right," he goes on, grabbing my arm with surprising gentleness. "That's what I've been saying all along. What's your name?"

"Jason. And this is my pal Cole."

"Nice to meet you guys. By any chance have you read Joan Hunter Holly's *The Death Dolls of Lyra*? It's about this doll-shaped fungus from outer space, well not exactly, but it talks about the same thing we're discussing, an uncontrollable force that for a long time remains hidden. By the by, I think I have a rash on my elbow. It's been bothering me for weeks. You're not a doctor by any chance, are you? Anyway, these are all metaphors for our loss of control as a society. As a *world* society." He stretches out "world" with a swirling drawl, so that it sounds like a freakily elongated "whirl."

I don't want to encourage this lunatic, but honesty gets the better of me. Besides, when else am I going to get the chance to discuss the fiction of Joan Hunter Holly? I glance at Cole, who gives me a go-for-it grin. "An excellent novel," I say. "The way it starts with those two extragalactic toy dolls is genius. And then how the fungus takes over the town and people go *insane*, marvelous stuff. By any chance did you get the rash when you read the book?" I smile impishly.

"Don't even," the second man squawks. He's as burly as the first, better groomed but worse dressed, and his voice has an implausibly high timber. Is he wearing pajamas? I can't think how else to describe his baggy attire.

"What do *you* think?" Cole asks the woman.

"I think Jon here should roll up his sleeve," she says with malevolent glee. "I'd like to see how bad that rash is. Holly, by the way."

"Nice to meet you," Cole says.

Jon doesn't take long to follow her ignominious suggestion. Fortunately for us, he can't peel the skinny sleeve up past the elbow of his flabby arm, and he gives up after a few seconds of huffing.

"If you really wanted to carry your premise to its logical conclusion," says the man who dismissed Jon's claims, and by extension mine, "you'd incorporate *Doctor Who* into your argument. There was an episode actually titled 'The Invisible Enemy.' Maybe the show's creators wanted to let us know they've observed this phenomenon you're insisting on."

"Excuse me, are you wearing pajamas?" I ask the second man.

He turns to me, expanding his chest in pride. "What, you've never seen Johnnie Fingers playing with the Boomtown Rats? I figure if he can get away with it, so can I. Anyway, to get back to the topic at hand. If invisible enemies are behind everything, how do you account for infant plastic surgery?"

"It's the parents who're doing it," Jon says. "Right in the open, nothing secretive about it. They say no harm comes to the babies because they grow right through the modifications. It's not real surgery, I guess. More like prosthetic extensions designed to make the babies look much older than they are. Like putty."

"Ewww," the woman exclaims.

"It's obvious," Jon ploughs on, "that the agenda is one of fear. Facing middle age and mortality terrifies people, and they feel not-quite-so-old when they don't have to confront the youth of their infants. There's only two logical ways to close the gap: make the old look younger or make the young look older. This unhealthy obsession with appearance is pushed on us by the media, which endlessly accentuates superficiality over substance."

"It's true that more and more people like to live in make-believe worlds," Mr. Pajamas says, perhaps not realizing that that's as good as any a description of the time spent living inside the world of a novel.

"Like the crap Codis peddles," says Jon.

Talk about silver platters. "You'll be pleased to know," I say, "that I quit them."

"Why did you subscribe in the first place?" Jon says.

"No, no, I worked for them."

"Oh!" Jon is enthused. "And then you quit—good for you! Rumors have been raging about how their voice-acti-vated computers secretly record users' conversations. Total invasion of privacy, it's unseemly."

I wonder if these computers are provided by another department within Codis. I don't remember them from my training days—but then again, that was years ago, and they've come out with new products since then, which they were perhaps too compartmentalized to train their EmuX specialists on.

"Sounds nasty," I say. "But EmuXs are even more insidi-ous."

"Excuse me, what now?"

"EmuXs—you know, the machines that emulate what it's like to live a fraction of a fraction of a second in the future, like the PPs do."

Everyone, including Cole, is giving me looks.

"Never mind," I say, defeated. This must be another change in this version of reality. *Good thing I quit my job,* I think with no shortage of self-directed sarcasm, *since it doesn't even seem to exist anymore.*

"Plus, their connection with Equimedian really stinks," Jon says. "Evil is a many-headed hydra, but there's nothing subtle or hidden about any of these buffoons."

"How long did you work for them?" asks Holly.

I give the group a rundown of my years with Codis and some of the things I observed during that time. Cole fetches us a second round of beers. I characterize my customers as mostly uninspiring, and I note that I find it especially depressing that Codis' popularity seems to be skyrocketing. "More and more folks preferring the virtual to the real," I muse.

After answering some additional questions about my career, we get back to science fiction and stay on the topic for at least an hour, during which round three of beer takes place. Cole finds the editor that he wanted to pull up with and then circles back to our group. I notice him yawning around one in the morning, and I'm happy to call it a night as well.

We excuse ourselves. Cole uses the bathroom first and then it's my turn. He signals that he'll wait for me by the front door.

From inside the bathroom the sounds of the party become waves lapping up against a faraway beach.

After peeing and flushing, I turn on the water to wash my

hands. Following a quick rinse I dab some water on my temples, splash a little on my face, and let the droplets bead down my neck and under my shirt. I hold my hands up, enjoying the sensation of water drops snaking down my arms.

I know Cole is waiting for me, and I don't wish to be rude, but something compels me to linger in this bathroom.

I dry my hands and notice that above the toilet there are three white metal shelves packed with books. I've never been one to read in a bathroom, and find the location of these paperbacks icky. And yet, out of habit, I find myself scanning the titles.

None of them are familiar, though unsurprisingly they appear to be science fiction and fantasy offshoots, mostly by British publishers. A trade paperback called *The Stone Book* catches my eye. Despite my wariness at the yuckiness of the situation, I pull it down, and find myself moved by a strikingly minimalist and melancholy wraparound cover. It shows the cross-section of a hill, with a man walking up towards the hill's crest while carrying a sack. A rear cover quote describes the novel as "weird, strange and simply beautiful." As the seconds pass, it becomes heavier in my hand, more real. *One paragraph*, I tell myself. *One line.*

I open it at random.

No matter how hard I try, my eyes are unable to resolve the symbols on the page into meaningful characters or words.

The letters won't stay still.

Indecipherable dancing symbols, like the ones in my trapdoor dream…

Like tiny worms, they wiggle.

I try, to no avail, to will my eyeballs into becoming their fishhooks.

I squint.

I rub my eyes.

Nothing.

The characters dance and dance before me.

∽

Ringing. More ringing. It won't stop. And then a second sound, an internal clangor, splits off from the incessant jingle. Grudgingly, I accept the return of reality. The words necessary to verbalize what's happening form in my consciousness as sleep evaporates in wisps: *The phone is ringing and I have a serious headache.*

I roll over and reach for the receiver. I'm not yet ready to open my sleep-crusted eyes, so I use my fingers to feel my way towards the sound.

Ouch. It's not only my head. My entire body throbs in protest.

Ring. Ring. Riiiiiiiing.

There it is. Damned phone. Vibrating against my fingertips now.

My arm twitches as I raise the receiver and pull it in the general direction of my face. "Hello?" I say, voice at least an octave lower than usual.

"Is this Jason Velez?"

The voice is so upbeat I could throw up. I clear my throat. "*What time is it and who the hell are you?*"

"I'm so glad we were able to get in touch with you," the voice continues, undaunted by my sluggishness and uninterested in my queries. "We got this number from your roommate Leon. My name is Gina, and I'm a representative of the Progress Pilgrims Lottery. I'm delighted to share with you that as of three minutes and ten seconds ago, you're officially a Progress Pilgrims lottery winner! Congratulations, Mr. Velez. A whole new future awaits you—and it begins right now!"

That gets my eyes open. I stare at the phone, as though it might spontaneously develop sentience and let me know what I should feel. "Whoever this is, did Leon put you up to it? Ramon?"

"I understand that this news might come as a shock, but this is no prank." The voice is sincere. "I'm going to ask you some basic questions to verify that you're Jason Velez. We'll need to confirm everything in person, but this is a preliminary check. Once that's completed, I'll be happy to tell you about some of the benefits of your prize."

Without wanting to, I automatically verify the information she provides, namely my address, phone number, date of birth, and driver's license number. She then reads me the lottery ticket number, which matches my recollection of the one I cast with Cole.

"Fantastic," she says, a chirrup of enthusiasm. "Naturally, you'll have to undergo some basic medical tests to ensure our modified PP tech won't pose any risks to your health, and then you'll need to complete a short guidance training. When these two trifling items are behind you, Mr. Velez, you can start to reap the benefits of your prize. You'll be able to experience temporal micro-displacement firsthand!"

Her voice compounds the throbbing in my head. I hold my hand over the receiver to muffle it and call out Jill and Tommy's names. No answer. I roll towards the edge of the couch, so I can, with some squinting, see the clock on the opposite wall. It's eleven thirty. Holy crap. My right eyelid flutters. I definitely need aspirin.

"Hello?" I say back into the receiver. "I'm going to need to check this out in person. Anyone could get a hold of my number and say the things you're saying."

"Mr. Velez, did I not correctly confirm your lottery ticket number earlier? How else would I have known that information?"

"That's why we're still talking, Gina." I'm not sure if I sound firm or mean. "Tell me where your office is, and I'll come down there."

"Mr. Velez," Gina begins, "based on our experiences with previous winners, you're about to gain a certain measure of celebrity from your newfound status. Reporters will likely start contacting you within the next few hours. Winners are officially disclosed on the mid- day news, you see, and newspapers are often curious as to winners' life stories. All this is a long way of saying that we recommend privacy and a certain guarded stance. Your relationship with the media is entirely your own, of course, but the initial tone of your interactions may determine what follows, so it's best to be savvy rather than getting caught off guard. We therefore offer a complementary service. To finalize the paperwork necessary for you to redeem your prize and begin the first phase of your temporal micro-displacement program, we're happy to send a driver to your address. The driver will escort you to our headquarters with a maximum of discretion. By the time the reporters get to your home, you'll be long gone."

"Next thing you know you'll be bringing in a man called Sloane to protect me." Blame Leon for my reference to this secret agent television show; who could have possibly guessed it would come in handy? I waltz to the medicine cabinet, find some aspirin and down two, then return to the phone. "What I'm saying is that this all sounds over-the-top, Gina. I'll take my chances with the reporters."

"Naturally, that's up to you."

"Then you'll give me your address."

"I can give you the address of a location where you can rendezvous with one of our mobile teams," she says, imbuing the words with nonchalance. "We don't, as a rule, disclose our HQ address, because leaks to the media can cause problems on our end. We house sensitive testing equipment there, and so on, and have already suffered various break-in attempts."

"As far as I'm concerned, you're just a voice. My mom told me never to get into cars with strangers," I say.

"Mr. Velez, I wholeheartedly respect your desire for caution, and I appreciate your skepticism. How can I help convince you that these measures are in your best interests?"

"Give me your address. Let me get there on my own. Then we can continue the conversation in person."

"Are you declining your prize?"

"I didn't say that."

"I can't disclose our address, for the reasons mentioned," she says, "But please, do ask anything else that comes to mind."

I throw on a brown, print floral shirt and some tan corduroy slacks, making myself halfway presentable. Would my matching two-button tan blazer be too much? Look at me, already thinking of media photographs. The blur in my right eye is pretty severe by now, and my headache has induced a rictus.

"Would you like your family notified?" she asks. "Some of our winners ask us to courtesy-call their loved ones with the good news while they are en route to our HQ. Others prefer no special contact."

"Since I'm not en route anywhere, I don't need you to call them. I'll tell them myself, when I'm ready. Which will be once I can prove it's true."

"Very well."

I pick at a bothersome eyelash and renegade hair chafing against the corner of my right eye. "Is there a cash prize associated with my win?"

"I'm afraid not, Mr. Velez. Though once you've experienced temporal micro-displacement, certain remunerative opportunities will become available to you. There's a whole host of jobs, for example, that require temporal micro-displacement and are thus not available to the general public. There are also tremendous investment opportunities in a variety of PP micro-displacement spin-off technologies."

I barely understand how the real stock market works, and what I do grasp already feels like hexing, or maybe hoaxing. I'm sure this thievery she's talking about is at least a hundred times more impressive. The PPs don't have to create money out of thin air, I realize. They can literally steal—borrow, I'm sure they call it—from the ever-immediate future. My gag reflex surges up. "What about medical technology?"

"Would you care to be more specific, Mr. Velez?"

"I have a cataract in one eye. The other may follow. Could PP doctors treat me?"

"I'm not familiar with the details of that particular condition," she says, "but you are eligible for a free consultation.

If they have the ability to help you, they will. They feel it's imperative to lead by example."

I think about my appointment with Equimedian. I made a plan to go with Kathleen and ended up passing out in my car and standing her up. Will this turn out any better? At least, I think, everyone knows about and accepts the PP lottery; Equimedian, though recently in the news, feels more sinister. Or am I simply justifying myself with this line of reasoning?

"How soon could I get that consultation?" I ask.

"Normally the earliest option would be upon completing the intro I referenced earlier. But given your special circumstances, I can make a note that you'd like the consultation as soon as you complete testing," Gina says. "The diagnostics take less than two hours. By dinner time today you could have both the testing and the consultation behind you."

I dwell on her choice words, "special circumstances." What does she mean by that phrase—the obvious desperation in my voice? My refusal to play along? Both?

What I really need right now, I realize, is someone inside the PP system to validate whether any of these claims are true.

I say, "If you can put me in touch with someone I know who is already micro-displaced, I might be persuaded to agree to your terms."

"You will be able to speak with anyone registered on the micro-displacement grid yourself once you are induced— sorry, induction, that's the technical term we use for the transition from our present to the PPs'. May I have the person's name?"

"Shanice Vega. As a matter of fact, she left a message for me not too long ago, which the folks at the lottery office were kind enough to forward. Can you connect me to her?"

I'm surprised by my own impetuousness. But now that the notion is in my head, I can't let it go.

"I'm afraid I don't have that ability," Gina says, summoning a convincing simulacrum of regret. "Messages may be sent from undisplaced individuals to those displaced only by a relay of Planck-scaled bridges, and that's a costly procedure."

"Cost be damned. If I can't talk to her, you can stuff your prize."

"Mr. Velez—"

"She married a prominent PP, so she shouldn't be hard to find. Aren't you an ambassador for the PPs? Isn't the entire point of this lottery to create goodwill amongst non-PPs?"

"The PPs do indeed wish to raise awareness about certain social causes, and to share their technology with others," Gina says.

"Are you in their employ? Who pays your salary, Gina?"

"I'm a government employee," Gina says. "The PPs help fund the lottery, which is federally administrated. But I'm not sure I see—"

"If the PPs sign your paycheck, then technically you're working for Shanice Vega. And she would want you to fulfill my request, even if it's expensive. Her message said that maybe there was a way for me to see her. She said I should contact the PPs, *and that's what I'm asking you to do.*"

After the longest pause thus far, she says, "Let me see what I can do. It may take a few minutes for this to get sorted out, so I'll call you back shortly."

"Good deal."

I pace in Tommy and Jill's living room, trying to get a handle on my thoughts. Then I hear keys in the front door, and Jill comes in, a tchotchke of some kind in her hand.

"Jason." She looks pleased to see me up and about. "We went antiquing. Tommy's parking, he'll be up in a minute. How are you? We didn't hear you come in last night, but it must have been late."

"Yeah," I say. "Stayed out later than I should have and probably drank too much. Thanks for letting me sleep in." I proceed to relay a condensed version of my exchange with Gina.

Jill sets down her knickknack, worry lines furrowing her brow. "I'm glad you didn't agree to be picked up by their car," she says. "Something doesn't feel right about all this."

"I know," I say. "On the other hand, what if it's true?"

"I suppose that's possible," she concedes. "You said she confirmed your identity?"

"She did."

"Still, you should be careful."

"I'm waiting for her to call me back."

"Okay," she says.

Tommy arrives, and she fills him in.

"There are things that are too good to be true," he says, "and then there are things that may or may not be true but are not good."

"What does that mean?" I ask.

"Even if it's not a scam, it could be dangerous."

"After everything you've been through, I'd hate to see you get taken advantage of," Jill adds.

"I appreciate the concern." I fight a spark of defensiveness. The epiphanies I experienced during my oceanic vision come back to me, warning me about old patterns. Jill is herself, no one else. She's not my mother. "I'll be cautious," I assure them.

A few minutes later, Gina calls back as promised. She informs me that her supervisor has approved an exception to the usual process and has put in a request for a communication to be sent through the timestream to Shanice Vega. There is a special PP officer that needs to approve it, but she should know soon.

"I think they'll say yes," she says. "It's mostly a formality. They trust that if a request is made, it's normally justified."

"Glad you were able to get this worked out. Now how do I leave the message for Shanice?"

"Make a note of the following number and password." She reads out a phone number and a six-character alphanumeric combination. "Call, enter the code, and leave your message. It's a secure voice box for PP communications. That way you're guaranteed privacy."

"Understood. I appreciate it."

"Since we've complied with your request, Mr. Velez, I assume that means you're ready to initiate the lottery claim process. I've taken the liberty of informing our driver who'll be at your location in twenty-five minutes."

"Um—"

"We look forward to meeting you in person. It's been a pleasure." Click.

Out of a sense of obligation—it would be absurd not to follow through and leave Shanice a message after all the verbal energy I've already expended on it—I dial the number

Gina provided and ramble on for about a minute and a half before bashfulness gets the better of me.

Immediately thereafter, I find myself dialing another number I shouldn't have memorized—I told myself I wouldn't—but which nevertheless arrives at my fingertips without consultation. After three rings, voicemail.

"Kathleen," I say. "This is Jason. Hey, just calling to apologize again. It's really unlike me to stand anyone up. Anyway, I think I was dehydrated. That's all. Lack of H_2O. Good ol' H_2O. You know how it goes." I cringe at my own inanities, but I can't stop. "I'm doing a lot better now. How are you? Make sure you get plenty of fluids." Somebody beat me over the head with a shovel, please. And yet on I go. "Anyway, something's happened. I'm not sure, but it looks like I may have won the PP lottery. Since we didn't get down to the Equimedian office, I was wondering if maybe you wanted to join me on a visit to the PP lottery headquarters. If not, I completely understand, but maybe we can meet soon anyway. Hope things are going well for you. How's everything? Don't get dehydrated. Okay, gotta go."

Appalled at my message, I put it out of my mind as quickly as possible. After all these calls, I should be sick of the phone, but in an effort to preclude introspection and cast a lifeline into a world of sanity, I call Cole. He expresses a healthy dose of skepticism at the turn of events.

"I think I want to look into it," I say.

"A head-on approach," he notes. "I think that's not a bad way to go. You know that article I wrote about our visit to the PP lottery center?"

"Sure," I say.

"The reporter behind the *New York Times* piece on Codis

and Equimedian reached out to me with some questions. He thinks there may be more to the story, that the PPs might be somehow involved as well. If I can come with you to claim the prize, I might just be able to get another article out of it—and maybe the jigsaw pieces will fall into place."

"Great. That means you'll join me?"

"I shall," he says.

"I've been told a car is on its way to pick me up."

"I'll come over."

Tommy and Jill are in the kitchen.

"Cole's on his way," I tell them. "As is a PP car."

"Jason," Jill chides.

"I know, I know. I promise we'll be cautious. Cole's going to be taking notes."

Fifteen minutes later I greet Cole downstairs. Waiting for the PP vehicle, Jill's admonitions echo in my mind. She has good instincts. Maybe we should listen to her. I glance up at the apartment. *Turn around*, I tell myself. *Go back up. Let this storm—whatever it is—pass you by. Don't get caught up in someone else's production.*

That's when a Cadillac limo arrives.

TWENTY-TWO

"MEDICI CRUSHED VELOUR fabric," the driver says. "How do you like it?"

I recline in the back seat. "Not bad."

Cole shrugs, unimpressed. "I've seen better."

We drive for ten minutes, heading out of the city. The limo's interior is freezing, though it doesn't seem to be affecting Cole. I hug myself. The driver-passenger partition, raised up two-thirds at the start of our journey, offers a limited view of our driver. I try to lower the partition using the control panel in front of me, but none of the buttons seem to do anything. From what I can tell, the driver has a bulbous nose and a round, stubbly, pockmarked face, likely connected to a large body. He's probably six feet and two hundred and fifty pounds. The softness of his voice belies the ways in which his bulk might be deployed if he were displeased.

"This Cadillac also comes in black, with a light gray Magnan knit interior," he says. "Or commodore blue with a matching padded cross grain vinyl top. But the bosses went with dark blue Medici."

"The bosses have interesting taste," I say.

The driver laughs. "Talking about bosses, last week I

watched a TV interview with the city's mayor," he says. "What a putz. Utterly clueless."

"How so?" Cole inquires.

The driver's face tenses, as though being pressed for particularities is the equivalent of a mosquito's irksome buzz. "One way or another everyone in the city is a schmuck."

Cole and I say nothing.

"But some people, they think they're *better* than others," the driver goes on. "You understand me?"

Again, we remain quiet.

"My ex-wife, she didn't understand," the driver expounds. "That's one of the problems with artist types. She claimed she was a writer. I never read a word of her stuff, so I can't be sure."

"Was her work published?" Cole says.

"Beats me," the driver says, as though it were an insurmountable mystery. "She was always talking about stories. I tried to explain to her."

"Explain?"

"That there's no such thing as stories," he says, lowering his voice. "If you write it down, it's real. It exists in the world. You're putting it out there. You have to be careful with that. There's no such thing as fiction. Words are real. What does *fiction* even mean?"

I can't tell if the driver is serious, but a distinct lack of cues indicating self-awareness or philosophical postmodernism makes the option unpalatably likely. Doing my best to marshal a rising impulse towards panic, I glance over at Cole, whose face is a study in disbelief.

"Fiction simply means the stories aren't about real events or real people," Cole says.

"That doesn't make sense." The driver coughs, which

comes across as a dogmatic underscoring of his thesis. "If you write it down, *it's real.* It exists."

"We understand what you're saying," Cole says.

The driver's next look, as glimpsed through the little partition crack, encourages us to remain silent.

We drive for another ten minutes. Still cold, I tap on the control panel I played with before and say, "Does this thing have a radio? Can I listen to the news?"

"Why'd you want to do that?" says the driver. Then he repeats: "*A radio.*"

"I like to stay informed," I say.

"Where we're going you'll be getting a ton of great information, my friend," he says.

Then he slides the partition all the way up.

Twenty minutes pass. Through the limo's tinted windows, it's easy to pretend the day has ended, and I have to make an effort to resist the dusky illusion.

As the limo slows at the approach of an intersection, I test the door to my right. It's shut and won't unlock. Cole tries his side and obtains the same result. After the light, the limo climbs an on-ramp and gets on the freeway.

Ten more minutes elapse.

"Is there anything to drink back here?" I call out.

The partition stays in place, and there's no sign the driver hears me, or that if he does, he's interested in responding.

"Hey," Cole says.

No response.

With enfeebling self-consciousness, I scoot forward and wrap my knuckles on the partition. It comes down an inch. "What gives?" says the driver.

Drawing strength from Cole's companionship, and

from my rehearsal of these words in my mind during the last ten seconds, I raise my voice. "Let's cut the crap," I say. "Where are you taking us?"

The driver stares ahead. In a deadpan voice, he says, "There's beer in the mini-fridge. I've unlocked it."

"We're not interested in beer," Cole says. "Listen to me. People are going to find out about this. I'm a journalist, and I'll tell the media. You need to stop the car and let us out."

"You're going to be getting so much good information," the driver says. "Now, look at me."

I do my best to hold my gaze steady as the driver cranes his neck back and gives us his undivided attention. At this range the man's eyes speak a history we don't want to know. The limo begins veering off to the side.

"Watch the road," I say. "You're going to get us killed."

"I know what my purpose is," the driver says, still looking at us, his back turned to the front windshield. "Do you know yours?"

I hesitate. That's all it takes for the driver to assume a sort of metaphysical victory. He turns around and raises the partition again.

"Where are we going?" Cole asks. He bangs his hands on the partition, without result.

"Son of a bitch," I mutter.

As time draws on, the seat's plush comfort, the rhythmic vibrations of the limo's humming engine, our steady speed along the freeway, all conspire to lull me into an irritating state of semi-awareness. Every once in a while, I exchange a few words with Cole, who is doing a better job at staying alert.

Eventually we slow down. Automatic gates swing open and allow the vehicle inside a compound. A minute later the sound of my door unlocking makes me snap to. As Cole and I open our doors, we're greeted by harsh, bright daylight amid a stark landscape.

I cover my face with my hands. The driver comes round to me, and I see that my estimate of his physique has been on the conservative side.

Without a word, the man depresses a switch on a small brown device in the palm of his hand.

"Really welcoming vibes," Cole says, pointing ahead.

I look at a large nondescript structure, a cross between an office building and industrial hangar, whose outside is a uniform dull gray and whose front façade is lined with tinted windows. A gravel path leads to the entrance, comprised of two sleek, barred metallic doors, about ten feet away. I complete a slow three-sixty. Cole and I are standing in the middle of a dusty field. We can make out the road the limo followed to get here, through the set of high gates. By the time my eyes follow the encircling fence back to the point where it disappears behind the building's contour, the building's metallic doors have swung open, and a familiar figure emerges.

"Welcome, Jason! Glad you could make it. And thanks for your messages." She waves with incongruous joviality. "I got the one you intended for Shanice, too. Sorry to say, she's not in a position to receive it. It's nice to see you again as well, Cole."

I want to move because movement of any sort might dispel the ludicrousness of the situation. But I'm here against my will, and I'll be damned if I take even a single step in the direction intended by my captors. Still, I have to respond. "Kathleen?" I say. "What the hell are you doing here? What is this? Know that Cole is a journalist. This story won't go untold."

"He's right," Cole adds.

"How dramatic! You two make a great duo. Please, come inside," she says. Four tall, lean men wearing sunglasses that completely obscure their eyes appear behind her. "Jason, my understanding is that you're here to claim your prize, and we'd love to get the process started."

"No." Despite the aridness of the surrounding field and the dry heat in the air, I tremble. "I decline. I want to go home."

Kathleen stays by the door and the four men advance. As they approach, I notice that beyond their identical plain-beige tunics they all seem to have identical builds.

Two of them get closer and one of them holds a glass up to my face. "Drink," the man says in a flat voice. "It was a long drive. This will perk you right up."

"No thanks." I cross my arms.

Cole says, "Why don't you get out of our faces?" The man ignores him.

"Follow us," he tells me.

The second man positions himself right behind me and brushes up against me. I feel his breath on my neck. The man starts walking, shoving me forward.

Cole tries to step aside but the other two men block his path. "You're coming with us," one of them says.

I turn and see Cole struggling. "On you go," says the man behind Cole.

"Where are you taking my friend?" I demand. "You're making a terrible mistake, believe me."

"He's just going to the waiting area," the man in the lead says. "No need for hysterics."

"Jason!" Cole calls out, as he's dragged towards a different door in the building. "We're going to be fine! These cretins don't know who they're dealing with!"

"Hang in there, buddy!"

A hand lands on my shoulder and pushes me forward. I comply.

"Nothing to be afraid of," the man at the front says. As we stride toward the door, he drinks the contents of the glass that had been proffered to me. "See?" A thin white residue sticks to his lips, and he doesn't bother to wipe it away.

"Jason, you look rested," Kathleen says. "That's fabulous."

"Are you kidding me right now? These brutes are dragging Cole off God-knows- where and you're commenting on my appearance?"

"We're all friends here," she says. "Please, this way." A badge in her hand activates a hidden mechanism in the doors, causing them to part open.

Inside, the air smells antiseptic and manufactured, like the polyurethane foam used in packaging. Buried beneath these aromas I think I detect other lingering scents I can't place. The ceiling lights, mounted in huge panels that also house small valve openings, are ultra-bright, and I feel my pupils contract. I'm left standing with Kathleen and the two goons in front of a large semi-circular foyer.

"Kathleen," I begin. "This is completely insane. What— what are you doing involved in all this? I don't understand. I thought you just moved to the city."

"I did," she says. "I came here with a purpose. It's no good drifting through life, you know. One must set a course and stick to it. Are you rudderless, Jason?"

"How about pissed off? Spare me the cheap metaphors

and tell me what the hell is going on. And since you have trouble comprehending, let me re-iterate: the world is going to find out about this."

"The world," she says. "*The world*. Yes. Precisely. That's exactly what we're hoping you can help us with."

"What?"

"Let's have a civilized conversation in the visitor's office. Maybe a few familiar faces will help calm your nerves."

She leads us twenty feet down the building's principal hall. On the way I deliberately falter and buckle my legs.

"Are you hurt?" As Kathleen bends down to help me back up, I surreptitiously swipe her security badge and slip it into my pocket.

"Only my pride," I mumble, feigning embarrassment.

At last we arrive at a windowless room. Inside, a man rises from a suede couch. He wears a slim, blue, yellow, pink and white-striped chambray shirt with a too-tight, fold-over collar. As the man's face draws closer to me, I recognize his beady eyes.

"Terence?" I whisper. "Don't tell me you're part of this outfit too. Jesus."

"I assure you, it's not what you think," Terence says.

Another man enters. "Good to see you here."

I size him up. He looks familiar, but I can't place him.

"We met before things were…altered," the man says, smiling. "Most people can't remember how it was before each change. But you'll find our group isn't exactly most people."

As he speaks, recognition finally dawns on me. "You're the guy who gave me the lottery tickets at that Mayflies meeting," I exclaim. "Gary something!"

"Indeed. Mr. Stanek, at your service. It was one of several catalyzing circumstances we had to enact in order to arrive at this juncture. Good thing we had that plan in place, too, because your responses to our other stimuli were underwhelming."

"Other stimuli?" I pull back.

"Our efforts with the Equimedian flyer were only partly successful," Kathleen says. "And you rudely rebuffed Terence's offer for the mutational narrative chips as well. You're more strong-willed than we anticipated, to be sure."

"Thanks a lot. Also, fuck you."

"Please, sit," Kathleen says.

Terence and Gary do so at once.

I continue to stand while the two nameless men and Kathleen sit on a sectional couch behind an oak coffee table.

"You sit, winner," one of the anonymous men says. I look at him closely for the first time. His eyes are perfectly obscured by his black glasses. His face is unnaturally smooth and pale: the gray, waxy pallor makes the skin look like it's at one remove from necrosis. The longer I stare, the harder I find it to actually identify any details in the man's doughy countenance. Is my eyesight deteriorating by the moment? Or is there something intrinsically non-specific, seemingly malleable, about this plaster-like face?

"I don't feel like a winner," I say. "Abject would be more accurate."

"We'll help you feel the way you *deserve* to feel," Terence says.

"Our PP here is telling the truth. You *are* a winner," Kathleen says. "I don't think you realize it yet. But we're going to help you with that."

"You're a Pilgrim?" I ask the man.

He appears to want to speak, but only a strange gargle arises from his throat. I take a step back.

"He's excited," Kathleen says. "It happens sometimes. The vocal cords are still a work in progress. Limited range, which is why he tends to speak in a monotone. His sense of taste is also, uh, underdeveloped. But he can almost score sixty on an IQ test, which is a phenomenal advance over where the PPs were a few years ago."

"The PPs are supposed to be some kind of geniuses," I say. "Is that what you're covering up—that micro-temporal displacement turns your brain into mashed potatoes or something?"

Kathleen throws her head back in amusement. Terence stifles a laugh.

"No," she says, "of course not. Induction is absolutely safe. These are not just any old PPs, Jason. They're part of an elite."

"An elite of rent-a-thugs," I say.

Gary says, "It's all about harnessing spiritual discipline. The ability to *truly* focus the mind."

"Spiritual discipline?" I challenge. Then I start and stop. "Oh my Lord. *The eagle and the dream.*"

"Bravo," Terence says. "Your subconscious mind realized it before your conscious brain did, which is why you put it into the news. The PPs and Equimedian are two aspects of a greater whole. PPs are the symbol of possibilities, Jason. They speak to the potential for reformation. Equimedian and its members are the ultimate representation of selfless-ness. This man here is one of its senior leaders."

The man rocks back and forth, a dull glee evident in his bland features. "We want help others," he says, his voice bereft of all affect. "We want introduce population to spiritual techniques for positive experiences." The little speech seems to wear him out, and he lapses into silence.

"Normalization through mass conversion," Gary says.

"Hold on a second," I interject. "You're saying things that don't make any sense. *I* didn't put anything into the news—that was a story that Jill told me about. I didn't even read it!"

"We know that you've become aware of certain changes in reality," Kathleen says. "It's happened three times so far, to be precise. Each time you lost consciousness, and when you came to, the world was different. After this most recent incident, that story was out there."

"I…" It seems pointless to deny what Kathleen is saying. "So what if there have been changes? I mean, what does that have to do with *me*?"

"We'll get to that in a moment," Terence says.

"Our plans are long term," Kathleen adds. "We've found that most people who undergo induction don't want to return to the kinds of lives they led before. It's like trying to cram a vastly expanded soul into a tiny heart-shaped-box."

"Sounds like tasting the future inflates the ego," I observe.

The Pilgrim's mouth opens and spittle accumulates at its edges. "Future?"

"That's our publicity for the PPs," Kathleen says, placing a consoling hand on his thin frame. "But our true interest lies elsewhere."

"In a very real way, the future is useless," Terence says. "An idealization. It promotes thoughtless ambition, unmeditated optimism. These are destructive forces. We wish to encourage reflection, consideration. We wish to learn from our mistakes so as to not repeat them. We *do* want a better future—but the future is an abstraction. Only a better *present* is achievable. Our goal is transcendence."

"Please do sit down," Kathleen says.

I don't move. "If the PPs don't tap into the future, what are they connecting to?"

Kathleen's eyes light up. "It's a question of linearity. Most people think of the future as the forward part of the arrow of time, stretching beyond where they are; they see the past as the segment of the arrow behind them, pointing in the opposite direction. But we've discovered that if you move far enough forward, you end up looping back. If you move far enough back, you end up circling forward. Time is a circle, Jason. It connects at infinity."

"Mumbo jumbo," I say.

"Your first and only tattoo was a symbol of infinity, was it not?" Gary says. "Even then, you were intuiting something about yourself. But you weren't ready to face it. Not then."

"This PP travels to the immediate past," Terence says. "He examines what has just occurred in glorious, diminutive detail. And with the help of others, he builds a bridge, extending that rear-looking view. Others do the opposite, pushing our temporal scaffolding ever forward. Eventually these two pathways will connect. Then we will have achieved nirvana. We've only received glimpses of it so far. But it's enough for us to have set up…all of this."

"So this group is behind the PPs and Equimedian," I say. "You engineered them somehow."

"Our scope is wider than that," Gary says. "Significantly wider," Terence notes.

"When Terence says that we've set up all of this," Kathleen says, "he means *all of this*. Everything. The world. What you think of as reality."

I utter nothing for several moments. "I thought *I'd* read too much science fiction," I finally say. "You people can't even tell the difference between fantasy and fact. You're truly wacko."

"I believe you still can't account for the changes you admitted to earlier," Kathleen says.

"It's perhaps, therefore, hasty to call us names," Terence says. "If you're going to use a label, though, the correct term would be Conceptualists. And we have the solution to your mystery."

"We have more than answers," Gary says. "We brought you here because we want to offer you a real chance to improve life in ways you can't even imagine. Not only for yourself, but for humanity as a whole."

"Here would be a grand way to start improving the situation: let Cole go. Then I'll hear you out."

Kathleen trades looks with the two nameless men, then likewise confers silently with Gary and Terence. I'm not sure in what direction the decisions are flowing, but don't particularly care as long as it's a favorable outcome.

"We know your friend means a great deal to you. If you join in our efforts, he'll be better off too. But for now," she says with an unmistakable air of finality, "he stays put."

TWENTY-THREE

"I MENTIONED BEFORE that Equimedian and the PPs were linked," Terence says. "There is a third element, a third vertex, if you will, in our little triangle."

My cheeks flush. "Codis," I say. "How better to prepare folks for what's to come? But your plan isn't working. *Something's* screwing it up, otherwise you wouldn't have invested so much energy in getting me here, and you wouldn't be wasting your breath with me right now." I feel my eyes bulge with disbelief. "Somehow," I say very slowly, "*I'm* a threat to you."

Kathleen crosses her legs. "You're a threat to yourself, Jason. We're concerned about your potential for self-destruction."

"You grandiosely call yourself Conceptualists, but you're afraid of a science fiction fan who does scut work for a tech company?" I laugh bitterly. "The only card you're holding in your hands right now is some kind of knowledge about me that I lack. But I must be getting closer and closer to such knowledge myself for you to have become this desperate and overt."

I study the nameless men. I presume they're observing

the conversation, but I can't really tell if they're even awake. They seem to have retreated to the role of spectators. Good. Maybe that means they'll be less of a threat.

"Let's talk about the changes you've been experiencing in the world around you," Kathleen says.

"Let's," I say. "Terence claimed that I put something into the news. I thought that was absurd at first. But maybe that's what this is about. Maybe I did and I just can't remember. Something or someone is altering my memories…"

Kathleen shakes her head. "Jason, things would be so much simpler if you'd trust us."

"I trust that you have an agenda, nothing more," I say calmly. "If the risk I pose to you simply involved information, you could eliminate me and dispense with the problem. So the news story can't be it. That's why you didn't bat an eye each time I said Cole was going to get our story out. You have the ability to counteract that somehow. But then why did you let me get away—if indeed I somehow did—with giving that scoop to the *New York Times*? And why wouldn't I remember it when I remember other things no one does?" I feel on the cusp of understanding. My hand eases into my pocket, fingers touching the edges of the stolen access card. Not yet. Not yet.

"The reason you remember things that no one else does," Gary says, "is the same reason that *we* remember those things along with you."

"You're becoming one of us," Terence says.

Kathleen smiles. "Congratulations, Jason. You're about to blossom into a full-blown Conceptualist."

"You seriously think I'm involved with the PPs?"

"Forget the PPs, forget Equimedian, forget Codis,"

Kathleen says, waving her hand. "Like I said before, we created those. They're our tools, in the service of our designs. Like us, you're something far more special, Jason. You have the ability to refashion the world. You have the gift to remake reality. All you need is to tap into the power of Conceptualism."

My face tenses so much that my jaw hurts when I speak. "You're saying," I whisper, "that *I* was the one who created the changes? That *I've* altered reality?"

Gary claps.

Terence says, "Your memories are memories of how reality was before you modified it."

"Which you've done three times," Kathleen continues. "As Conceptualists, we're sensitive to these changes. You've produced sounds, if you'll forgive the analogy, that only we Conceptualists can hear. Reality was reset three times by you. And that's interfering with the order of things."

For the first time in what seems an eternity, one of the nameless men speaks. "Order," he says. "Equi-librium."

"This reality," Kathleen says, "as our friend is so concisely pointing out, didn't arise by chance. It's the result of our concerted efforts. There are several hundred of us working in unison throughout the globe, and it's taken us a long time to fine-tune our abilities and embrace working together rather than at cross-purposes. Generations, in fact. Throughout that time, we changed reality thousands of times, tens of thousands. We created social systems that we thought would be perfect, but there were always flaws that grew beyond repair and ruined the fabric of civilization. Trial and error, Jason. Trial and error is what we used. And at long last we arrived at this reality, the world into which you were born.

You may think it has problems, and you're right, but every problem exists for a reason. Forces counterbalance other forces precisely so that long-term stability is attained. We tried worlds in which a tiny elite existed and remained inaccessible to ninety-nine-point-nine percent of humans. Those structures proved untenable. They were ultimately wrecked by the stresses of disparity.

Societies are like springs—they can only stretch so far. So then we tried the opposite, worlds without a concentration of wealth or poverty, ever regulated for parity. Those didn't work either. Humans rebel against stagnation and even the suggestion of a status quo. They require the belief in improvability. And so we arrived at the present middle path. In this reality we avail people of a chance to dream of a better future; we permit many to simulate that future; and, finally, a highly publicized few are chosen to experience it. In this way we provide the greatest social gift of all: motivation. So you can appreciate that when we talked about offering you possibilities, we weren't exaggerating. We're willing to admit you into our cadre, to allow some minor, subtle tweaks that won't affect our overall plans but will give you everything you dreamed of. You want perfect vision? It's yours. Wealth? Status? Reputation? Name your terms. In exchange, we'll put certain parts of your mind… to sleep, so to speak, so that you won't make further undesirable changes on your own. I can't see how this wouldn't be satisfactory for all parties involved."

Something clicks inside me.

I survey the room in an all-encompassing moment and bolt towards the door.

Before anyone else can react, I flash Kathleen's badge on

the sensor and, arms pumping forward, I devour the twenty feet to the building's main entrance. In the dim background of my awareness, I think I hear people screaming.

A foot from the main metallic doors a cluster of men similar to the nameless Pilgrims swarms around me.

"Back off!" I demand, turning my back to the door.

A pungent aroma, as of rubbing alcohol, manure and talcum powder, assails my nostrils. Somewhere I've smelled something similar, and have been, as I am now, repulsed, but I can't afford the luxury of distraction in trying to recall where that was.

I wave my hand with the card, and the metal doors recess into the building. Hot outside air pushes in, promising freedom.

"Mr. Velez," one of the men says. Though he's raised his voice, it carries no sense of urgency; merely empty, emotionless volume.

A klaxon blares. Kathleen and the others catch up with us. "I understand we've given you a lot to chew on," she says, "but it'll make sense in time."

Security personnel barrel towards us, and I see a weapon being drawn. I grab the Pilgrim nearest to me and throw him into the crowd, creating a domino-chain of toppling Pilgrims. As part of the same uninterrupted movement, I spin around and rush through the open doors.

TWENTY-FOUR

I SPRINT TOWARDS the compound gates. I still have Kathleen's badge, and I reason that she must have the highest level of clearance available, which is unlikely to have been disabled in the last thirty or so seconds. I wave the badge at the rectangular sensors, and the gates recede.

Once I'm past the fence, my burning lungs force me to stop and catch my breath. *Now where are you gonna go?* I wonder.

I hear tires squeal, and automatically assume they've sent a car after me. But something's wrong. The sound seems to be coming from the side road, not from inside the Conceptualist enclosure.

It gets louder by the second, and a cloud of dust engulfs me.

"Jason!"

I recognize the car a few feet from me, but my eyes have a hard time accepting its reality. "Jill?" I cry out. "Is that really you?"

"Get in!" Tommy yells from the passenger side. The rear door pops open.

I dive in. Jill starts up the engine before I've even shut the door, which I slam a moment later.

"Jill was so smart to have us follow you," Tommy says. "Man, are you okay?"

"You guys are incredible," is all I can muster. Then my relief is suddenly replaced by an anguish that has nothing to do with the gates. "Stop the car!" I scream. "We have to go back for Cole!"

"We can't risk it," Jill says. In the driver's mirror I see her eyes glistening. "We have to get out of here. Then we'll call the cops and get Cole out."

"Good thinking," Tommy says.

We rush through, dust cloud in our wake as we hit the pedal on the dirty road towards the nearest freeway onramp, some two miles away.

"Your timing was impeccable," I say.

"We didn't want the limo to know we were trailing it, so we took the exit after yours," Jill says. "Then we had to backtrack, but there were no connecting streets, so we had to cut through a field. I thought the tires wouldn't take it, but Tommy had faith we'd get through."

"One of my talents," Tommy said. "Wishful thinking whenever it's useful."

"I might know a thing or two about that," I say.

Jill continues to tear up the road. It takes me about five minutes to accept the fact that after getting out of the compound like greased lightning, nobody appears to be shadowing us. Still, I stay sharp, scanning the highway for any suspicious cars.

"Check this out," Tommy says.

He flings back a pouch. I open it and find a camera.

"That's right," he says. "I took pictures. If they try to make a move on us, we can disclose the location of their hush-hush center."

I think about what Kathleen and the others told me. If even a fraction of it is true, Tommy's pictures won't make any difference in the world. But it's a valiant, thoughtful gesture and I don't wish to appear unappreciative. "Pretty slick," I say, and pass the pouch back to him.

"So how was it in there?" Jill inquires.

I describe the conversation as best I can, thankful for the opportunity to verbalize my experience and fix in place certain details that would otherwise likely fall through the capricious sieves of memory. I make a new connection, too. Those familiar smells as I dashed out, I realize, were similar to the ones in Shawn Gerber's apartment. Which leads to the realization: *the nameless men were clones.* Their similar appearances and emotional registers, the sameness of their tunics, make sense now.

As I relive events, I have a strange thought. "Disorientation and shock—I felt that. Outrage at having my freedom violated—also. But you know what else? A sense of smallness. Being held against your will somehow feels petty, *banal.*"

I proceed to fill them in on some of the Conceptualist's claims. Naturally, they share my disbelief.

"I doubt if any of it's true," I say. "I think they're just off their rockers."

"Did they offer any proof?" Jill asks.

"No," I admit. "Their story is a convenient way of explaining my memory issues, I suppose, but I'm suspicious of my prominent role in it."

"They clearly did go to a lot of trouble to get you in that place, though," Jill says. "If they were lying, I wonder what they were really after."

"I guess it's possible that *they* believe I'm somehow important even if I'm really not. Maybe that part was genuine."

Tommy says, "Either way, we definitely need to go to the police."

"I agree." I pause. "But we can leave out their crazy story. Conceptualists? A reality-altering cabal? Repeating that nonsense would make us sound like loons. Our focus needs to be on credibility, so we can get Cole out."

The engine kicks into even higher gear as Jill pushes the car's speed.

The scenery becomes more familiar and an imaginary belt previously constricting my waist eases by a notch. I start making out little towns, gas stations, more frequent exits, and other signs of civilization. When we enter the city proper, that imaginary belt eases another notch.

We head directly to the police station and file our report.

Phone calls are made, inquiries placed. We wait. The belt tightens up. We are asked for additional information. We fill out forms. Then we are asked for the same information again. More calls are placed. We wait some more, and the belt is back to its original, gut- squeezing circumference.

"I need…" I say, and don't bother to finish the sentence. I get up and walk outside.

When I re-enter the station twenty minutes later, Tommy comes up to me. "We're going home. Apparently Cole's been released. He's saying it was all a misunderstanding and doesn't want to press any charges against the PP lottery."

"Where is he?"

"He was driven home," Jill says. I can tell that, like me, she's skeptical. "I want to talk to him," I say.

It's the first thing I do when we get to Jill and Tommy's place.

Cole picks up right away. "Look," he says, "I want you to know I really appreciate that you guys went to the cops."

"Cole, what happened in there? What did they do to you?"

A ruminative pause. "Nothing I care to discuss right now."

Fear of retaliation? I wonder. Is our conversation being eavesdropped on? What have they threatened him with?

"I'm sorry we didn't break you out ourselves."

This pause isn't as long as the previous one. "Don't worry about it," he says. "You did the right thing."

Still, regret claws at me. Cole has been there for me always, and now I can't help but feel like I failed him. In the process I've let myself down. Phone in hand, I slide onto the couch.

"Is there anything I can do?" I ask.

"Everything's gonna be fine," Cole replies. "I just need some time."

"I'll check in on you soon."

"Thanks pal. I know I can always count on you." Silence. Then one of us, I'm not sure who, hangs up.

Tommy orders Chinese take-out, and I sit, waiting without any appetite for the food to arrive, out of words, out of steam, out of place.

◆

Dawn reaches into the living room with pinkish rays. I'm not ready for another day, but here it is.

"Hey."

Jill sips coffee by the kitchen counter, and Tommy fills up a bowl with cereal. They look like they've had one night's sleep between the two of them. I refrain from trying to imagine my current appearance.

Jill pours me coffee. While drinking it, images from yesterday's odyssey play in my mind, out of sequence, only partially in focus, like some avant-garde collage. I think again about Kathleen and Terence and Gary's crazy claims. How far does their reach extend? What was truth and what were lies? Merely recollecting yesterday's sordid misadventures pecks at my wellbeing, like those eagles picking at Prometheus' liver.

Breakfast is a quiet affair. Afterward Jill and Tommy follow their morning routine and eventually leave for their respective jobs.

I pace around the apartment.

I realize I still need to return the car to Codis. If it's true that they're in league with the Conceptualists, I certainly don't want to be involved with them. Still, there's no way around it. I have no proof of anything, and it's my responsibility to return their property, which is late as it is. So I force myself to repress the wretched feeling in my stomach and drive the vehicle to the service office at which I used to be employed. I hand over the keys to the proper person and complete the required paperwork. I don't bother to visit any of my old co-workers, and I make sure as hell to avoid Mr. Wirt, just in case.

When I return to the apartment, the first thing I see upon entering is a note that's been slipped under the door.

For Christ's sake, I think. *Not more of this covert bullshit.*

Heaving a sigh, I pick it up and read it to discover that that's exactly what it is.

Anonymous handwriting spells out the following words: *Statler Hilton. Noon.*

Turning it around, I see that it's a ticket for a mega-convention being held at the Statler. The con started yesterday and lasts three more days. I check the time. If I leave in the next ten minutes, I can still make noon.

Oh hell.

And so I go. Because maybe, I figure, it's someone who wants to tell me something important and prefers to seek me out in the anonymity of a crowd rather than at my temporary lodgings. It could be Cole. It's only been a day, but perhaps he's ready to talk.

The sheer number of attendees sends claustrophobia coiling through me within minutes. Custodians and Mayflies and dozens of other out-of-state groups have converged for this uber-gathering, in which several top-name Hollywood people and a few commercial writers are Guests of Honor.

I stumble and stagger around, not recognizing anyone and realizing I have no way of identifying whoever summoned me here. Where specifically should this rendezvous take place? I study the main entrance, but don't spot any familiar faces. The dealer's room is probably my best bet, so that's where I head.

There I find myself buffeted by anonymous hordes in even greater concentration than out on the main programming floor. Through sheer proximity, I involuntarily eavesdrop on conversations that sound simultaneously boorish and affectedly highfalutin. I've already walked by at least three people whose breath smells like that of a sick cat on a diet of expired tuna, and a half-dozen others who feel perfectly content to graze my skin as they mosey on by.

I could try to escape these crowds by attending one of the panels, but that's definitely not why I'm here, and if the person who wrote the note is on one of them, I've no way of telling which one. So I wander around some more. Signings? Look at those lines. I pass stalls with toys, film memorabilia, even one booth advertising itself as an emporium of Top Trumps, the silly collectible cards.

About twenty minutes in, I realize something else is nagging me. I'm having to keep myself at a safe distance from the used-book stalls to avoid temptation. I've not successfully severed my umbilical cord from all this, it seems. Instead, it feels like I've entangled myself with that cord and turned it into a noose. Every few steps closer to the source of my formerly oxygenating delight—those vibrantly-colored magazine covers and irresistibly-titled novels—makes it harder to breathe. I start to perspire, feeling trapped in some in-between limbo, still drawn to these books but no longer able to get my kicks from them. Sad in a way. When the chance to pick up books like Ron Goulart's *Broke Down Engine and Other Troubles with Machines*, Michael G. Coney's *Brontomek!*, Michael Moorcock's *The Condition of Muzak*, D. G. Compton's *The Continuous Katherine Mortenhoe*, Richard Cowper's *Kuldesak*, Angela Carter's *The Passion of New Eve*, Mark S. Geston's *The Siege of Wonder*, Harry Harrison's *Montezuma's Revenge*, Kit Reed's *The Killer Mice*, Stephen Goldin's *Assault on the Gods*, Harry Mathews' *The Sinking of the Odradek Stadium*, Michael Bishop's *A Funeral for the*

Eyes of Fire, and Lee Killough's *The Doppelganger Gambit* no longer quickens your blood, you know you've reached a terminus of one sort or another.

I circle the book tables as if in a collapsing orbit. Overhearing a reader berating a bookseller for the scientific infelicities of a recently published novel on display at the seller's booth, it strikes me that despite their intelligence, these fans have little idea of what's going on in the actual world. I mean, I'm certainly no expert. But these people have never heard of Conceptualists, have no clue of the web connecting Equimedian and Codis and the PPs and cloning and who knows what all else. These fans are open to *so* many future possibilities that they've failed to be vigilant about the here-and-now. And I'm to blame just as much, if not more. I was part of Codis; a tool.

"There he is, in the flesh," someone says.

An older man approaches me, waving a magazine. "Would you mind signing this for me?"

"You must have the wrong person," I say. "I'm not a writer."

"Your name badge." His determination is undaunted. "Jason Velez, right? You wrote this review."

He hands me what looks like a badly stapled-together pamphlet called *Aura*. I study the blurry table of contents and see my name there. And then I remember. This is the fanzine for which I wrote that review, over which I labored for hours, penned by a me who now feels like a different person. *At least*, I try to console myself, *I put forth my best effort*. I hope to have done well by Cole, honoring him with the opening line. Except that as I lean in and flip the pamphlet to the fifth page, on which begins my review, I see no mention of Cole's name in the first line.

Or in the next.

Or in the one after that.

In fact, the first few lines are not my work at all, but a hodgepodge of thoughts and ideas bandaged together by something I'd be reluctant to term grammar and sprinkled with a hearty helping of typos. In the second paragraph, I recognize mangled fragments of my writing, with more typos to boot. In disgust I skim the rest of the piece, which doesn't take long because of how severely truncated it is, and find that the final statement not only contradicts what came before, but represents an incomplete thought.

As if that weren't enough, it's hard to escape the review's focus: nitpicking. "I'm sorry," I say, cringing. "I can't sign this."

"But—"

"It has my name on it, but this isn't what I wrote."

"What are you saying? I'm a good friend of Margot, the editor, and her integrity—"

"If you'll excuse me, I have somewhere to be," I say, and start walking away.

"Ah yes," he calls out after me. "The haughty pride of the amateur!"

I storm out of the dealer's room to one of the less-congested corridors that connects with the gaming room. That's when I see him.

"Hey Jason," he says, signaling me to step inside. He holds the door open to a programming room, apparently unoccupied. "Step into my office."

"Mr. Wirt? What are you doing here?" After a brief hesitation I enter the room and the door swings shut behind us.

"You obviously got my note," he says. "That's good."

"I don't understand. Why did you—"

"A panel will be starting here at the top of the hour, so we don't have much time. What did they tell you?"

"What did *who* tell me?"

"Don't be coy with me, Jason. The group leaders. I know they sent a car for you and drove you down to HQ. I've been with Codis for seventeen years and they've never invited me. Believe me, I've asked."

"Figures you've been spying on me," I say, without hiding my disapproval. "Why should I tell you anything? You're not my boss anymore. Even if you were, what I do in my spare time is not your concern."

His face reddens. "All that time under my wing," he says. "Do you know what kind of interference I ran with upper management to protect you? I was hoping that at least you'd give me the benefit of the doubt."

I think back to our conversations during the last month or so. Somehow he must have learned that I became acquainted with Equimedian—or maybe I mentioned the PP lottery tickets at one point.

"Whatever you did for me, I don't owe you a thing," I say, angling towards the door. "I recommend you reconsider."

He extracts something from his back pocket. As he holds it up in the air, I recognize the colors and writing.

My Equimedian flyer.

Anger bleaches me. "You crook," I say. "You were in with Andre to break into our apartment."

"Unlike you, I've put my years with Codis to good use. I've taught myself a thing or two about surveillance," he says. "You haven't had a private conversation for a long time, Jason. None of my employees has. And guess what? My search finally paid off. Now tell me what happened when you called this number. Did they give you instructions? Some kind of code? By the time I got the flyer the number was disconnected. Were they the ones who set up the visit to HQ?"

I stare at him, my tempest of anger dissipating. I feel now only enormous pity for this twisted, broken man. I remember a time in my life, decades ago, when I succumbed to the same sickness to belong to a group. I think about the eventual price that fateful decision exacted. If I hadn't been so desperate to join Dustin Shea's gang, if I hadn't been so insecure and consumed by a longing for approval, would Boglins still be alive today? "The reason they'll never want you, Mr. Wirt," I say, "is that you have nothing to offer."

I open the door and march down the corridor, find the nearest exit and depart the hotel.

Though externally calm, I'm too mentally agitated to negotiate the kind of proximity to others that's inimical to the subway, so I walk to Tommy and Jill's. This forty-minute hoof somewhat ameliorates my inner turmoil.

Seconds after opening the door to their apartment, I know something's wrong. Tommy's standing by the phone.

His complexion is blotched, and part of his face is bruised.

My remaining regrets and self-centered worries evaporate like dew under harsh heat. "What the heck happened?" I ask.

"They took her," he says, sounding as if pebbles are lodged into his sternum. "The fuckers took her."

"Jill? *Who did?*"

"They claimed they were government agents. A task-force I've never heard of before. Flashed a badge, as well as several pretty pieces. Two guys wearing suits. They said they had to take her in for questioning related to PP trespassing charges."

"We should go to the station."

"They wouldn't say where they were taking her. I called the station and they said she's not there, that they don't know anything about this." He slams his fist on the counter. "I told them to take me in her place, that she hadn't done anything. I tried to fight them off."

I think about my absence from this apartment at a critical time. Could I have done something to help? Jill and Tommy rescued me. They invited me into their home. And in exchange I've brought mayhem down upon them and absented myself when I would have been most useful. Bile rises up within.

All this wanton suffering for what? *For what?*

I can't escape a crushing sense of *betrayal*. Not by Mr. Wirt.

Not by Codis.

Not by science fiction.

By my own thoughtlessness.

TWENTY-FIVE

THE VOICE COMES in the middle of the night. All is ashen and gray, willowy and fluid. I don't know who's speaking to me, though it's somehow clear that I am the voice's intended recipient. More disconcerting than the sense of no-space is feeling trapped in that interim state of awareness—not asleep, but brain not fully booted up—in which the specific descriptive and individuating labels of who *I* am remain just beyond my grasp. The feather of self-identity tickles me, but there's no release.

"This is not a dream," says the voice. I muse whether a dream-voice wouldn't say exactly that. "We are in a safe place," it continues. "You can relax."

"Everything around me is…" I say. "I see only a haze."

"We are momentarily sheltered from the ravages of time."

"Of time," I repeat. I consider this. "If that's true, then how can discrete events happen in this place? Wouldn't each thought last forever, and no time at all? How can we have a conversation?"

"The human brain is not suited for multi-temporal simultaneity," the voice says. "Our conversation has already progressed, and ended, and started, all in a zero-instant. Your experience of it in separate, sequential stages is an illusion. When you open your eyes, none of this will have happened in the world *out there*, though it will be real to you."

Somehow, I don't question this. Instead, I focus on the qualities of the voice: merciful, wise, but also firm and admonitory. "Who are you?"

"Think of me as a position without coordinates," the voice says, "a depth to which no surface adheres." With these words, a fraction of familiarity *seeps through*, as though the voice has chosen to reveal a tiny glimpse of its true nature. If I were to attribute a gender to it, I'd say it was female.

"Why have you sought me out?"

"Because there is something I want to share with you," the female-approximate voice says, "and sharing is one of my talents."

Unpleasant memories of the PP compound and the Conceptualists' bizarre claims surface. Have they kidnapped me again and drugged me? Is this a form of brainwashing? Perhaps I should be resisting. I don't need more private worlds, more distortions of what people call reality.

"Leave me alone," I say. "I have enough to deal with."

"This concerns your friend Jill. We know—*I* know—that you care about her."

I look this way and that, to no avail. The smeared, foggy nature of this enclave becomes trying. "You're acting like this is some kind of a game," I say, frustration unleashed. "*Stop it.* Tell me whatever it is you want to say and let's be done. What about Jill?"

"A game," the voice reflects. "Perhaps that's not a bad

way of thinking about me. A gamester, if you will, with access to many domains."

"Is Jill okay?" I press.

"One of the domains I can peer into is what you call the future," she-voice says. "And Jill's is not a bright one."

"Show me."

Show me she does.

I see Jill in her bedroom, alone. The door is closed. She lies down on her bed. Her face betrays nothing. Then she reaches for the nightstand, grabs a small pharmaceutical bottle, and empties its contents into her mouth. Dozens of pills, like miniature white pebbles, slip into her mouth. She puts the bottle back on the nightstand and closes her eyes.

I want to save her. More than anything else. But some force of cosmic inevitability stops me. I try to bargain. I plead to be permitted to hold her, to console her as her pulse weakens and her breath fades and her consciousness eclipses into final night. I want to speak to her one last time, to bring her a measure of solace in those parting moments of surrender and quiescence. Again, I'm helpless.

Instants later, mind still reeling from what I've seen, we're back inside our featureless precinct, our temporal smudge.

"I can't accept whatever that was," I say. "Jill is the most resourceful, persevering person I know. She'd never kill herself."

"The endurance of her spirit appears to be rooted in the conviction that she can make a difference in the world," the voice says. "Remove that faith, and her will implodes. At the hands of the same individuals who asked you to join them, she'll come to believe that her actions don't matter. Why go on if everything you achieve can be undone in an instant by agents beyond your control and understanding?"

There's something eerily familiar about this voice. I say, "There must be a way to prevent this from happening. Tell me how."

"I don't have that ability."

"You can show me how my best friend kills herself, but you can't help me change the outcome? What kind of a sadist are you?"

"Jason, Jason," the voice croons. "I'm trying to help you."

The repetition of my name, that particular tone—more linguistic clues. "Help me?" I ask, in genuine dismay. "What do you want me to do?"

"Your revulsion at Jill's fate is reasonable but misdirected. Don't blame me, and don't blame yourself."

What can I do, sequestered in this etheric bubble? Who or what *should* I blame? A tremor passes over me.

"Interesting. You are more sensitively attuned than I expected," the female voice says.

"Attuned to what?"

"The changes," she says. "We think of them as *revisions*."

"Gee, that's helpful," I gripe. "How about explaining what the heck you're talking about?"

The voice becomes alluring now. "A few weeks ago you experienced a wipeout. You stayed up all night reading. Remember it now."

I think about that night. It comes back to me with piercing clarity. I was reading Daniel F. Galouye's *The Infinite Man* and shortly after finishing it I lost consciousness. I didn't fall asleep—it was a different kind of breach of my awareness.

"When I came to," I say, "my surroundings looked the same. But things had changed. Wristplexes were gone. My friend Jill had been single, and now she was dating Tommy. Other smaller items."

"Precisely. It was soon after that you sold something you'd previously considered enormously valuable."

"Yes," I say. "My science fiction book collection." I struggle to articulate my memory. "I felt like I could no longer trust myself with science fiction. In a way, I suppose, I stopped trusting science fiction itself. It doesn't lead anywhere real. I wanted to take a forward step. I wanted more reality, not less."

"We are sympathetic. In a sense, science fiction lays waste to today by claiming undue influence over tomorrow," the voice says. "Perhaps that is science fiction's greatest sin. Not to rob you of the thrill of what's to come by obsessively anticipating it—though that dilution and pre-emptive appropriation is bad enough—but to then claim that it came *because* of the hand-waving. Seen in this way, futurity is a wrapped gift, and science fiction the uncouth child who spends countless hours guessing at the contents of the box, whining in disappointment when she eventually opens it, and then arguing that the contents of the box were the result of her fantasy."

I've heard everything the voice has just said, but my attention has been stuck on that opening phrase, "undue influence over tomorrow." I've heard it before. From someone who could never understand my obsession with science fiction…

A chain reaction occurs inside my mind, two moments of a soundless explosion:

The rueful "Jason, Jason."

The phrase, "undue influence over tomorrow."

I cry out, *"Shanice?"*

The voice replies with the same placidity it has demonstrated from the start. "Shanice is to me as Earth's aurora borealis is to the Milky Way."

"A tiny part of you, then," I marvel. "But nevertheless present."

"Yes. Her human memories reside here, along with those of many others. This information occupies a small chamber of my consciousness, which is split among many bodies and dimensions, all of which contain a myriad of other chambers."

"How are you related to the PPs?" I ask.

"The PPs exist near a certain beginning," the voice says, "and I exist near a certain end. They believe time is a circle, which is a crude first-order approximation to the truth. We perceive a much finer geometry at work."

"I suppose even science fiction, with all its grandiose visions, wouldn't help me understand," I say.

"Don't let your present limitations discourage you. The game continues. If you make sufficient moves, Jason, you may yet infer its rules. As a gamester, I will try to assist you."

The enfolding light, now pastel, ripples, and I wake up on a couch.

I'm in Jill's apartment. The window shades are drawn and the living room smells like a fresh pot is brewing. Feels like mid-afternoon, but for all I know it could be morning.

With some effort, I rise.

Furniture has been moved around, decorations changed. Some objects on the kitchen counter I can't identify.

"Hello?" I say.

I'm here, the voice says, startling me. I turn around.

No one in the living room and kitchen but me. "Where?"

You don't need to use your vocal cords, Jason.

This has to be a dream. Or perhaps it's a dream-creature that has somehow crystallized into the real world, like one of the dream people bent on destroying Project Ephialtes in Jerry Sohl's *I, Aleppo.*

No dream, the gamester voice says. It replays parts of the conversation we had in the timeless place.

That doesn't prove anything, I think back. *If I'm having a conversation with myself, before as now, then I'd remember what I talked to myself about.*

Then consider this.

I levitate two inches above the floor.

Before I have the chance to freak out about it, the soles of my feet touch down again, as smoothly as they detached when I went up.

That's... certainly impressive, I grant. *But I could merely be willing myself to hallucinate. Still, let's say for the sake of argument that it's really you. This mental communication is really invasive and freaky.*

You will endure, the voice says.

I hear the bedroom door swing open and Tommy enters.

My God, he looks old.

"You woke up," Tommy says.

"I was hoping this was all a dream. Right about now I could really use a trapdoor."

"What?"

"Never mind," I say.

"Usually you nap for at least an hour. Everything okay?"

"I'm hearing a voice inside my head and it won't stop."

"That's probably grief," Tommy says. "I hear it too. I hope it quiets down for us eventually."

"I'm not being metaphorical."

He shrugs. "So you need more rest."

"I'd like to talk to Jill," I say. "This concerns her."

"That isn't funny," Tommy snaps. Then he reaches into a drawer. "Take another one of these. The doc said up to three a day is okay."

I study the white pill. "What the hell is this?"

"Anti-anxiety medication."

"What happened to Jill?"

"You know," he says. "She was here yesterday."

"Don't start," Tommy says. "I can't do this today. Pill, nap."

"Stop talking to me as though I'm six years old."

"You want adult conversation? Jill's dead. She killed herself. Then you tried to kill yourself a year later. You concussed your head, inducing memory loss. I've been taking care of you for the last four months. Now finish your nap."

His matter-of-fact manner hits me with sledgehammer force. I hear a sound I haven't heard in years, somewhere between a hum, a low-pitched trill, and a lisp. This I know is entirely in my head. It's the sound of cruelty, of violence without reason. It's the sound that Dustin Shea used to make when he would fly toy airplanes into imaginary combat.

"I didn't…," I mumble. "I'm not… How is…"

Tommy shakes his head at me, maybe in sadness, maybe frustration at my perceived regression and disorientation. Then he disappears back into his room.

I want to get out of here, I think to the voice. *Take me back to my world, my life.*

This is how your life plays out, the gamester responds.

I refuse to believe it. Something changed while we were in the bubble. You admitted that yourself. And if it changed in one direction, it can change in another. Take me back.

I'm not the ghost of Christmas yet-to-come, the voice says.

You acknowledged being able to see the future, I point out. Then I sit down on the couch and close my eyes.

Think, I tell myself. Sherlock Holmes reasoned that when the impossible is eliminated, whatever remains, however implausible, must be true. What if the initial premise is incorrect? What if the impossible *can't* truly be eliminated, because 'impossible' is simply a construct based on the information available at the time? Then perhaps it's best to eliminate everything. Surely it's easier to hold unreality at arm's length if you give yourself a safety berth from reality too. This reasoning makes perfect sense for about half a second and then collapses into absurdity. If I can't believe anything, then I'm back where I started, unable to make a move.

Action requires energy. And my brain feels so crammed and cluttered right now that the only practical response is inaction. I should conserve my strength. Think about nothing. Drift off. Ease myself into a dream state.

I tug at this possibility. Dreams. Trapdoors. There's something to the notion, beyond the obvious temptation of sleep and escape. In dreams begin responsibilities…

You're on the right path, Jason, says the voice.

Whether as a result of my volition or of its own accord, I feel the voice fade. The gamester has left me, at least for now.

Where was I? Dreams. Yes. My dreams are records of my awareness, of my perceptions. Maybe my dream history can shed light on that which I can't access through my conscious mind.

The most memorable dreams I've had in a long time are unquestionably my three trapdoor dreams. I need to focus on their details.

A common element to all three was the sense of displacement, of turbulence, of falling and moving uncontrollably. What differentiated them? During my first dream I observed indecipherable symbols floating in the air around me. Trying to read them caused me pain.

During the second I sensed others watching me; I longed to make contact with them, but the speed of my fall made that impossible. In the third dream I saw myself wearing a backpack, and I wished to open it, convinced it would contain useful tools. Again, pain interfered.

What's the common thread?

A sense of dissatisfaction with my life's choices, perhaps—my desire to achieve things beyond my abilities. Maybe, if I'm less gloomy about it, a reminder of my untapped potential.

If I think of each dream's images as representations, perhaps I can ascribe them more specific meanings. The enigmatic symbols, for instance, might be stand-ins for communication. Or for language. Hmmm. Perhaps writing? Storytelling? Maybe science fiction. Science fiction around me; its true meaning elusive. And the observers—other entities. Consciousness? Beings? Minds outside of my own mind? My desire to connect with them—relationships. Yes, that feels right. A longing to connect with other human beings. And the backpack, with its mysterious tools. Technology. Work. Right. Codis. My job.

I feel closer to comprehension.

My confidence grows.

But what am I trying to truly explain with these dreamscape-culled ideas? I have to be specific.

I've experienced three ruptures in my awareness. The voice used the word "revisions." If I'm to believe the Conceptualists, I am responsible for three alterations to reality as we know it, each change accompanying one of these ruptures.

And now I realize I have three dream images to work with.

The first rupture occurred in the wake of staying up reading science fiction and thinking about what it means to me.

The second rupture happened right after my oceanic vision, on the street with Cole. I remember feeling like I'd had insights into my relationships with others.

The third rupture, in the vehicle, unfolded right after learning that my work as a Codis employee was part of someone else's master scheme.

The intensity of these three experiences… it was more than passing out. Closer to passing *through*… And each time, after coming to, the world was modified.

I feel so close now.

What do the three ruptures have in common besides the physical sensations and loss of consciousness?

Insights. In all three, moments before the event, I felt like I understood something profound to me.

My passion for science fiction—rupture one.

My relationships—rupture two.

My job—rupture three.

The three trapdoor dreams—each one symbolic of a particular insight.

Pressure rises in the back of my skull.

Three trapdoor dreams; three trapdoors between realities unlocked.

A new sense of freedom overtakes me. Admitting that I'm part of something that can't be fully grasped by my own mind, not truly, is liberating. Yes. Existence is fundamentally incomprehensible. Accepting that brings peace.

The voice of the gamester returns. *That's it*, it says. *One more revision—but this time you'll be awake.*

I open my eyes, still on the future couch in Tommy's apartment. I yell out his name but I'm not sure if I'm projecting my voice or merely mouthing the words. And yet I hear Tommy's name echo over and over, ricocheting through the living room's niches, or perhaps merely contorted spaces within my own brain. The name shoots back at me, determined to enter my vocal apparatus, rest, and then be spit out again, starting the whole cycle over. Tommy can you hear me, looped in an infinite regress.

I stand up while remaining seated, run around the room without moving an inch, and cry the purest tears I've ever cried in complete and magnificent dryness.

The gamester speaks to me and I speak back, but the conversation appears to unfold in silence, and the words—including my own—are beyond me.

Then our exchange finishes, with a finality suggesting only the start of something far more intense.

You're ready now, the gamester says. *In we go.*

But I—

gateway windows theworldmenders
whatentropymeanstome

profundis transfigurations concreteisland theexilewaiting
themortalimmortals moonstar onestepfromearth
flightfromrebirth thievesworld
agalaxyofstrangers thisdarkeninguniverse
tunnelthroughthedeeps tothelandoftheelectricangel
intheenclosure   thebloodychamber   szygy
theinvertedworld   manplus   theembedding
nodirectionhome   ardoronaros
thegamesman   wildsmith
afterthingsfellapart   crackpot
domino   icecrown
starbrat   highrise
redshift   herds
phaseiv   cinnabar
catchworld   thegodwhale
stolenfaces   fireworks
overlay   bibblings
ausuallunacy
…
… deathanddesignationamongtheasadi
…
… hellosummergoodbye
… thedevilisdead amazeofdeath
… starshadows
.. somethingfrom...
anexerciseformadmen

V. The Man Who Folded Themselves

TWENTY-SIX

JASON CAME TO in the middle of the sidewalk two blocks from his apartment. His first sensation was one of hyper-reality. When he opened his eyes, he found that he could only see through one of them, but even that didn't blunt the intensity of his feeling present, alive and in the moment. He blinked several times, but the near-zero visual acuity in the bad eye remained. He realized a skinny-faced woman with long hippie hair was crouching beside him. She placed her cool palm on his forehead and asked if he needed medical assistance.

"I think I'm going to be all right," he said, despite apparent evidence to the contrary, and slowly he lifted himself up and started walking.

Some instinctual part of him accessed the correct combination of public transportation—two subways and a bus—to get to his parent's home, though he was startled several times en route to discover that specific stops had different names from the ones he remembered.

When Jason rang the doorbell, his mom opened at once. His dad turned off the television and joined her. Jason's mom used a look to communicate something to his dad and his dad nodded, almost imperceptibly. He gave Jason a strong hug.

They had dinner in the living room, an entrée of pineapple chicken and a side of small talk. Jason kept waiting for the illusion of the experience to crumble, to wake up and find himself in some other place, some other time, perhaps an altogether different person. But reality maintained its cohesion. Few things had ever felt as good as settling into that certainty.

During dessert Jason's mom said, "Your luck will turn around soon, you'll see."

"Luck?"

"You know, with your job search," she said.

"Oh," Jason said. "Right. Let's hope."

"We're happy you're with us," Jason's dad said. "We know things are tough out there. With the energy crisis the job market is a far cry from what it was a year ago. Carter really needs to get his act together. So you shouldn't feel embarrassed."

"I… wish I was more tuned in to what's going on," Jason said meekly. He needed to read newspapers and visit the library. He knew he had catching up to do.

"Chin up and soldier on," his dad said.

Jason sighed audibly and said, "Thanks. I feel like I've already been imposing." His choice of words had the desired effect.

"Nonsense," said his mom. "It's barely been two weeks since you moved out of Leon's place."

That night Jason slept unexpectedly soundly and had no dreams he could remember.

The following day he began job hunting. Though his

own internal narrative was more or less continuous with what he remembered from his last *revision*—minus approximately two weeks—he soon realized that the broader world story contained sizable differences. At one employment agency Jason asked about Codis and received a puzzle look in response to his query. A quick consultation at the local library revealed no mentions whatsoever of the PPs, of their lottery, or of Equimedian, as though these entities had simply never been. Not surprisingly, there were no wrist-plexes or EmuXs here. There was no telebox. There was no Moon base and there had been no Mars landing. There were no clones. And, as a doctor soon confirmed, Jason had a fully-formed cataract in his right eye, and should not expect any improvement.

At a nearby electronics store, Jason examined a variety of products that had launched recently, like the Apple II computer and the Sony Walkman. His years of work at Codis enabled him to figure out their operation and basic mechanisms. Within a week Jason had leveraged his tech skills to get hired as a junior associate at a store called Tech HiFi that offered a multitude of music-geared marvels. Manufacturer names like Crown, Infinity, Micro Seiki, Ortofon, Tandberg, Phase Linear, Hitachi, Thorens, Collaro, ERC and Audio-Technica became second nature in a month. He had accustomed himself to countenances devoid of decorative tats several revisions ago, and now adapted to aesthetic changes in his co-workers' dress styles.

He spent the next six months learning the ways of this world and establishing a simple routine from which he derived stability and purpose. He rose early, made himself a cup of green tea, went for a walk, took the subway to work, performed his duties diligently and enthusiastically, rode the subway back home in the evening, had dinner with his parents, had a shower, and went to bed early. He read primarily newspapers and watched only the news on television. Each day, during quiet moments, a feeling of gratitude arose within Jason. It felt good to work at a job that brought musical joy into the lives of others, and it felt even better to have reconnected with his parents. Along with this wellbeing, a memory tickled at his consciousness. It involved his interaction with the gamester immediately preceding his passage to this reality, but try as he might he could not access details or understand why it beckoned. *Don't stress out about it*, he told himself. *If it's important enough, eventually it will come to you.*

During this period, he avoided social engagements with the exception of a lunch or coffee break with work pals. He relished his downtime to think, to process, to just be himself, still, unoccupied. His parents received several inquiries from concerned friends in the science fiction community, and they politely asked the inquirers to respect Jason's need for space.

After feeling like he had a solid grasp on things, Jason decided he was clear-headed enough to wade back into social waters. He looked up Jill Hann but found no trace of her. Next he tried Tommy Kappel. It took several weeks of dogged effort and zero results to convince him that they were no longer a part of his journey, and he mourned their loss—particularly hers—deeply. He wrote down everything he remembered about her and vowed to honor her memory with his actions. Next he sought out Cole Wellmann, who proved easy to locate. Cole made no reference to the limo ride or to being held captive, since these events were not a part of his history here. Indeed, he bore no grudges against Jason, and their relationship resumed smoothly. Cole had just come back from Europe and shared plenty of fun stories. "Not exactly paradise, but stimulating" was the phrase he used to describe his recent, budget-conscious one-week stay in Paris, which had in turn led to an even cheaper week in Amsterdam and finally an ultra-penurious tour of Eastern Europe. "Not exactly paradise, but stimulating" was a phrase, Jason thought, that might equally apply to the last six months of his own life. Cole gave Jason a copy of his promised commune memoir, which Jason read with delight, further teasing out differences between this world and the ones he'd known.

The next step was a science fiction gathering. He waited for a somewhat subdued meeting on a rainy day. During the event, Jason met an amateur physicist and presented to him in conversation a thinly fictionalized version of his life's events, claiming they comprised the plot of a science fiction novella published in an obscure magazine. The armchair physicist told Jason that the protagonist's experiences and memories didn't track with reality's "world lines," and it was another phrase that stuck with Jason. A second party led to Jason re-establishing contact with, of all people, Keshawn Lee. They got along splendidly. One evening a few days later, right around sunset, Jason accepted Keshawn's invitation and spent an hour rifling through his dusty pulp collection. Jason's response to these artifacts was no longer endorphin-producing. He could appreciate their art and popular appeal without a rush, without the need to possess them himself. Observing that internal change made him smile as much as the artwork and memories of the magazine's stories themselves did.

He was pleased by something else. The titles and authors were familiar to him, unchanged from the previous realities he'd experienced. All science fiction texts he'd read or discussed with others had been constant. Jason realized that must have been his doing too.

Even when unconsciously reshaping reality in substantial ways, he'd wanted to preserve the comfort of the known, and there was at this time in his life nothing better known to him than science fiction.

After Keshawn there followed conversations with others from the same circle, including Keshawn's girlfriend Christina. She mentioned a difficulty with her LP player at home and Jason fixed it for them.

Eventually Jason felt that he was ready for a challenge he'd been putting off: Leon Edel, he of the aquiline nose and blue eyes and preternaturally tanned skin and perfect complexion and occasionally-overbearing-but-well-intentioned-manner. Over the course of several hours and as many beers, they caught up. What Jason perceived didn't stir in him any longing for a deeper friendship, but it was nevertheless satisfying to reconcile and accept Leon on his own terms. Jason had no intention of moving back in with him, and perhaps this lack of pressure facilitated things.

Summer gave way to fall, and in time followed winter, and then came the rebirth of spring, but in his new contemplative approach to life, Jason didn't let himself be fooled by the regularity of this cycle. If there was one thing he was sure of, now more than ever, it was that he was on a one-way trip, each day unique and irreplaceable and expired for good upon passing. Everyone, whether they cared to admit it or not, was subject to this same truth. The journey was unstoppable and finite. So be it, thought Jason. He was dealing with it one moment at a time, and he held on to the self-awareness of his own mortality as a compass needle simultaneously pointing everywhere and nowhere. It imbued him with a kind of ambivalent poise, as though he might be on the edge of a cliff, soon to soar through an unknown abyss, but also at the foot of a great mountain, setting off for the climb of a lifetime.

His parents and Cole and Keshawn and Christina and Leon and others sensed that things were different—that this *Jason* was different from the version they'd known before.

Over the course of a year, he saved enough to put down a deposit on an apartment of his own. After he moved out of his parents' house, he continued to have dinner with them twice a week and preserved other elements of his routine. On the weekends he took himself to museums and film theaters. After a second eye exam confirmed what the most recent one had established, he decided he could use some distraction, and on a whim attended a shindig hosted by that indefatigable Custodian, Ramon Cloutier.

On the way to the gathering, for nostalgic reasons, he stopped at a used bookstore where he'd spent a lot of time over the years. As when going through Keshawn's pulp magazines, he was relieved to find himself free of the endorphin response. He perused for about ten minutes, idly, calmly, and was about to leave when he spotted a bright yellow spine that caught his interest. Here was a British first edition hardcover of Daniel F. Galouye's *Counterfeit World*. He took it in his hands, read the cover blurb and opened it up. Considering the effect that Galouye's *The Infinite Man* had had on Jason, maybe this one was worth picking up… As he turned to the first page, he noticed a neatly folded piece of paper, crisp and unsullied by age. He unfolded it and read: *We won't give up so easily. If you pay attention, you will see the signs and realize that the world you have brought into being isn't sustainable. When you are ready to join us, we will find you.*

As though having come in contact with a fungus, Jason stuffed the paper in the book and jammed it back on the shelf, wiped his hands on his sides, and shivered.

"Can I help you?" the store manager asked, frowning.

"I'm afraid not," Jason said, and made a hasty exit.

He headed straight for Cloutier's party and once there, downed two drinks in five minutes. He milled around for a while, doing his best to put thoughts of the Conceptualists out of his mind. In time a newer member of the group asked Jason point blank what had caused his absence from science fiction. "I heard rumors about your health from some of the old-timers," the young man said. "I hope you're okay."

"Health was definitely part of it," Jason said. "I have a full-blown cataract in my right eye, and it's made things interesting to say the least. Depth perception, for example. Yesterday I was distracted by the radio when I poured myself my tea and I ended up spilling it on the counter."

"Ugh."

"I also lost a good friend," Jason said, thinking again about Jill. "I'd known her since we were kids." Jason's eyes watered up, so that the vision in his left eye became as cloudy as that of his right. He dabbed at the tears and wondered how he could be comfortable making these personal revelations to someone he'd barely met, or for that matter if it was in good taste, but he decided honesty superseded other considerations just now.

"I'm so sorry," the man said, adjusting his glasses. "Was she…?"

"No," Jason said. "We were really just friends."

"No, what I was trying to ask was if she was… part of this scene?"

Jason smiled. "Nah." He drank. "Truth be told, part of my absence was figuring out whether *I* belong here." Jason waved his hands, indicating the people around them, the apartment, the city, maybe the cosmos itself.

"You're here," the man said. "I suppose that means something."

"Maybe." Jason glanced at his watch. He felt tired. It would be a long walk home, but he'd endure it rather than take the subway. Today he wanted to feel the bracing night air on his face. "I'm sure we could talk about the value of science fiction for hours," Jason said. "In my own case I've learned to become wary of solipsism."

"What do you mean?"

"If I read too much of the stuff, I start to experience the world exclusively through that lens. But instead of the world becoming a larger place, science fiction shrinks down to my size."

"I'm finding out the writers are an interesting bunch," the man said. "A lot of money issues. Bohemian, often derelict lives. Their visions of wonders come from dark places."

"Maybe as a reader that's been my process in reverse," Jason said.

The man repositioned his glasses on the bridge of his nose. "I read a story recently in which it turned out that our entire reality was an advanced simulation being undertaken by far-future post-humans who were recreating the distant past for fun. They were super-mutants or something."

Jason thought about this, and again felt the call of the night. "On the other hand," he said, "couldn't we also be the crazy future dreams of a prehistoric shaman?" He smiled. "Look, it's been great talking to you—Ian right?"

"Yep," the man said. "I enjoyed it too."

"I'm going to call it a day," Jason said.

He took the stairs down to the street and walked to the corner.

The light took forever to change, and while he waited, Jason's mind returned to Ian's word: "super-mutants." It made him remember Terence Nylunds' idea about mutational narratives. Maybe that part hadn't been gibble-gabble after all. *Maybe that's why things are always changing*, he thought. The three discontinuities he'd experienced were clearly connected to three distinct conceptual breakthroughs he'd had. But what if the discontinuities didn't result from *him* reshaping reality? What if after each conceptual breakthrough reality reassembled itself in such a way as to prime the following breakthrough? A tantalizing possibility occurred to Jason. *Maybe the notion of conceptual breakthrough is* itself *the remolding agent of reality.* He crossed the street, and decided he'd stop at an all-night donut store on the way home.

If he was right, he mused on the next block, the possibilities were staggering, because the number of conceptual breakthroughs lying in wait was vast. The realization slowed him, as though physically anchoring his body with its import. He'd heard something like this somewhere before. If only he could zoom in on the memory. The idea had been expressed in a place that seemed to exist outside the ordinary confines of…

And then he knew. The memory of the conversation he'd had with the gamester right before his most recent transition crystallized in his mind. It had happened over a year ago but felt utterly fresh. Jason had asked the gamester how many more trapdoors there were. *I've already opened the three that corresponded to my dreams*, Jason had said. *What's next?*

Consider the possibilities, the gamester had replied, and thinking on it now filled Jason with the same chilling awe as did the night sky. *Reality itself can be perceived*, had said the gamester, *as that form of mutational art created by consciousness. Mutational art removes the finished product, such as books, from the participant's experience, and instead offers a series of inspiring influences—like the music that inspired writers—to generate individual "narratives" by anyone who experiences them. Do you see what has happened here, Jason?*

Yes, Jason had said. And for a time-defying instant he had understood it perfectly. *The representational, like a text, has been replaced by the non-representational, like music. In the same way, the process of awareness, instead of producing a fixed continuum—what we would normally call reality—offers a series of inspiring influences called perceptions, used to generate individual narratives.*

The gamester had sounded pleased. *Precisely.*

We think reality should be representational of itself, Jason continued in a heady rush, *existing in a closed and perfect loop. But awareness, by definition, renders, it non-representational.*

The gamester's ensuing silence had served as all the assent that Jason needed.

De te fabula narratur, Jason thought now. *Of you the tale is told. Of you, and you, and you…*

He stopped outside the donut shop's façade and marveled, in the refreshing night air, at its flamingo pink and emerald green neon sign.

He remembered being irrepressibly curious, despite his insight, and asking the gamester one final question before their jump.

Is there truly no limit? Jason had wanted to know. *Or is this talk of boundless possibilities merely a consoling metaphor? Where does wonder end?* he had asked.

And the gamester had replied: *With your capacity to produce it.*

ABOUT THE AUTHOR

Alvaro Zinos-Amaro is a Hugo- and Locus-award finalist who has published over fifty stories, as well as over a hundred essays, reviews, and interviews, in a variety of professional magazines and anthologies. These venues include *Analog, Beneath Ceaseless Skies, Galaxy's Edge, Nature, Vastarien: A Literary Journal, The Los Angeles Review of Books, Locus, Tor.com, Strange Horizons, The Year's Best Science Fiction & Fantasy, Cyber World, This Way to the End Times, The Unquiet Dreamer, Nox Pareidolia, The Book of Extraordinary Femme Fatale Stories, Multiverses: An Anthology of Alternate Realities*, and many others. *Traveler of Worlds: Conversations with Robert Silverberg* appeared in 2016. Alvaro's debut novel, *Equimedian*, and his second book of interviews, *Being Michael Swanwick*, were published in 2023.